Praise for the Billionaire Boys Club novels

THE WRONG BILLIONAIRE'S BED

"Just thinking about it puts a smile on my face . . . In short, this is a really fun, entertaining, engaging book, and I can't wait to read (and reread) the other billionaires' stories."

—*Heroes and Heartbreakers*

"An awesome quick read that touched my heart and stirred my spirit. Buckle up and take the ride—you'll enjoy every peak, valley, twist, and turn." —*Cocktails and Books*

BEAUTY AND THE BILLIONAIRE

"Clare really knocked it out of the park again . . . This series has been a pure and utter delight." —*The Book Pushers*

"I am in love with this series." *Read for Fun*

"Sexy and f *mexy Books*

"I loved this *artbreakers*

STRANDED WITH A BILLIONAIRE

"A cute, sweet romance . . . A fast, sexy read that transports you to the land of the rich and famous." —*Fiction Vixen*

"[Clare's] writing is fun and sexy and flirty . . . *Stranded with a Billionaire* has reignited my love of the billionaire hero."

—*The Book Pushers*

"Clare's latest contemporary is gratifying for its likable but flawed hero and heroine, [and] sexy love scenes." —*Library Journal*

continued . . .

Praise for the Bluebonnet novels

THE CARE AND FEEDING OF AN ALPHA MALE

"Sizzling! Jessica Clare gets everything right in this erotic and sexy romance . . . You need to read this book!"

—*Romance Junkies*

"What a treat to find a book that does it all and does it so well. Clare has crafted a fiery, heartfelt love story that keeps on surprising . . . matching wit and warmth with plenty of spice . . . This is a book, and a series, not to be missed."

—*RT Book Reviews* (4 ½ stars)

"Very cute and oh so sexy." —*Smexy Books*

"[Clare] did a fabulous job of creating a very erotic story while still letting the relationship unfold very believably."

—*Fiction Vixen*

"A wonderful good girl/bad boy erotic romance . . . If you enjoy super-spicy small-town romances, *The Care and Feeding of an Alpha Male* is one that I definitely recommend!"

—*The Romance Dish*

THE GIRL'S GUIDE TO (MAN)HUNTING

"Sexy and funny." —*USA Today*

"A novel that will appeal to both erotic romance fans and outdoor enthusiasts. Set in the small town of Bluebonnet, Texas, this rollicking story of a wilderness survival school and a couple of high-school sweethearts is full of fun and hot, steamy romance." —*Debbie's Book Bag*

"Clare's sizzling encounters in the great outdoors have definite forest-fire potential from the heat generated."

—*RT Book Reviews*

"A fun, cute, and sexy read . . . Miranda's character is genuine and easy to relate to, and Dane was oh so sexy! Great chemistry between these two that makes for a *hot* and steamy read, but also it is filled with humor and a great supporting cast."

—*Nocturne Romance Reads*

"If you like small-town settings with characters that are easy to fall in love with, this is the book for you."

—*Under the Covers Book Blog*

Titles by Jessica Clare

The Bluebonnet Novels

THE GIRL'S GUIDE TO (MAN)HUNTING
THE CARE AND FEEDING OF AN ALPHA MALE
THE EXPERT'S GUIDE TO DRIVING A MAN WILD
THE VIRGIN'S GUIDE TO MISBEHAVING

Billionaire Boys Club

STRANDED WITH A BILLIONAIRE
BEAUTY AND THE BILLIONAIRE
THE WRONG BILLIONAIRE'S BED
ONCE UPON A BILLIONAIRE
ROMANCING THE BILLIONAIRE
ONE NIGHT WITH A BILLIONAIRE

Billionaires and Bridesmaids

THE BILLIONAIRE AND THE VIRGIN
THE TAMING OF THE BILLIONAIRE
THE BILLIONAIRE TAKES A BRIDE

The WRONG BILLIONAIRE'S Bed

JESSICA CLARE

BERKLEY SENSATION, NEW YORK

THE BERKLEY PUBLISHING GROUP
Published by the Penguin Group
Penguin Group (USA) LLC
375 Hudson Street, New York, New York 10014

USA • Canada • UK • Ireland • Australia • New Zealand • India • South Africa • China

penguin.com

A Penguin Random House Company

THE WRONG BILLIONAIRE'S BED

A Berkley Sensation Book / published by arrangement with the author

For information, address: The Berkley Publishing Group,
a division of Penguin Group (USA) LLC,
375 Hudson Street, New York, New York 10014.

ISBN: 978-0-425-26915-2

PUBLISHING HISTORY
InterMix eBook edition / October 2013
Berkley Sensation mass-market edition / April 2015

PRINTED IN THE UNITED STATES OF AMERICA

10 9 8 7 6 5 4 3 2

Cover photos: Crystal chandelier © logobloom / iStockphoto;
Abstract lights © Kulish Viktoriia / Shutterstock.
Cover design by Sarah Oberrender.
Interior text design by Laura K. Corless.

ONE

The three teens sat on the end of the rickety wooden dock at the pond.

"Today's my thirteenth birthday," Daphne Petty told the boy at her side, giving him a coy look and winding a bright red lock of hair around her finger. "You know what that means, right?"

"That it's Audrey's birthday, too?" Cade glanced around Daphne's shoulder to smile at the quieter twin.

Audrey gave him a shy smile, flustered that he'd remembered her. She sat on the opposite side of her vivacious, flirty twin, saying nothing. That was usually how it went. Daphne commanded attention and Audrey just sort of stood by her side. Not that she minded much. Daphne was also the bad twin, and Audrey liked being the good twin. You got into trouble a lot less when you were the good twin, and if there was one thing Audrey hated, it was being in trouble.

"That's not it," Daphne said with a pout. She nudged his shoulder. "Pay attention to me."

Instantly, Cade's amused gaze went back to Daphne. "I am paying attention to you."

"No, you're paying attention to Audrey. Don't you like me, Cade?" She continued to twist that lock of hair around her finger, imitating a move they'd seen their older sister Gretchen pull, to great effect. Gretchen always had interest from boys, and Daphne wanted to learn everything she knew.

"I like both of you," Cade said in a cheerful voice, then ruffled Daphne's hair like she was a child. "You two are my friends."

"Best friends," Audrey said shyly, swinging her legs.

Daphne rolled her eyes at her twin. "We can't be best friends with a guy. Guys can only be boyfriends."

Cade choked on a laugh. "You two are too young for me. I'm fifteen now. You just turned thirteen."

"Well, it's my"—she turned to look at her twin—"our birthday and you need to give us a present."

Cade tugged on the frayed collar of his shirt. It was faded and worn, much like everything he owned. No one talked about it, but the Archers were the poorest family on a rather low-end block of the neighborhood, poorer even than Audrey and Daphne's parents, who worked long hours for little pay. "I don't have money, Daphne. I can't get a job until next year, remember?"

"It's okay," Audrey said. "You can give us something that doesn't cost anything."

"Like?"

A kiss, Audrey thought dreamily, staring at Cade's handsome blue eyes and blond hair.

"You could teach us how to make out with a boy,"

Daphne said slyly, that wicked tone in her voice. "I need to practice so I'm ready for my first boyfriend."

Cade sputtered. "Make out? I don't think so. You two are like my little sisters."

That was not the first time he'd referred to them as his little sisters. It crushed Audrey's heart a bit, but she could tell her twin was undeterred. Daphne usually didn't take no for an answer.

"Maybe just a hug, then?" Daphne asked sweetly.

"Of course," Cade told her, leaning in and reaching an arm around Daphne.

Daphne immediately wrapped her arms around Cade and thrust her mouth against his, trapping him into a surprise kiss. Audrey's jaw dropped in shock as her twin kissed—no, *mauled*—the boy she knew that Audrey had a crush on. Their friend.

Cade made a noise of surprise and tried to pull away, but Daphne clung to him like a leech.

"Daph, stop it," Audrey hissed. Anger began to bubble inside her. How dare Daphne make a scene with Cade. It was bad enough that she monopolized him constantly. "Just stop it!"

But Daphne didn't stop. She made a loud *mmmmm* in the back of her throat, just to goad Audrey.

So Audrey shoved her twin into the pond.

Daphne fell with a splash and a yell, and Cade barely managed to scramble backward onto the dock. He stared at Audrey in surprise.

That was okay, because Audrey was pretty surprised at her actions, too.

Dang it. There went her impulsive temper. Audrey tried to keep it under control, she really did, but sometimes it got the better of her.

Like right now.

Daphne surfaced in the pond's scummy water, screeching as she flailed. "Audrey, you suck!" she yelled. "Cade, help me out!"

"That was not cool, Audrey," Cade told her, leaning over the side of the dock and extending a hand to Daphne. When she continued to flounder in the water, he sighed and looked over at Audrey, who sat on the dock, frozen in horror.

She tried so hard to be the good twin, she really did.

"Here, hold this," Cade told her, and pulled off his T-shirt. Then he jumped into the water and grabbed Daphne, who went into his arms, sobbing, and began to pull her to the nearby shore.

A moment later, both of them were dripping on the bank of the shore. Audrey now stood on the dock, clutching Cade's shirt and mortified by what she'd done. She'd pushed her twin in, all because Daphne'd been kissing the boy Audrey wanted.

But it wasn't just any boy. It was Cade. Audrey had adored him for what seemed like forever, and Daphne only wanted him because Audrey did. That was how it always went.

"You came for me," Daphne sobbed, clinging to Cade.

"Of course," he soothed. "I'll always come for you, Daph. You know I will."

It was true. Though two years separated them in age, the three of them had roamed their neighborhood for years, fishing for crawdads, playing in the pond, and riding bikes. It never failed that Daphne would get into some sort of scrape—like the time she'd pulled up a manhole and climbed down—and Cade would have to come after her.

Daphne caused trouble, and Cade rescued her. And Audrey stood by, because she was the good twin.

Until today, of course, when Audrey's temper got the better of her, and she'd suddenly become the bad twin in a blink.

Daphne wiped streaming hair off her brow and scowled at Audrey. "I'm going to the house and telling Mom. You'll be sorry, Audrey." She turned and stomped off, heading back to the neighborhood.

Audrey sucked in a breath. She was totally going to be grounded.

"Looks like the birthday celebration's going to end early," Cade told her, heading down the dock and reaching for his shirt. He pulled it over his head and then ran his fingers through his wet hair.

"It's okay," Audrey said. "She'll forgive me. We're twins. We can't stay mad at each other."

Cade smiled, reaching out and ruffling Audrey's hair. "Well, since you're twins, I can't give one a present and not the other, can I?"

And he leaned in and kissed her on her freckled cheek.

Audrey flushed bright red, her mouth gaping.

Cade pulled back, tousled her hair again, and grinned. "Happy birthday, Audrey." When she continued to stand there, he added, "You should probably go home and check on Daph."

Audrey nodded, then raced after Daphne. Her cheek throbbed in the perfect, perfect spot where he'd kissed her.

Sure enough, Audrey was grounded that day. Daphne had sobbed her story to their parents, who were appropriately horrified. Audrey was sent to bed early, without TV or computer, while they let Daphne stay up late, feasting on birthday cake. Daphne was upset, and that was almost as bad as getting in trouble on its own.

As of that day, Audrey learned two things.

One, that she was never going to slip up and be the bad twin again.

And two, that she was absolutely, without a doubt, in love with Cade Archer.

Twelve years later

Audrey glanced in the bathroom mirror, smoothed a stray lock of hair into her tight bun, and then straightened her jacket for the eighth time that morning.

Time to approach the boss.

She left the bathroom, her nerves tingling with a mixture of dread and wariness. Not that her outward expression showed it. She was very good about remaining calm and in control in a stressful situation, and this was definitely a situation. Her low heels clicking on the marble floors of Hawkings Conglomerate's headquarters, she swept the mail out of the delivery basket and returned to her desk. Once she'd sorted all the envelopes for Logan's personal attention, she rubber-banded the rest and set them in her mailbox to attend to later.

Her hand paused over the tabloid on her desk. After a moment's indecision, she folded the magazine in half lengthwise and tucked it under her arm. Then, with mail in hand, she headed to Logan Hawkings's closed door and rapped twice.

"Enter," he called.

She did, her stomach churning just a bit.

He didn't look up as she approached, continuing to

type on his laptop. As was their usual routine, Audrey moved to his outbox and picked up any outgoing memos or faxes that he needed her to handle. She slipped his personal mail into his inbox, picked up his faxes, and glanced over at him. But she couldn't make her mouth form the request.

So she stalled. "Coffee, Mr. Hawkings?"

"Thank you."

She moved to the Keurig machine in her adjoining office and brewed him a cup, waiting impatiently for the machine to finish. Once it was done, she sweetened it, added creamer, and stirred, all the while mentally cursing herself for not broaching the conversation yet. She returned to his office with the cup in hand and set it on his desk.

Again, he didn't look up.

"Dry cleaning today, Mr. Hawkings?"

"No." He picked up the mug and gave her a suspicious look. "Something wrong?"

And here she thought she'd hidden it so well. Audrey clutched the folded tabloid in her hand, hesitating in front of his desk. "I . . . need some time off work."

Over his coffee mug, Logan frowned. "Time off?"

Just as she'd thought, it hadn't gone over well. In the three and a half years since she'd been working for Logan Hawkings, she'd never missed a day of work. She was here before he was, left after he did, and took her vacation time concurrent with his so as not to disrupt his schedule.

She was the model employee. She kept things quiet and running as smoothly as possible for Mr. Hawkings. When he needed something handled, she took care of it.

And she never, never asked for time off until today.

Audrey swallowed. "I'm afraid so."

"How much time off?"

"I . . . don't know. It's a personal matter." And very quietly, she unfolded the tabloid and offered it to him.

Logan tossed it down on his desk, eyeing the picture on the cover. The headline was a bold yellow that screamed out of the grainy photo. POP PRINCESS CAUGHT IN A COKE-FUELED ORGY! PICTURES ON PAGE 17! And there was the unmistakable face of her twin, blade-thin, her hair matted and dyed a hideous shade of black, a dopey smile on her face as she snorted lines in a club bathroom and leaned on an equally dopey-looking pair of men. Audrey didn't know who they were. She never knew who Daphne ran with anymore. Daphne's manager handled all that . . . theoretically. She suspected Daphne's manager took care of his own needs first, and Daphne's second.

Logan glanced at the magazine, then back up at her. "Your sister?"

She nodded succinctly. "I understand that this is an inconvenience, but I've taken extra precautions to ensure that your schedule is not interrupted. I talked with Cathy in personnel, and she's agreed to send a temp for me to train on daily duties."

"It's fine."

"I'll make sure she's prepared before I leave. I'll have my phone with me so you can contact me—or she can—if you need something. And I've made sure that your address book and calendar are up to date. The meeting next week—"

"It's fine, Audrey. Take the time you need." He folded the magazine and offered it back to her. "I take it you're getting her some help?"

She took it from him, her fingers trembling with a rush of relief. "She refuses to go to rehab, but she's agreed to go away for a time if I go with her. No parties, no drugs.

I'm basically going to chaperone and try to get her to sober up." She hesitated. "It might be a few weeks. It might be longer. If that's a problem—"

"It's fine."

"If you need personal errands run—"

"I said it's fine, Audrey." Now he was getting annoyed with her. She could tell by the set of his eyebrows. "If I have personal errands, I'll ask Brontë to step in and help. It's not a big deal. Take the time that you need. Your family comes first."

Words that she'd never thought she'd hear billionaire Logan Hawkings say. His fiancée must have mellowed him quite a bit. She nodded. "Thank you, Mr. Hawkings. I'll make the arrangements with Cathy."

"Close the door when you leave." He turned back to his computer and began to type again.

She quietly exited his office, then shut the door behind her. Only when it was shut did she allow herself to lean against it, the breath whistling out of her in relief.

That had gone much better than she'd anticipated. Mellowed out, indeed. Two years ago—heck, six months ago—Logan would have given a few thinly veiled hints that if she'd valued her job, she'd find a way to make things happen. He paid her very well, after all, and if she couldn't find a way to perform her job to his satisfaction, he'd find someone who could.

Of course, that was BH—Before Hurricane. And before Brontë. Still, Audrey hadn't relished asking him for the favor. Logan knew she was twins with Daphne; he'd met her at a rather unfortunate dinner party once. Most people didn't know she had a twin, and Audrey didn't volunteer the information. She'd learned the hard way that the conversation usually went in one of three directions:

Scenario one: Oh, my God. You're related to Daphne Petty? *The* Daphne Petty? The singer? Can you get me her autograph? Free tickets? A visit to my kid's birthday party?

Scenario two: Daphne Petty? Really? You don't look anything like her. She's so thin and glamorous. You're . . . not.

Or scenario three: Daphne Petty? You poor thing. Is she really like that?

Scenario one was simply annoying, but she'd learned to deflect it a long time ago. No, she couldn't get free swag/tickets/CDs of Daphne's latest. No, she couldn't have Daphne show up at someone's birthday party. She kept business cards of the manager of Daphne's fan club and handed them out when pressed.

Scenario two was irritating, but again, she'd learned to deal with it a long time ago. Stage Daphne dressed in wild, colorful outfits and thick makeup. She never left her car without six-inch heels, a thick fringe of fake eyelashes, and her hair dyed some trendy shade. She'd gone Hollywood thin years ago at her label's suggestion (though secretly Audrey suspected drugs more than a healthy diet) and it was just another way that Audrey no longer looked like her twin.

Audrey's hair was straight, smooth, and a pale orange-red that hadn't faded when childhood did. Her skin was still lightly freckled, which was only obvious when she didn't wear makeup. She never wore much, either, because it would have looked out of place with her conservative business suits. And she was several sizes larger than Daphne. Where her twin had been a svelte size two, Audrey was soft, curvy, and just this side of plump. She didn't wear false eyelashes or six-inch heels. She looked like Daphne, but only if one squinted hard and compared photos.

She was used to being insulted about her looks and being

asked for favors. But worst of all was scenario three: the pity. The look she'd come to recognize all too closely in the last two years. The look on someone's face as they recalled one of the more recent tabloids with Daphne's escapades splashed across it, her stints of jail time, her public fiascos, the rumors of drugs, alcohol, men, and excess. The train wreck that bright, wild Daphne Petty had become.

And Audrey hadn't been able to do a thing about it. She'd stood by, helpless, as her headstrong twin pushed her away and embraced all that her fast-paced lifestyle had to offer.

It was killing her. And that was why Audrey hated the pity more than anything else. Because she desperately wanted to do something about it, and now she had the chance. Daphne had called her last night at three in the morning, crying, from the back of a squad car. She'd called Audrey instead of her handlers, and though she'd been in LA instead of someplace that Audrey could have actually helped out with, her sister's misery had broken her heart.

Daphne was reaching out to her. She wanted help. Not rehab, she said, because that would be all over the tabloids and she'd already been to rehab twice, without success. Just a chance to get away and reconnect with her old life, with Audrey's assistance. This time, Daphne swore, it was going to be different. This time she'd leave behind the drugs and alcohol, if Audrey would just help her. She didn't trust anyone else.

And so Audrey had promised to help. She'd go away with her twin. Put her life on hold and come to Daphne's aid once again. She'd soothed her weeping twin on the phone, and then quietly contacted Daphne's management about the most recent visit to the police station. Like most of Daphne's incidents, they were able to make things disappear and Daphne was released from custody and flying to New York in the morning.

And then Audrey would start the slow process of finding Daphne again. Hopefully.

Audrey nibbled on a pretzel stick, flipping the pages of the latest romance novel she'd picked up at the supermarket. She checked the clock, then sighed and dug back into the pretzel bag. It was late and she was in her pajamas. Daphne's plane was supposed to have landed hours ago, and she had promised—*promised*—to come straight to Audrey's apartment from the airport. Audrey had volunteered to meet her twin, but Daphne had demurred, laughing it off and claiming she knew her way around New York just fine.

Except that the later it got into the night, the more positive Audrey was that her twin had made a few pit stops along the way. And it made her furious.

Sometime after one a.m., she heard a knock at her door, and then a giggle. Stifling her irritation, she headed to the door and checked the peephole. Sure enough, there was Daphne, along with a stranger. Audrey unchained the door, flipped the lock, and flung the door open to glare balefully at Daphne and her companion.

Daphne leaned heavily on a tall, skinny man wearing black clothes and enormous plugs in his ears. He had several brow rings, neck tattoos, and a bright green faux-hawk. Daphne was, as usual, a disaster. Her jeans and T-shirt were stained, her hair was in a messy braid that hung over one shoulder, and the small suitcase at her side had shed clothes all down the hall. They both listed to the side and couldn't stop giggling despite Audrey's clear displeasure.

They were drunk. Sloppy drunk.

"You were supposed to be here hours ago, Daphne," Audrey told her. "Where have you been? I've been worried sick."

Daphne shrugged, pushing her way into Audrey's apartment. "The flight sucked and made me all tense, so Stan and I went out for a nightcap."

Audrey eyed Stan as Daphne staggered past her. When her date tried to follow, Audrey put a hand on his chest, stopping him. She gave him a polite smile. "Thanks for bringing her home."

He grinned, showing a gold tooth. "Don't I get to come in, too?"

"No, you don't."

He looked as if he'd argue, but then began to head back to the elevator, too wasted to even realize he'd just abandoned his famous hookup. Audrey quickly shut the door and rebolted it, then turned to glare at Daphne.

Her sister was passed out, face down, on Audrey's couch.

"I don't believe you, Daph," Audrey said. "Drinking? Weren't you coming out here to clean up?"

"Tomorrow," Daphne mumbled from the couch cushions, not bothering to get up. "I'm starting tomorrow. Quit yelling."

"I'm not yelling!" Audrey bellowed, then winced when the neighbor pounded on the wall in response. Frustrated, Audrey grabbed Daphne's suitcase and hauled it to the bedroom. *Fine then.* Daphne wanted to be like that? Audrey wouldn't give her a choice in the matter. She'd simply have to take control—again—and save Daphne from herself.

Tossing the suitcase on her bed, she returned to the living room to grab Daphne's purse. On the couch, her sister snored, oblivious to Audrey's movements. Audrey snagged the purse, returned to the bed, and dumped the contents out.

The usual clutter fell onto the bedspread—half a protein bar, three lipsticks, a few pens, hair clips, and credit cards. Several prescription bottles fell out as well, and Audrey bit her lip, frowning as she read the names. Two of them weren't even Daphne's prescriptions.

She flushed those, along with the small baggy of white powder she found. Daphne would be pissed when she woke up, but Audrey didn't care. Next, she searched the luggage and found several more pill bottles under different names, more drugs, and a thick packet tucked into the liner of her suitcase. It all went into the garbage, and with every item tossed, Audrey grew more and more determined.

Daphne wanted Audrey's help in getting clean? She was willing to help, all right, but she was pretty sure Daphne wasn't going to appreciate it. And that was too damn bad for her twin, because Audrey was in this for the long haul.

She returned to the living room and watched Daphne, snoring, on her couch. Makeup was smeared across Daphne's delicate features, and her mouth hung open, slack, as she slept.

Audrey *would* get her twin back. No ifs, ands, or buts. Daphne would be furious and threaten her, but it didn't matter.

Audrey had to do this once and for all, because it felt as if she'd already lost Daphne.

TWO

Daphne was still seething with outrage, even twenty-four hours after she'd woken up and found that Audrey had gone through her things and rid them of any whiff of drugs.

That was just fine with Audrey. She didn't care if Daphne was mad. She suspected Daphne was going to get a lot madder before they returned from their mini-vacation. A month in the family lake house? With no one around but the two of them? No drugs and no alcohol? They were bound to butt heads, and that was fine with Audrey. She expected it.

What she hadn't expected was that, several hours into their drive upstate, Daphne would turn down an unfamiliar highway.

Audrey frowned and reached for the map in the glove compartment of Daphne's tiny roadster. "I think you missed the turn."

"Nope," Daphne said, staring straight ahead at the road.

"I'm pretty sure this isn't the way to the cabin."

"That's because we're not going to the cabin."

A sinking feeling moved into the pit of Audrey's stomach. Her twin was giving up already? This was just like every other time. "Daphne, you promised."

"Correction. I promised I'd go away for a month with you to try and start over," Daphne said, her eyes shielded by enormous designer sunglasses. Audrey couldn't read her expression. "But my manager expects me to be at the lake house, which means the label's going to put pressure on him. And do you know what that means? It means the paparazzi are going to show up at some point when I'm looking my scuzziest and attempt to get something they can sell to the tabloids to drum up some publicity. And I don't want that."

Audrey couldn't blame her twin, though she was still a bit leery of any change in plans. Daphne needed to be in a controlled environment. "So where are we going?"

Daphne glanced over and gave Audrey a sneaky smile she recognized all too well.

"Oh, no," Audrey moaned. "What did you do?"

"Something that should make you pretty happy, if you're still carrying a torch for a certain someone."

Audrey wanted to throw up and throttle Daphne at the same time. "Please don't tell me we're going to Cade Archer's house."

"We're not," Daphne said.

Relief set in.

"We're going to his lodge in the mountains."

There went the relief, right back out again. "Seriously, Daphne? You called Cade and arranged this?"

"I did. He said he'd always be there for me," she said

stubbornly. "I'm cashing in that chip. I thought it'd be fun to be just you and me and Cade for a few weeks. He's so busy all the time he could use a vacation, too. And I thought if he was there, maybe I could help you lock him down."

Audrey put her head in her hands and stifled the moan that threatened to escape all over again. "Daphne, we're not doing this so you can try to hook me up with our childhood friend. We're doing this to get you clean and get your life back on track."

"I know that," Daphne said irritably, reaching for her pack of cigarettes. She'd already gone through them, and she sighed at the empty packet and pitched it out the open window. "Gimme a new pack of smokes out of my purse, will you?"

"You shouldn't smoke."

"Oh, you're right," Daphne said sarcastically. "Let's stop by the nearest gas station and I'll ask where I can score some rock instead. Leave me fucking something, Audrey. All right? You can nag me about the other shit but smoking is off limits."

Wordlessly, Audrey handed her twin the new pack of cigarettes. "Just promise me that this vacation is going to be about you and making healthy choices for your life."

"I promise," Daphne said, shoving a cigarette between her lips and punching the car's lighter in. "You know what's different this time? I want it for sure. This time I mean it."

You say that every time, Audrey thought with a sigh. But she couldn't help but feel a little flutter of excitement in her belly. Cade Archer was going to be spending the next few weeks with them. Sweet, caring Cade Archer. He'd gone from a considerate, thoughtful, handsome teenage boy who she'd had a crush on to a gorgeous and near-perfect billionaire with a kind heart. And she was still ridiculously in love with him.

Self-consciously, she flipped down the mirror on the passenger side and checked her hair. She wished suddenly that she'd worn something a bit more exotic than a plain black sweater over a purple tank top and jeans. Since she was on vacation, she wore no makeup and her hair was pulled into a loose, carefree ponytail. Too casual. She wanted to look good for Cade. After giving her twin another frown as Daphne chain-smoked her way down the highway, Audrey relaxed and tried to think of what she could say to Cade to make it seem like a wonderful surprise to see him.

If she rehearsed, maybe she wouldn't blurt out her love for him as soon as he came into sight.

While their family had a modest cabin on a bit of lakefront property as a timeshare, Audrey had to admit that if they wanted privacy, Cade's hunting lodge was the way to go. She didn't think he actually hunted, but the name had stuck. It was in a remote portion of the Adirondack Mountains off a heavily wooded road. It backed up to a lake, but the difference was that their parents' cabin shared the lakefront with dozens of other small cabins. This lake and all the surrounding property had been bought up by Cade, and it was isolated and quiet.

Perfect, really, Audrey thought. She'd been to the lodge once, and only for a short period of time. She hadn't been invited—rather, her boss, Logan Hawkings, and his buddies had a weekend getaway and she'd had to bring some work for him. She'd glimpsed the cabin, admired the scenery, and then driven straight back to the city.

But it was clear from Daphne's knowledge that she'd been here before. Audrey cast her twin a suspicious glance. She hadn't needed the map, and she'd clearly been in contact with Cade for quite some time. Exactly how many times had Daphne been to this cabin without letting Audrey know about it? A flare of hurt rose through her that her twin would be so secretive. Once upon a time, they'd shared everything. It just reinforced that Daphne had turned into someone who Audrey no longer knew.

"Huh," Daphne said as they turned down the long, graveled driveway and the lodge came into view.

Audrey glanced up, her train of thought disappearing. "What is it?"

Daphne nodded ahead. "That. He's here already?"

There was a sleek, shiny Lyons convertible in the driveway, cherry red with tricked-out rims and a personalized license plate. A little ostentatious for Cade, Audrey thought with a wrinkle of her nose. Maybe he liked a little flash with his cars? Anything was possible. He was a generous, low-key man, but perhaps he had a weakness for finely tuned, expensive cars. Lots of men did.

The lodge itself was nothing short of spectacular. Built in an A-frame style, it nestled amongst the trees on stilts, a curved wooden deck flowing around the exterior. The front of the lodge seemed to be made entirely of windows to let the light in, and smoke curled from the chimney.

"Someone's definitely here," Audrey commented, heading around to the trunk of Daphne's car to grab their bags. She pulled out her overnight bag and turned to hand it to her sister.

But Daphne had wandered away, holding her cell phone up into the air, trying to get reception.

"Daph?"

She glanced back at Audrey, then put the phone to her ear, waving a hand at her. "You go ahead. I'm going to make a call."

Audrey gave her an exasperated look. "Please don't tell me you're calling someone about drugs already."

Daphne made a face. "I told you. I'm fine. And I'm not calling about drugs. I just have to make a call, all right? Get off my back." She made a shooing motion with her hand. "Why don't you go say hello to Cade? I'll be in in a minute."

Audrey hesitated, but when her twin continued to ignore her, she shouldered the bags and headed up the steps. She couldn't watch Daphne every minute of this vacation. If her twin was calling for drugs, there'd be no saving her. As it was, she had to have a little bit of trust for her sister.

And she did want to see Cade.

The front door to the cabin was unlocked, and Audrey knocked as she opened it. "Hello?"

Silence.

Audrey stepped into the lodge, admiring her surroundings. A plush rug covered the wooden floor, and three rustic couches framed a massive stone fireplace that flickered with logs and a small fire. The walls were not adorned with animal heads but instead had ornate, wire art pieces that somehow matched the rustic decor. The clock over the fireplace was designed to look like a rusty wagon wheel. *Charming enough*, Audrey thought. The kitchen was off to the far end of the house, and down a nearby hallway she could see several bedroom doors and a set of stairs leading up. A den? Game room? Interesting.

Still no sign of Cade, though. Audrey set the bags down near the entryway and wandered a bit farther into the house, trailing her hand along the back of one of the couches.

A feminine giggle touched her ears.

Frowning, Audrey glanced back outside, but she could see Daphne in the distance, her phone held up to her ear. It wasn't her twin. Had Cade brought someone? Dread sunk into her and she stepped quietly forward. When the giggle sounded again, she followed it, smoothing sweaty hands down her jeans. She'd thought about her reunion with Cade on the car ride here. She'd planned on being so very casual. Smile and exclaim about how good it was to see him again, and hug him tight. She'd engage him in conversation, reminding him of what close friends they'd been once upon a time and how different she was from her train-wreck twin. And maybe, just maybe, things could lead somewhere else if given time.

None of her plans had ever factored in another woman.

Clenching her fists, Audrey headed to the back door, where the sound of the giggles emanated. She heard a low, constant rumble like the sound of a generator . . . or something else. To her annoyance, the back door had no window and she was unable to see outside. What if she was interrupting something awkward? Should she leave? If she did, though, Daphne would just come barging in and announce that Audrey was spying. That would only make things worse. Best to just open the door and get it over with. Taking a deep breath, Audrey threw open the door and stepped outside.

Three things were immediately apparent.

One was that the sound she'd heard? The low rumble? It was coming from an enormous jetted hot tub.

Which was currently filled with two naked people: a man and a woman.

Neither of whom were Cade Archer.

The couple was kissing passionately. She could see the long, slim back of the tanned woman as she pressed against the man's chest, her arms wrapped around him. He'd stopped kissing her, though, and was staring at Audrey in surprise. They were bare chested and though she could see nothing untoward, it was pretty obvious what their goal was.

Audrey cleared her throat.

The woman jerked around, saw Audrey, and then slapped the man she was mauling. "You told me you weren't seeing anyone else!"

He winced, rubbing his cheek. "I'm not. I don't know who she is." He pinned Audrey with an irritated look. "Who are you?"

They were both glaring at her like she was the intruder. Worse, like she was a bug. A really unattractive bug. Audrey bristled. "I should be asking that of you, shouldn't I? This is Cade Archer's private getaway."

"So it is," the man drawled lazily. He looked familiar, but she couldn't put her finger on as to why. "Which makes me wonder why you're here."

"I'm supposed to be here," Audrey said in a clipped voice. "My sister was assured that the cabin was available for her use for the next month."

He gave Audrey a wink and pulled the topless woman back against him. "We'll be done with it in a few hours."

Ugh. Audrey couldn't hide her expression of distaste. "I hope you'll drain the water from the hot tub when you're done. No one else is going to want to swim in your DNA."

He chuckled.

The woman scowled at him, pushing off his chest. "You didn't set this up as a threesome, did you?"

"Of course not, Camilla."

Audrey rolled her eyes. "I can assure you that the last thing I plan on doing is crawling in that hot tub with the two of you."

"Reese." The girl pouted, sinking into the bubbling water. "I thought this was going to be our private weekend."

"I thought so, too," he told her, still watching Audrey. She was irritated to see that he was still grinning like he was amused, his mouth framed by a rakish goatee.

"Sorry," Audrey said crisply. "This cabin is already reserved. I'm sure the two of you can find someplace else to go and make out like teenagers."

"Reese," Camilla nagged again.

Audrey's memory jarred, and she narrowed her eyes at the man. His hair was slicked down and he had a goatee, but . . . She raised a hand in her vision, covering the lower half of his jaw, and gasped. "Reese Durham."

"You said you didn't know her," Camilla said, splashing him.

"I don't," he replied, shielding his eyes. "Cut it out."

"I'm Logan Hawkings's assistant," Audrey said in her most efficient voice. That was where she'd seen him before. Normally she'd seen him in a suit and clean shaven, his hair perfectly parted. He was one of Logan's cadre, one of the six men she privately referred to as the "deadly half dozen," since they always seemed to hang out together. She'd seen him plenty of times in and out of the Hawkings office and at business functions. He'd clearly never noticed her before.

Then again, she'd never seen him shirtless and wet.

"Who's out there?" Daphne hissed from behind the door.

Audrey glanced back at her, noting the strained, pale face of her twin. "One of Cade's buddies is here with a date."

"Shit." She didn't think it was possible, but Daphne got even paler. "Can you get rid of them? If the paps find out I'm here, they're going to be crawling up my ass the entire time."

The worry in her twin's face was enough to spur Audrey into action. "Go upstairs," she whispered. "I'll get rid of them." Turning back to the two in the hot tub, she pulled out her phone.

"What are you doing?" Reese asked in a warning tone.

"Documenting this rendezvous," Audrey said blandly, turning on the camera and beginning to take pictures. "I'm sure someone out there will be quite interested in private photos of billionaire playboy Reese Durham and his date—"

"Don't you dare," Camilla screamed, lurching from the hot tub at the same time that Reese did.

Audrey ignored them, continuing to take pictures. "If you're not going to leave, I'm going to have to—" Her words cut off as a wet man grabbed her arms and tried to wrestle the phone from her. "Don't touch me!"

"Give me that damn phone."

"No!" She held it out from her body as Camilla wrapped a towel around her torso and scuttled past. As he reached again, Audrey continued to maneuver, holding the phone out of his grasp by wiggling and bending. It was childish and ridiculous . . .

And she was determined to win, damn it.

His arms were long and so was his reach, so she turned her back to him and bent over her phone, protecting it. To her shock, strong arms wrapped around her torso and she was hauled against the wet, naked body, his hands clutching perilously close to her breasts.

"Give me the phone, little assistant," he murmured, sounding more amused than outraged.

She wriggled against him, trying to free the arms that he had trapped. They were at an impasse. He pinned her arms to her side, which prevented him from reaching for the phone, but prevented her from doing anything with it, either. "Let me go."

"Nope. I can do this all day."

She shifted and, to her horror, she felt something hard against her hip. Audrey drew in a scandalized breath. "That better not be your dick I feel against my leg."

He chuckled. "Can I help it if you're squirming?"

"You are a loathsome man!"

"Hey, if you chased my date off, I'm happy to trade out and give you a chance—"

That did it. She dropped her phone on the ground. "There. You win. Happy? My phone's gone. Now let me go."

Just as quickly, he released her and scooped up the phone. Before she could protest, he tossed it into the hot tub, and Audrey made an outraged sound. "That was my phone!"

"That was my hot ass you were taking pictures of," he said, heading to grab the other towel on the railing. She noticed—to her relief—that he was wearing a pair of Speedos. And that he had an amazing butt and muscled back. *Damn it. His ass was hot.* "And Camilla would not appreciate her father seeing pictures of us together, and neither would I. He'd think that I was going after his daughter just for a business deal."

"A business deal?" Audrey echoed, confused. "Who is she?"

"That was Camilla Sellers, daughter and only heir to the Sellers empire. And I *am* only after her for a business deal," Reese said in a devilish voice, wrapping the towel around his waist. "But I just don't want her father to *think* that."

"You're a pig," Audrey said, plucking her now wet sweater away from her body. It was clinging to her breasts like a second skin, and she hadn't missed the appreciative look that the lecher had sent in her direction. "I'm going inside. And you're buying me a new phone."

"Anything you say, Ms. Assistant."

"My name," she bit out, "is Audrey. Not Ms. Assistant."

"You're rather mad," he said in an amused voice.

"You mauled me and threw my phone into the hot tub. Why wouldn't I be furious?"

"You were kind of being an ass," he said lazily, leaning against the hot tub and regarding her.

"I was not," Audrey said.

"I don't recall Logan's assistant being quite so mean. Or having such red hair." He gave her an up-and-down look, his gaze settling on her breasts. "Or such a rack."

"Ugh," she snarled. *God, he was revolting.* She threw open the door and stomped back into the lodge, scanning the room for her twin.

Daphne was nowhere to be seen. That was good, at least. That meant she'd avoided Camilla and hadn't seen her capable, uptight twin getting mauled by a wet jerk.

The sound of tires screeching out front made Audrey run for the window, her heart pounding. *Oh, no, no, no.* Surely Daphne hadn't run away yet.

But the car that was peeling out of the gravel driveway was the bright red Lyons convertible, with Camilla's blonde hair ruffling in the breeze.

"Well," said a male voice behind her. "Guess you're stuck with me. There went my ride."

THREE

Audrey turned and regarded the man standing behind her, determined to keep a lid on her temper. He lounged against the door, towel low on his hips, arms crossed over his chest. He was handsome, in that cocky, knows-all-the-ladies-want-him sort of way. The goatee on his tanned face was scruffy and he wasn't classically handsome like the statue of David or a model. He was a bit too blue-collar and rough seeming, but what he lacked in the looks department, he made up for in sheer charisma. Even though she was furious at him, she couldn't help but weaken every time he gave her that sly little half smile.

And that made her more than a little furious with herself.

So she forced herself to be calm. Cool. Collected. The smile she gave him was professional. "I'm sorry, Mr. Durham—"

"Reese."

"Mr. Durham," she emphasized. "But Cade promised to let us have use of this cabin for the next month and you're not invited."

"Us?" His thick brows went up, and a delighted look crossed his face as he glanced toward the stairs. "Loverboy hiding up there? Letting you fight all his battles for him?"

"No, and it's none of your business who I'm here with. The important thing is that you leave."

"My clothes were in that car that just drove off."

Audrey gritted her teeth. "You're lying, aren't you."

"Wish I was. Did you say Cade was headed this way? I can borrow some stuff from him." He scratched his bare chest idly. "When he gets here."

And he continued to lean against the wall as if he had all the time in the world.

This . . . was frustrating. Audrey crossed her arms over her chest and then flushed when his gaze automatically went there. She'd forgotten that her sweater was wet and caused her breasts to be a little too outlined in the damp material. She clasped her hands in front of her instead, concentrating on the problem. How did she get this man out of here without him noticing that her famous sister was here?

"What if I drive you back to the nearest town and you buy yourself some clothes and call a taxi?" she suggested.

"Nah." Again, he scratched his chest, drawing her attention there. She hadn't noticed it earlier, but he had a dark tattoo over one rather well-defined pectoral, as well as a sprinkling of dark chest hair that narrowed to a tight vee close to his—

She jerked her head back up, her cheeks burning. That had been dangerously close to checking out his package, and she refused to do that. Refused.

"How about I call you a cab?" she asked desperately.

"No cab's going to want to pick up a naked man."

"You're not naked."

"I can be."

"Are you just deliberately trying to be infuriating?"

"Maybe." And that bastard grinned at her. "I have to admit, I'm enjoying myself. Kind of nice having the tables turned and someone else is caught off guard, isn't it? Consider this payback for your little hot tub ambush." He strolled past her and sat down on one end of the couch, then planted his large, bare feet on the rustic coffee table. He looked for all the world that he was ready to settle in for the evening.

He also looked like he was in danger of losing his towel.

"You know what? I'm calling you a cab," Audrey said, her voice high-pitched and a little louder than usual. "I don't care what you want. This cabin is going to be ours and you weren't invited."

"There's no landline," Reese told her, not bothering to get up from the couch. "And your phone is in the hot tub."

"Then I'll use your phone."

"It's in my pants." He grinned. "Guess where those are."

"In the car?" she asked weakly, then slumped on the corner of the couch opposite from him. "This is a nightmare."

"Hey, look at the bright side. You have pants."

Audrey rubbed the bridge of her nose. "Will you shut up for five minutes? Please! You're driving me mad!"

He laughed.

"Audrey?" Daphne's thin voice came from the stairs. "I thought I heard someone talking. Is everything okay? Did you get them to leave?"

Audrey stared at Reese in horror and then bolted from

the couch, running for the stairs. She had to get to Daphne before Reese saw her.

To her intense frustration, Reese dashed after her and nearly skidded into her back when she halted at the base of the stairs.

Daphne stood on the steps, her hand to her forehead. Her thin face was ghost pale and her fingers were trembling, her eyes sunken. She stared at Reese for a moment, then focused back on Audrey again. "Who's that?"

"One of Cade's friends," she said, forcing a bright smile to her face. "It's all right. He's promised not to say anything about you being here. Cade will take care of it." And she leaned in and pinched Reese's arm, hard, as if daring him to say anything to the contrary.

"That's right," Reese said. His voice had taken on an oddly gentle tone, very different from the constant obnoxious teasing he sent her way. "I'm staying a few days, but your secret's safe with me. No worries."

"Thank you," Daphne said quietly. Her fingers brushed her forehead again. "I think I'm going to take a nap, Audrey. I'm not feeling so hot."

"All right," Audrey said. "Do you need anything? A glass of water? Aspirin?"

Daphne shook her head, turning and heading back up the stairs. "Just want to sleep."

"Just yell if you need anything," Audrey called after her, and remained where she was until Daphne disappeared. As soon as her twin was gone, she turned to Reese, grabbed him by the arm, and dragged him back toward the living room. To her satisfaction, he didn't fight her. When they were a safe distance away, she dropped his arm and whispered, "You cannot say a word of this to the papers."

Reese gave her an odd look. "So you're *that* Audrey.

Gretchen's sister Audrey." He was looking at her as if seeing her for the first time.

Her face burned. She knew what he was referring to. Last month, Gretchen and her new boyfriend, Hunter, had given a dinner party. Audrey had been invited but Daphne had showed up at Audrey's apartment at the last minute, high as a kite and upset about the cancellation of her latest tour by her label, who didn't think she was healthy enough to perform. Audrey'd had no choice but to take Daphne with her to Gretchen's party, and all of Logan Hawkings's rich and powerful friends had been there—including Cade Archer and Reese. At the party, Daphne had drank copious amounts of wine and embarrassed the hell out of herself—and Audrey.

It wasn't surprising that Reese hadn't remembered her until he'd seen her with Daphne. She was a pretty forgettable sort. She didn't dress flashy, didn't call attention to herself. Still, the fact that he remembered now and was thinking of that party? Humiliating. Audrey's cheeks burned in memory. "Gretchen's sister Audrey," she affirmed. "And you can't say a thing about Daphne being here. If the paparazzi get wind of this, she'll get more stressed than she already is."

"She's not stressed. She's strung out. Didn't you see how her hands were shaking? She needs a doctor, Audrey."

Her hands clenched all over again. The last thing she needed was a bossy jerk butting into their business. "Don't you think I know that? She won't see one. This is the only thing she'll let me do for her."

"Stop asking her and just do it. She clearly isn't in a position to make decisions for herself."

"You don't understand. She's my twin. If I betray her, she'll never forgive me." Daphne had cut Audrey out of her life once, for a year, and it had been awful. She'd been worried sick for Daph the entire time. If staying in Daphne's life meant giving in on certain things, then Audrey would. If she wasn't in Daphne's life at all, she couldn't help her.

He shook his head, then rubbed a hand through his wet hair. "She needs rehab more than she needs a vacation. You're not doing her any favors here."

"Look, will you please just go? Just forget you saw us here. I'll call you a cab and you can go back to chasing after Tiffany and her father's money."

"Camilla, and I'm staying." He headed back to the couch and lounged on the end of it, locking his hands behind his head. "She's going to need a few days to cool down and it's time I had a vacation. Besides, you're going to need my help."

"I don't need your help."

"You will if she's looking that bad already," he cautioned.

"Cade's going to be here soon," she said desperately. "He'll help me with things."

He looked at her, then shrugged. "Still not going."

"There aren't enough rooms."

"There are three. One for me, one for Cade, and you and your sister can share." He wagged his eyebrows at her. "Or you and I can share."

"Or you can leave," she snapped. When he put a finger to his lips and pointed at the ceiling, indicating that she should be quiet for her napping sister, she had to bite down on her lip to keep from screaming.

This man was going to drive her absolutely insane. Where, oh where was Cade when she needed him?

It was, quite possibly, the longest afternoon she'd spent in quite some time. With her twin upstairs napping and no one around except for Reese—who she didn't want to talk to—Audrey sat on a corner of the sofa and drummed her fingers, waiting for Cade to arrive.

She couldn't go upstairs and unpack at the moment. Daphne looked exhausted and Audrey didn't want to wake her. She could have read one of her romance novels, she supposed, but Reese was lurking in the too-small lodge and she had no wish to hear smirky commentary from him about what she was reading. So she sat and waited, drumming her fingers on the arm of the couch. If she'd had her phone, she could have gone through work email and routed it to the temp covering her job. But her phone had been thrown into the hot tub and was completely and utterly destroyed.

Reese had disappeared and reappeared some time later in what must have been Cade's clothing—a T-shirt that was a few sizes too small and a pair of pajama pants that looked to be about four inches too short. She'd almost laughed aloud at the sight—almost—except that when he turned, that tight T-shirt displayed every single muscle in his well-defined body, including a pair of the most sculpted arms she'd ever seen. When his hand slid over his stomach, idly scratching at his skin, her gaze had followed, riveted.

It suddenly hadn't been a laughing matter anymore.

She'd gotten up and went outside, admiring the view that the cabin offered. They were perched in the trees and atop a hill, but behind the cabin she saw a dirt path leading to a small dock and a crystal clear lake surrounded by trees. This was by far the prettiest vacation spot she'd ever been to, and she supposed that money could buy just about anything after all.

Someone came up behind her as she gazed down at the lake. "So," Reese said, leaning on the wood railing of the balcony. "You avoiding me or are you planning a secret skinny-dipping rendezvous later?"

She took it back. Money couldn't buy a personality for Reese Durham. Audrey cast him a scathing look. "Don't you have a rock you could crawl back under?"

He chuckled, amused by her irritation. "Hey, if you didn't want me here, you shouldn't have ran my date off."

She ignored him. It seemed to be the best policy at the moment. Instead, she focused her attention on the lake and the lovely weather. It was brisk but clear, and there was no snow (for which she was thankful).

Inside the cabin, a male voice called out, "Hello?"

Cade was here!

Audrey's heart pounded in her chest and she jerked upright. Automatically, her hands went to her hair and she smoothed a few stray locks down, then bit her lips to plump them. She glanced over at Reese and noticed he was watching her with great interest, one eyebrow raised.

She ignored his inquiring look and headed into the house, her heart pounding with excitement. Cade was finally here.

Standing in the doorway, looking just as gorgeous as the last time she'd seen him, was the man she was in love with.

Cade Archer.

Audrey gave a small little sigh of pleasure at the sight of him, noticing the fine cut of his gray suit and the matching tie. Cade wasn't as tall as Reese or Logan, but he was well built and oh so handsome. Dark blond hair clung to his elegant skull and his blue eyes brightened at the sight of her.

He held his arms out in greeting. "Audrey! Look at you. You look terrific."

She rushed into his arms, feeling the blush heat her cheeks and didn't care. She clung to him, enjoying the warmth of his arms around her, smelling the fresh dry-cleaning scent of his clothing.

Her Cade.

He pulled her away and smiled down at her upturned face. "I'm so glad you and Daphne decided to come to the cabin."

"Well, you know Daphne," she said, delighted at his obvious pleasure. "Once she gets an idea in her head, she won't let go of it."

"She's not the only twin like that," Cade said easily, then glanced around the room. "Speaking of twin, where is yours?"

"Sleeping," Audrey said with a small grimace. "She wasn't feeling so well."

His sparkling gaze turned somber. "Is she . . . all right?"

Audrey nodded. "For now. She says this time she's going to change. She promised." She didn't add that Daphne had promised that many times before, and then just as quickly broke her promises. This time, Audrey vowed, it'd be different.

Cade nodded. He rubbed Audrey's arm as if to reassure her. "Well, it's going to be good to have all three of us together again. Just like old times, eh?"

"Just like," she said, and was horrified to hear a girlish giggle escape her throat. God, was that pathetic sound coming from her?

Cade didn't seem to notice it, though. He continued to smile at her. "How have you been? It feels like forever since we've seen each other."

"We saw each other last month at Gretchen's party," she told him, then grimaced. "Briefly."

"Mmm." His face fell a little and his smile faded a bit as they both recalled Daphne's actions at that party. Once again, Daphne hadn't listened to a thing that Audrey had said, and Cade had come to the rescue, scooping Daphne into his arms and removing her and Audrey from the party.

A throat cleared.

Cade looked up and he tilted his head and stared over his shoulder, as if not quite believing his eyes. "Reese!" His gaze went back to Audrey, and then a sly, almost disbelieving look crossed his face as he pointed at her, then Reese. "Don't tell me. The two of you—"

"No!" Audrey's horrified response blurted from her and she raised her hands. "Not in a million years!"

Reese chuckled, approaching Cade, and gave him a man-hug that involved a half handshake and a slap on the back. "Good to see you, bro. I was here for the weekend with a . . . friend when these two showed up and my friend retreated, along with my ride back to civilization."

"And he was just about to call a cab," Audrey interjected.

"No, I wasn't," Reese said easily. "I'm staying for the weekend, if you don't have a problem with that."

Please, please have a problem with that, Audrey thought quietly.

But Cade, ever the gentleman, looked thrilled that Reese was there. "You know I don't have a problem with it. I told you that any time you wanted, the cabin was yours to use. And we'll be glad for the company. Isn't that right, Audrey?" Cade looked over at her.

"I thought so," Reese said, giving her an I-told-you-so look from Cade's side.

She was trapped. Hell. Audrey forced her tight, professional smile on her face. "As long as you're okay with someone taking up one of the rooms, I don't have a problem with it."

"Not to worry," Reese said, elbowing Cade as if they were frat brothers. "Audrey told me she wouldn't mind cuddling with me if things got too tight in Daphne's room."

Audrey gave a shocked gasp. "I did not!"

Cade laughed and slapped Reese on the back. "Count on you to romance all the women within minutes of making an entrance."

"He's not romancing me," Audrey pointed out, trying to keep smiling. "And he's joking. About all of it."

Cade just chuckled, and then rubbed his face. He gestured outside. "I parked behind you, if that's all right."

"That's perfect," Audrey said, then blushed at how infatuated she sounded. "Perfectly fine," she amended in a brisk voice.

He grinned. "I'll just go get my bags, then."

As he disappeared back out the front, Audrey followed to the doorstep, watching him move as he jaunted down the steps of the lodge and out to his car. He drove a Lyons, too, but she wasn't surprised to see that it was a dark blue sedan. That was more like Cade. Practical and elegant.

"Well, well, well." Reese's voice thrummed in her ear. "Just look at you."

She turned and scowled at him. "What?"

"You're glowing." His grin cut across his entire face.

"You're positively beaming now that Cade's here. You're lit up like a firecracker."

The flush on her cheeks threatened to grow hotter. "I'm just thrilled to see an old friend."

"Don't think I didn't notice how you weren't exactly quick to let go of him," Reese said. "And I'm pretty sure I saw you sniff his jacket."

"I did not."

"Yeah, you did." He rubbed that scruffy goatee on his chin thoughtfully. "Does Cade know that you're in love with him?"

Her irritation turned to panic. "What are you talking about?"

He made a silly, high-pitched giggle that sounded shamefully like the one she'd burbled just moments ago. "You're perfect, Cade," he mimicked.

She smacked his arm. "You're a horrible man. I wish you'd go drown in the lake."

He waggled his eyebrows. "I see someone's in a rush to try out her CPR skills. Baby, if you want to give me mouth to mouth, all you have to do is ask—"

"Please, shut up!"

"No can do. As Cade's best buddy, it's my duty to let him in on any secrets I might think he'd have interest in. And do you think he'd be curious to know that the good, sweet little twin is in love with her childhood buddy?"

She gasped, mortified to hear that out in the open. "It's not like that!"

"Too far back? Since your teen years, then?"

"No! You've got it all wrong."

"Do I?" He gave a lazy shrug of his big shoulders in

that too-tight shirt. "I guess we could always run the idea past Cade and see what he thinks."

She clenched her fists. He was turning her reunion with Cade—her first chance to spend some real, quality time with him in years—into nothing short of a nightmare. How weird would it be around Cade if he knew that she was secretly in love with him? How would he act toward her?

She suspected he would be kind and understanding . . . because Cade always was. He'd try to let her down easy, and it would break her heart. "Please," she gritted. "Please don't say anything at all."

He rubbed that scruffy goatee again. "I might be persuaded to keep my silence."

Audrey gasped. "Blackmail?"

"Now that you mention it, blackmail does sound pretty interesting." He grinned, white teeth flashing in his face. "What do you say me and you rendezvous later tonight for a moonlight kiss?"

"You know I don't want to kiss you! You're the last man on earth I'd want to kiss right about now."

"I know," he replied, his voice smug. "That's why I suggested it. It'd be more fun to tell Cade all about your secret. Maybe I could pass him a note like we did in grade school. 'Audrey's in love with you. Do you love her? Check yes or no.'"

She glanced at the doorway and noticed Cade was starting to head up the steps. Panic overtook her. "No notes. Don't tell him anything. Please!"

"Rendezvous then? Tonight?"

She had about two seconds to decide. Her mind whirled frantically for a moment, and then she turned and smacked Reese on the shoulder. "I hate you so much."

"So that's a yes?"

"It's a yes," she whispered, practically exploding it at him. "Now just shut up! Please!"

He winked at her and made a zipping motion over his mouth, just as the door opened again.

"Here, let me help you with that," Audrey said to Cade, rushing forward to take a few of the bags from his hands. He had an overnight bag slung over one shoulder and multiple plastic grocery bags piled onto each arm. "It looks like you stopped at the grocery store."

"I did. Wanted to make sure things were as easy for you and Daph as possible."

"You're so thoughtful," she said softly to him, taking a few of the bags.

"You're a real prince charming," Reese teased, but grinned and made the zipping motion again when Audrey glared at him.

He'd keep the secret, all right. He'd just needle the hell out of her with the information since he had it. God, she hated the man.

"I cleared my schedule," Cade was saying as he headed into the kitchen with the rest of the bags. "So as long as you and Daph need me, I'll be here for you."

Thankful tears burned her eyes. Getting Daphne clean would be hard enough on her own, but with Cade here, she had her best friend and support system right at hand. She couldn't have asked for better. "It's so good that you're here, Cade. I'm so glad to see you." And then she added, "I'm sure Daphne will be thrilled, too."

Cade gave her a gentle smile, ruffling her tight bun. "You know I'll always be there for you in your hour of need, Audrey."

His words were like sweet music to her ears. It was just a shame that he'd tried to ruffle her hair like when she was a kid. She ignored that part, focusing on the delicious words instead, and her heart melted just a bit more.

Things would be wonderful now that Cade was here.

So far, this weekend was turning into a huge bust.

Reese tugged at the too-tight sleeves of his borrowed T-shirt and sat on the end of the couch, watching as Audrey—snarling, angry Audrey with the tight bun and even tighter mouth—fluttered over Cade and giggled at everything he said.

It would have been downright amusing if it hadn't hurt his ego, just a touch.

Reese was the playboy of their club, after all. The others joked that if they needed a woman seduced, all they had to do was send her to Reese, and she'd be melting as soon as he smiled. His charm had gotten him into many a sealed boardroom . . . and plenty of beds. He'd been planning on using that infamous charm on Camilla Sellers, heiress to Sellers Hotels and daughter of the man Reese was currently going back and forth with in regards to an investment opportunity for a series of cruise lines. Reese wanted to expand his empire, and Sellers was looking more and more like the way to go. The fact that his daughter was twenty-five, gorgeous, and clearly interested in Reese was just a bonus. She didn't sit on the board . . . yet. But she definitely had her father's ear, and while Reese romanced her, she could be talking him up to her father, convincing him that a partnership with Durham Industries was the way to go.

Cade might think it was underhanded, but Cade had already made his fortune. Reese, as always, was still trying to catch up to the others in regards to funds. He'd relied on his easy charm for years, back when charm made up for the fact that his wallet was empty.

This weekend had been planned with dual purposes in mind. He'd wanted to get away and spend some time with Camilla, to get to know her better and to feel her out on how her father's business was leaning in regards to the cruise lines. And he'd been getting to know her quite well in the hot tub, edging into conversation about hotels and cruise lines . . . until sour Audrey had showed up and kicked up a fuss.

He could have cheerfully strangled her in that moment.

To make matters worse, Camilla had ran as soon as Audrey had pulled out the camera phone, ruining his plans. It was going to be impossible to romance Camilla into opening up about Sellers Hotels, especially when she was clearly terrified of her father finding out about their flirtation. Audrey's bullheaded charging into his seductive getaway had ruined more than just his weekend plans. He'd have to start over with Camilla, break down her defenses gently, and then lay the foundation for suggestion later.

But he hadn't showed any of his outward irritation at Audrey, because he'd gotten quite good at hiding that sort of thing years ago. Women—all women—responded best to a flirty laugh and a teasing voice.

All women, except this one. For some reason, the more he'd teased, the more annoyed and flustered she'd gotten. Which had made his bruised ego feel better, so he'd continued to tease and prod at her with his words, enjoying her reactions. She was as tense and rigid as that tight little bun that sat atop her head.

Until Cade had arrived. And then her tense frowns had turned into smiles; her narrowed eyes had changed and she'd begun to bat her lashes. And she'd blushed prettily when Cade had hugged her, and she'd even sniffed his jacket.

It was obvious to anyone that she had a crush on the man. And just as obvious when she'd turned and glared at him that she hated Reese.

It was fascinating to him. Normally he could charm the pants off any woman he put his mind to. And since she'd ruined his weekend, well, he'd go ahead and ruin hers. He could use a good diversion, and driving rigid little Audrey up the wall would do just fine.

She wasn't his type, after all. Though her hair was an interesting color, the tight set of her mouth and paleness of her skin were very different from the tanned, golden beauties he was used to dating. So was her figure. He normally dated women who were extremely conscious of every bite they put into their mouths. Audrey clearly was not. Where her twin was nearly skeletal from her drug use, Audrey's figure was lush and curvy. He'd thought her simply boxy and a bit frumpy in her loose-fitting clothing, until he'd gotten her wet and her sweater had stuck to her body. Before she'd pulled the fabric away from her chest, he'd caught a glimpse of large, rounded breasts above the hollow of her stomach, and he'd realized that her clothing was masking a very attractive figure.

His interest had grown exponentially.

Of course, her constant simpering over Cade was irritating. It was that reaction—so different to the one she'd given him—that had caused him to suggest their little deal. At first he'd mentioned it simply to get under her skin. But the more flustered she'd become, the more he'd wanted to hold her to it.

After all, she was now responsible for his weekend entertainment, since she'd chased his away.

Unless Cade was interested in her, too. If that was the case, he'd back off and let his buddy have the curvy little minx. He regarded the two of them putting away the groceries. It was a cozy scene; they laughed and chatted as they packed away cans and boxes of food. And he watched Cade's reactions to Audrey. They were pleasant, and his smile was easy and friendly. Whereas Audrey seemed to punctuate every sentence with a bright red flush that made the faint freckles on her cheeks stand out.

He was pretty sure there was interest, but it seemed to be only one-sided. Still, he decided to test the waters. He headed into the kitchen and hopped up on the counter, letting his legs dangle over the side. It was, coincidentally, the counter above the spot where Audrey had been putting away groceries. For her to continue to do so, she'd have to reach between his legs.

Audrey gave him a cross look. "Move."

"You have to ask nicely," he told her.

Irritation flared on her face again, just before she tamped it down into her serene, professional expression that would have fooled anyone who didn't notice the rigid set of her mouth. She looked over at Cade. "Your friend is determined to get under my skin this weekend."

Cade chuckled, shaking his head. "Reese is a flirt, Audrey. Pay him no mind." He shot Reese an amused look and handed Audrey a canister of oatmeal.

That wasn't the look of a man concerned about his woman. Whatever Cade felt for Audrey, it didn't extend past friendship, which meant she was fair game for his teasing.

Reese crossed his arms over his chest, grinning at Audrey. "Play your cards right and I can get under a lot of things."

Her color flared again, and her mouth went even tighter. She shoved the canister of oatmeal at his chest. "You know what? You can put this away. I'm going to go check on Daphne."

As she stomped away, Reese clutched the oatmeal to his chest and chuckled.

Cade simply shook his head. "You definitely bring out raw emotion in people. I don't think I've ever seen Audrey so flustered."

"It's probably the combination of the two of us," Reese told him, bending over and tossing the oatmeal under the counter like he was throwing a football. From the sound of things, it knocked a few other items over, which was fine with him. More to aggravate Ms. Uptight when she returned.

Cade gave him a puzzled look. "The two of us? What do you mean?"

"Nothing," Reese said blandly. If Cade didn't have a clue that Audrey had a crush on him, he'd keep it that way. The last thing Cade needed was more stress. He'd seemed a bit tense lately, which wasn't like him. "How you hanging in there?"

"Good. Work's been busy but numbers are good. I'm scheduled to go to Africa in a month to oversee a few of the clinics we've set up with Doctors Without Borders and determine the needs of the communities. I don't have to go, but I want to . . . as long as things are good here." Again, that line of tension crossed his face, and he set down a box of cereal, then gave Reese a dark look. "How is she?"

"Audrey? You saw her."

"No. Daphne."

Aha. So the white knight had arrived to the rescue of a very different twin. Suddenly, a few things locked into place. It explained why, despite Cade's busy schedule, he was here hanging out with a pair of childhood friends.

He was in love with a twin, all right, but it was the wrong one. For some reason, somewhere along the way, Cade Archer—good-hearted, generous, white knight Cade Archer—had fallen for the messed-up, drug-using, infamous twin.

He didn't know who he felt sorrier for—Cade, for his choice in women, or Audrey, who clearly had a crush on a man who wouldn't notice she was there except in a friendship capacity.

"She's a fucking mess," Reese said bluntly, and hated the way that Cade's brows furrowed even deeper. "That girl needs a year of rehab, not a vacation in the woods."

"Daphne's stubborn," Cade told him with a tense look. "Audrey's tried to get her into rehab before, but she just runs away. Her label's not much help, either. I think someone there keeps supplying her with the drugs. I imagine a constantly available stream of her favorite addictions keeps her under their control more than threats of a contract breach does." He didn't look very pleased at the thought.

"She's famous," Reese told him. "She runs with all kinds of crowds. She can probably get drugs anywhere and everywhere."

"That's why I'm here," Cade told him, and rubbed a hand on his nape, as if weary. "Audrey had mentioned concerns, but I didn't realize. Thought the tabloids were just full of their usual bullshit. Then when I saw her at the party, I realized that they were all true. And I couldn't leave her like that. So when she reached out to me, I suggested she come here. Maybe if . . ." He paused, then gave Reese a tense look, daring him to contradict him. "Maybe if I'm here, it'll make a difference."

"Maybe," Reese said. He wasn't sure. The girl seemed

pretty messed up to him. But if Cade wanted to ride to the rescue, he wouldn't be able to dissuade him. "You just let me know if you need help with things."

"I will. Sorry your weekend was ruined. Sounds like Audrey has some impeccable timing."

Reese grinned. "Camilla will get over it. In the meantime, I plan on making Audrey regret that she interrupted my rendezvous."

"Don't do anything I wouldn't do."

Reese snorted. "Buddy, everything I do is something you wouldn't do."

"She's a friend," Cade cautioned, ever serious. "A childhood friend. Don't hurt her. Despite her bluster, Audrey's got a really good heart and she's sensitive."

The woman was about as sensitive as a bull in a china shop, but he didn't disagree with Cade openly. "I just plan on teasing her a bit, man. She's safe with me." *Safe enough, anyhow.*

He didn't mention their little blackmail-directed rendezvous scheduled for later that night. While he still considered that teasing, he wasn't sure that Cade would.

"Good," Cade said with a grin. "I'm glad you're here. It'll give us a chance to hang out, and I'm guessing we'll need another set of hands around, if Daphne ends up being half the handful I think she'll be."

Reese was pretty sure that Daphne would be more than just a handful, but he said nothing to Cade. No sense in starting an argument. "It'll be interesting."

He just wondered what good ol' Audrey would think when he didn't leave immediately. Maybe he'd stick around for longer than the weekend, just to crawl under that woman's skin. He had to admit that the idea had appeal, and his work was covered thanks to a few rather aggressive hires to handle the day-to-day aspects of Durham Industries.

Which left him plenty of time to torment Audrey Petty.

She'd fall under his spell eventually. Reese Durham always won over the women he had his eye on. And until she did, she was going to be mighty fun to play with.

He always did enjoy the chase a bit more than anything.

FOUR

Audrey set four places at the wooden table, laying down the plates and ignoring the large man who hovered nearby, supervising.

"You're so incredibly domestic, Audrey. First dinner and now the table?" Reese tsked and shook his head, pretending to be impressed. "You're going to make Cade a lucky man."

She glared at him, clenching the last plate in her hand as if she wanted to strike him with it. "Will you shut up, already?" Audrey glanced around the room, making sure that Cade was nowhere to be seen. "He'll hear you."

"Sorry," he said in a tone that indicated that he wasn't sorry at all. "I thought I'd help you set the table."

"You're clearly being such a help," she said in a nasty tone. "What with your standing around and being in the way."

He chuckled. "What can I do to help you, then?"

Go away. Go away and never come back. "Go tell the others that dinner's ready."

"That, I can do." Reese strolled out of the small kitchen, whistling, and Audrey gritted her teeth again. At least he'd listened to her for once.

It had only been a few hours and he was already driving her crazy. The man seemed determined to make her lose her temper. Not only was he constantly hovering around and making cracks, but he seemed to delight in doing nothing more than heckling her.

She wished that Cade had stuck around, but once he'd unpacked, he'd taken a walk around the lake. He'd asked Audrey to go with him, but she'd declined, wanting to stay close to the cabin in case Daphne needed her. She'd suggested that Reese go instead, but he claimed to be tired and laid down on one of the couches in the living room.

Of course, no sooner had Cade disappeared than Reese had been back up again, bothering her and asking her questions. How long had she been in love with Cade? Had she ever told him about it? Had she ever seen him naked? Did she get jealous when he dated other women? Did she date other men?

She'd ignored his questions and gone into the small kitchen, determined to make dinner. It was something to keep her busy. The only problem was, she wasn't much of a cook. When they were younger, her older sister Gretchen had always cooked for the family, and she was wonderful at it. Living in New York City, Audrey had never needed culinary skills, not when there was a restaurant on every corner. But the groceries that Cade had brought seemed to be healthy, wholesome foods, and she guessed that someone would have to cook for them.

And given that the men had disappeared from the kitchen, she supposed that fell to her.

There'd been a recipe for meatloaf on the back of one of the packages of meat, and so she'd decided to make that for them. It didn't look so hard. They were missing a few of the spices, but she figured that she'd just add some extra salt and pepper. When she pulled it out of the small oven, it looked good and smelled even better. Pleased, Audrey set the pan down on the table and returned to the kitchen to make a small tossed salad to accompany it.

It wasn't high-class cuisine, but it was a nice-looking dinner. She wanted things to be comfortable for her twin while she was struggling to get clean, and a wholesome dinner with friends would be a great start. If she could keep Daphne distracted and relatively content, this could work. And with Cade at her side, between the two of them, they could keep on Daphne at all times.

This was going to work, Audrey decided.

While the food was cooling, Reese and Cade returned and washed up and sat down at the table. A moment later, Daphne descended down the stairs, each step shaky and weak.

Audrey's heart sank. It had been less than a full day and her twin looked like hell. Dark circles lined Daphne's eyes and her entire body shook with small tremors. Her steps were small and shuffling, and she seemed thinner than ever.

Audrey went to Daphne's side, wrapping an arm around her. "How are you feeling?"

Daphne brushed off her arm irritably. "Don't touch me. Hurts."

Immediately, Audrey released her, feeling contrite. "I'm sorry. What can I get you?"

"Glass of water," Daphne said, and licked her lips. Audrey noticed that they were dry and cracked, as if she'd gone weeks in the sun. Was detoxing supposed to be this hard on her twin? Audrey had never done drugs, so she didn't know, but she was concerned.

"I'll get it for you," she told her. "Go sit down at the table."

"Not hungry."

"Well, sit down with the others at least. I'm sure Cade will be happy to see you," Audrey said, keeping her tone bright and cheerful. "Go say hello to him."

Cade got up from the table and approached Daphne, extending his hands to her. "Hey, beautiful."

Daphne managed a tiny smile and put her trembling hands in his. "You're such a tease," she told him. "I look like shit."

"You're too hard on yourself," Cade told her quietly. "You're going through a hard time." He took her hand and gently guided her toward the table, then pulled a chair out for her.

Audrey smiled at the sight. Having Cade here was wonderful. He always knew what to say to her twin to make her behave, to make her respond, and he always treated her like a lady, even when Daphne was at her lowest. "I made meatloaf and salad, Daphne," she said, setting the glass of water down in front of her. "Do you want to try it?"

"You should," Cade said softly. "Your sister worked hard on it."

Daphne shrugged her thin shoulders. "I'll try and eat." She glanced over at Reese, who sat on the opposite end of the table. "Hey. You're the guy from the hot tub, right? You're still here?"

"I am," Reese said pleasantly, glancing at Audrey.

"Your sister offered to give me a ride back to town but I was enjoying her company so much that I thought I'd stick around."

Audrey snorted. She wished it was that easy to get rid of him. She finished dishing a small serving onto Daphne's plate and then took Reese's plate and began to slop a large amount on there. The meatloaf seemed a bit . . . pink in the middle, but she figured if you could have a steak rare, you could have meatloaf rare, too.

When he raised an eyebrow at the amount she piled on his plate, she gave him a saccharine smile and thumped it down in front of him. "I figured you probably have a caveman-like appetite to go with that caveman personality of yours."

"Is that a hint for me to drag you off into my cave?" He waggled his eyebrows at her.

She shot him a withering look. "Not in the slightest—"

"Well," Cade said, interrupting. "I'm starved and it smells great, Audrey. Thank you so much for fixing dinner."

"She'll make someone a terrific wife someday, won't she?" Reese said casually.

Audrey froze, then turned to glare at him.

He gave her a wicked smile, unfurling his napkin and placing it on his lap.

"That she will," Cade said, missing the tension between the two of them. He glanced at Daphne fondly, then smiled at Audrey when she set a plate of food down in front of him.

"Eat, everyone," Audrey told them, serving up her own plate and then sitting down. "You don't want it to get cold." Her gaze slid over to Daphne. Her twin had a fork in hand but she had yet to take a bite. Instead, she was poking at the food with the fork tines, dismantling it and shoving it around her plate. Wasn't she hungry? She hadn't eaten earlier, either. She cast a concerned look at Cade, who shook his head, indicating that she should leave Daphne alone.

A choked sound came from Reese, and Audrey looked over just in time to see him spit a mouthful into his napkin. His eyes began to stream as he coughed.

Her eyes widened. "Did you swallow wrong?"

"Yeah. I tried to swallow. That was the problem."

"Spitters are quitters," Daphne said from the far end of the table, her voice low and tired.

Audrey looked over at Cade, who had a pained expression on his face. As she watched, he reached for his water glass and politely coughed into his hand.

A hint of a smile touched Daphne's mouth. "You guys shouldn't have let Audrey cook. She kind of sucks at it." She pushed the meatloaf around on her plate a bit longer. "Glad I'm not hungry."

It couldn't be that bad. Casting another angry look at Reese for joking around when her twin clearly needed to eat, Audrey took a tiny bite of the meatloaf. Wet, half-raw hamburger meat and onion touched her tongue. The salty, greasy taste was overwhelming. With a gagging noise of her own, Audrey quietly followed Reese's lead and spit into her napkin. "I must have missed something on the recipe."

"Like the instructions?" Reese told her.

She tossed her napkin down on her plate. "I didn't see you volunteering to do anything in the kitchen, did I?"

"Is that a challenge?" he told her. "Because I'm up for it. You want to make a bet on who can make a better dinner?"

"I'm not betting anything with you, idiot," she bit off, and then glanced over at Cade and Daphne, mortified at her outburst. "Sorry," she said, bringing her voice back down to a modulated, calm tone. "I'm just a bit frustrated."

"So you don't think I'm an idiot?" Reese teased at her side.

"I didn't say that," she said tightly.

Daphne sighed heavily and drank her water.

Cade pushed his plate aside and focused on his salad. "Well, the effort was appreciated nevertheless, Audrey. I appreciate you. Maybe it'll taste better as leftovers."

She beamed at him, feeling warm at his praise.

"Fuck leftovers," Reese said. "Mine's going in the garbage. The maggots can have it."

Immediately, Daphne plunked her water glass down. Her face turned green and she bolted from the table.

Audrey cast a withering look at Reese as she got to her feet. "Can't you watch your mouth for five minutes? Look what you've done."

"I don't know," Reese said blandly. "I kind of think she did it to herself."

Tamping down her outrage, Audrey followed Daphne through the lodge. She found Daphne huddled on the floor in the bathroom, her face in the toilet as she vomited. Audrey sat down on the bathtub rim and pulled her twin's stringy, dyed hair out of the way, rubbing her back as she threw up.

When nothing else seemed to be coming up, Daphne rested her cheek on the side of the toilet and gave a weak sigh. "I hate this."

"I'm sorry," Audrey said. "I wish I could help."

"You can. Go to town and score me something. Just a little something to keep me going."

"No, Daph—"

"Not much," Daphne said, her voice desperate. "Just enough to take the worst of the edge off. It'll help me cut free if I don't feel quite so shitty."

"I can't. Even if I knew where to get drugs, I wouldn't get it for you." She shook her head. "I won't do that to you."

Daphne turned and gave her a vicious shove, knocking Audrey into the tub. "It's your fucking fault," she snarled. "I had enough drugs for this month and you fucking flushed them. You trying to kill me? I can't go cold turkey." She began to sob, laying her cheek back down on the side of the toilet as dry heaves began to take over her again. "I need my pills. I can't do this."

"It hasn't even been a day yet, Daphne." Audrey struggled upright and sat on the edge of the tub, then began to stroke Daphne's back again. "Be strong."

"If I was strong I wouldn't be here," Daphne sobbed. "Take me back to the city. Please. I've changed my mind."

Hurt and despair welled up inside of Audrey. Daphne was giving up already? It hadn't even been a full twenty-four hours and Daphne was determined to give up. This was just like every other time Daphne had tried to get clean. She'd talk a good game and then when things got difficult, she'd cave in. "If I take you back to the city, you'll end up just like you were before," Audrey whispered, her heart aching as she continued to stroke her twin's back. Daphne was so thin she could feel every bump of her spine, and it made her want to weep with frustration.

If this didn't work, her twin would die. It was only a matter of time before Daphne showed up on the cover of a tabloid with the headline "OVERDOSED."

"I hate you," Daphne cried. "I can't do this."

A shadow fell on the doorway, and Audrey looked up

to see Cade standing there, a stricken look on his face. "Is she all right?"

"She's fine," Audrey began, only to be interrupted by Daphne's retching cough, and then more dry heaves.

Cade knelt beside Daphne and brushed his fingers over her sunken cheek. "You okay, Daph? What do you need?"

"Need my pills," she sobbed, making small whimpering noises in her throat. "Something. Anything. I hurt so bad."

"What were you taking before you came here?" Cade asked her.

"Everything," she wept.

Audrey felt sick to her stomach. What kind of trouble was her twin in?

"What did you need to have, though? Which ones could you not live without?"

"Coke," Daphne sobbed, and wiped her running nose with the back of one hand. "And my pills."

"What were your pills?"

"Xanax. I need them," she said in a trembling voice. "They keep me calm."

To Audrey's horror, Cade produced a prescription pill bottle and held it out. As she watched, Daphne's hands formed small claws and she reached for the drugs, only to have Cade hold them out of reach again. "Just one, Daphne."

"Just one," Daphne agreed, breathing heavily. She held her hands out, and Audrey was horrified to see how much they were shaking.

"Cade, no—" Audrey began, but he shook his head at her. She pursed her lips and sat in silence as Cade carefully fished one pill out and handed it to Daphne, who gobbled it down like it was candy. Then, she lay her cheek back down on the side of the toilet and sighed, closing her eyes.

Audrey was not so happy, though. "Can I talk to you, Cade?"

They left the bathroom and walked away a few feet, and Audrey had to clench her fists at her sides to keep from shaking him. "What are you doing, Cade? We brought her here to get clean!"

"I had a talk with her manager," Cade said in a low, easy voice. "She's been taking a lot of Xanax over the last year or two, and it's dangerous to stop her cold turkey. Her manager keeps a supply at hand, and I talked with a few of my doctors about the side effects. They feel that weaning her off slowly is safer than stopping outright." When Audrey continued to frown at him, he added, "I've also flown in my personal physician to stay at a nearby cabin in case we have any emergencies. I want what's best for her, too, Audrey. You know I do." He reached out and rubbed her shoulder. "Trust me."

That hand caressing her through her sweater was so comforting. "I do trust you, Cade. I'm just . . . really concerned about her. It's so hard to see." A sudden rush of tears flooded to the surface, and she pressed her palms to her eyes. "I'm just so worried."

"I know it is," he said softly. "But I'm here to help." He glanced at something behind her and nodded. "Why don't you go take a walk with Reese? Get some fresh air?"

She glanced behind her and, sure enough, Reese was hovering nearby. The ever-present smirk was gone from his face. He looked somber. She didn't want to go anywhere with Reese, though. She needed to stay right here, especially when Cade was touching her. She wanted to throw herself in his arms for a hug, but she forced herself to stay right where she was. "I can't leave. My sister . . . Daphne . . ."

"I'll take care of her," Cade said. "Go on. You look rattled."

"Yeah. Come on, Audrey." She felt Reese's arm settle at her waist. "We'll go for a walk around the lake and you can give me that kiss you promised."

Horrified, she stared up at Cade and twisted out of Reese's grip. "I did not promise him that!"

Cade only chuckled. "You two have fun."

"We will," Reese said with a smirk. "And she did promise me that. Or don't you remember, Audrey? I seem to recall a conversation we had—"

She clapped a hand over his mouth. "*Shut up!*"

Something warm and wet stroked over her palm—Reese was licking her hand. A bolt of sensation shot through her body, and Audrey jerked her hand away, dazed.

That had felt . . . good. A little too good. Her eyes narrowed and she waited for Reese to say something now that she'd retracted her hand, but he only smiled down at her.

"You have your phone on you? I can call you if something comes up," Cade said easily, ignoring her reaction to Reese.

"Mine's in the hot tub," she said, lowering her hand and glaring at Reese. "Someone threw it there earlier."

"Do I want to know what you two were doing in the hot tub?" Cade asked.

"Nothing!" Audrey retorted.

"I don't have my phone, either," Reese said. "It left with my date. Don't worry, though. We'll be fine." He looped an arm around Audrey's shoulders and grinned. "I'll take good care of her."

Reese was pretty sure that this weekend was a recipe for disaster. He could just see it now. Mix one junkie pop star with a do-gooder billionaire who's hiding a secret crush on her. Add in the lonely twin sister crushing on the billionaire, and make all three parties completely unaware of one another's interests. Stir with that giant stick up Audrey's ass. Watch fireworks explode.

At any other time, he'd find the combination utterly amusing. Hell, Cade was a big boy. His buddy could take care of himself. And he figured that if Daphne was old enough to get hooked on all the drugs that the tabloids said she was on, she was responsible for her own fate. He didn't have much sympathy there.

But the factor that was bugging him in this was Audrey, and he wasn't quite sure why.

Maybe it was the fact that she got so flustered when he flirted with her. Maybe it was the way she carried herself, so incredibly stiff and rigid that sometimes he wondered if she even knew how to relax. Maybe it was the way her full mouth thinned out at the sight of him, and it only encouraged him to be even naughtier.

Hell, it was probably all of that.

But sympathy for the little ice queen who was bound to get her heart broken in multiple ways? That one had been harder to explain to himself. He told himself that he liked a challenge, that he was simply bored and looking for a diversion, and her prickliness was definitely a diversion. But when she looked up at Cade with those wide, shining eyes and that soft smile? Like he was Sir Galahad reborn and had arrived to save the day?

Reese had to admit, he got a little jealous. Not of Cade, of course. Cade was oblivious to Audrey's devotion, seeing it only as the affection of a friend, or worse, a little sister. It was the way she gazed up at him as if he were her hero. As if, now that Cade was there, everything in her world would be all right. Like everything was good again, simply because he'd arrived.

And Reese had realized that no one ever looked at him like that.

Which was not to say that he didn't get female attention—the opposite, really. Women had ceased to be a challenge long ago. Throw a little flirtation their way, laugh at their jokes, flatter them, pay attention to them, and he'd have a woman eating out of the palm of his hand within hours.

It was no challenge whatsoever. And once they found out he had money? It just became even easier. He was good looking and knew how to charm. Women often looked at him as if they wanted to devour him whole, or test out how he was in bed.

No one ever looked at him like Audrey looked at Cade. Like he was a motherfucking hero.

And for some reason that bothered Reese and challenged him all at once. Audrey cast him withering glare after withering glare, but because Cade helped her put away groceries and rubbed Daphne's back while she barfed, he was worthy of adoration and blind devotion?

The competitive side of Reese made him want to see if he could get Audrey to look at him the same way. And it had been that competitive side that had made him speak up and insist on the kiss she'd promised him.

Audrey had turned bright red of course, the freckles

standing out on her skin. And she'd huffed and blustered, but had been quick to escape once Cade turned his questioning gaze on her. Yeah, she didn't want to explain that one to Prince Charming, did she?

Oddly enough, it made him feel protective of stiff little Audrey. Perhaps she had a naughty side after all, and was doing her best to hide it from Cade. *Not to worry*, Reese thought to himself. *If there's a wicked side to you, I'm just the man to find it.*

Even her steps down the dirt path to the lake were jerky and irritated, he noticed with amusement. She walked a few paces ahead of him, arms crossed over her chest, back ramrod straight. It was cute, much like the way a pissed-off rabbit would be cute. Fluffy and harmless.

He let her continue on for a few minutes, and when they got to the dock at the edge of the lake, she turned to glare at him, shivering a little. She hadn't worn a jacket and it was bitterly cold outside with the night wind. "Is this enough of a walk for you? Or should we go back to the house and see if you can humiliate me again?"

"Here." Reese shrugged off the jacket he'd borrowed from Cade's closet and offered it to her.

She took it, giving him a wary look. "You're not cold?"

"Nah." He watched her as she shrugged it over her shoulders, holding it tight to her body. "It's a little small for me."

"All of Cade's clothing is a little small for you," she told him, her gaze straying to the too-tight fitness club T-shirt he wore.

"Yeah. These jeans are seriously crushing my balls. I'm gonna be gelded before the weekend's over."

She got that weird look on her face that told him she was probably blushing in the moonlight, though it was too dark to tell. "Well, maybe you being gelded wouldn't be such a bad thing," she told him in that prim little voice, "considering your reputation."

"I'd be depriving the world of greatness if that happened," he drawled, enjoying when her posture got just a little stiffer.

"You have a very high opinion of yourself."

"Someone should."

"Yes, I suppose someone should," she said, and gave a haughty little sniff.

Time to wipe that smugness from her face. "So, you ready to give me my kiss now?"

Even in the shadows, he couldn't miss the withering glance she shot at him. "Do you know how much I hate you right now?"

"Don't know, don't much care, but I'm sure you'll tell me."

She was mutinously silent.

"It won't be that bad," he teased her, crossing his arms over his chest and leaning up against a nearby pier beam. "I'm told I'm quite a good kisser."

"You do have quite the ego," she muttered. "Did it ever occur to you that I don't want to kiss you? That I'm not bowled over by your so-called charm?"

"Is it because you think you won't be any good at it? Performance anxiety?"

She sputtered.

"That's it, isn't it? I can give you lessons, you know. So you're good and ready by the time Cade pulls his head out of his ass."

Audrey's gritted teeth flashed in the moonlight. "I despise you."

"So, lessons?"

"Not in your wildest dreams," she bit out. "That wasn't part of our negotiation. Our agreement was one kiss in exchange for your silence."

He rubbed his chin as if pretending to consider this. "I'm pretty sure we didn't give specifics."

"We should have!"

Reese gestured at her. "Let's set the groundwork, then. You tell me what you thought our kiss should entail and I'll tell you what I thought, and we can meet in the middle."

The look she gave him was wary, but hopeful, and she clutched the borrowed jacket tighter to her shoulders. "That sounds reasonable."

"I'm a reasonable man."

She snorted with disbelief, and he had to grin at that. Perhaps that stick wasn't crammed so far up her ass after all.

"A kiss on the cheek," she offered.

"Get real," he told her. "We both know that wasn't the bargain. I'm talking an honest-to-goodness kiss."

"You didn't specify where. I should get to choose where I'd want to put it, and I'm saying there."

"Well, since we're picking body parts out of the air, I'll say that I want the kiss on the head of my cock." At her outraged gasp, he continued blandly, "So I guess we can meet in the middle and settle on the mouth."

"You're despicable."

"Yeah, yeah. You're the one who started the bidding low, sweetheart. I had to go high to counter it."

"I'm not your sweetheart! Fine. On the mouth. But no tongue!"

"Oh, there'll be tongue," he told her. "But if it'll make you feel better, I'll lead."

"You'll lead?" There it was again, that weird, half-startled, half-mortified look on her face that told him she was probably blushing again. "What do you mean by that?"

"I mean my tongue can do all the work. You can just let me be in charge of any tongue action."

She shook her head again. "I'm pretty sure I didn't agree to tongue."

"It's not a kiss if there's no tongue."

"Gee, you sure didn't seem to be thinking that when you suggested I plant a kiss on your dick!"

He laughed, surprised and amused by her retort. He liked her, stiff shoulders and all. "Now now, how do you know I wasn't referring to tongue?"

She made a choked sound of fury.

"Don't distract me from our bargain," he teased. "Let's keep things on track here. How long?"

"How long, what?"

"How long should the kiss be?"

"I don't have a timer!"

"Should you get one?" He gestured at the cabin up the hill. "I can go back to the house and tell Cade that we need one to make sure we get the kiss right—"

Her hands went to his chest, stopping him as he pretended to get up. "You're not going anywhere."

A smile tugged at his mouth. "Whatever you say."

"I sincerely wish that were the case," she told him pertly.

He laughed again. "So we agree to three minutes on the kiss?"

"Three seems like a long time." She gave him a skeptical look. "I vote one."

"Three."

"We're settling on two, then." When he didn't challenge that, she added, "What about hands?"

He raised an eyebrow at her. "You want to start the bidding on that one?"

"No thank you. I learned my lesson with the lips bargaining." She put her hands on her hips, challenging him. "I just wanted to know where hands factored into this equation."

Reese grinned. *Quick learner.* "I suppose we can leave hands off the table for now. Unless you object."

"Hardly." She contemplated for a moment, and then gave him a narrow-eyed look. "Did we leave anything out?"

"You tell me." He was enjoying this far, far too much.

"I feel like if I miss something, you're going to use it against me."

He laughed. "Double entendre?"

"See, there you go again."

"Hey, I'm ready whenever you are." He gestured expansively. "Just waiting for you to get a move on."

"Me?" She sputtered again. "Why do I have to make the first move?"

"Because you lost the bet. Those were the rules." He crossed his arms over his chest. "Now quit stalling."

"I'm not stalling!" Her shoulders rose in a huff.

"Aren't you? Because I can go back inside if you want to call this whole thing off. It's clear to me you have no intention of going through—"

His words cut off because she surged forward and put her hands on his cheeks, pulling his mouth in against hers. Her lips brushed his, and then he felt the barest flicker of tongue against his mouth.

And holy fuck, that was hot.

Reese had been so surprised at her impulsive move that he hadn't had time to anticipate the feel of her mouth against his. He was surprised by the utter softness of her lips, the sweet, delicious give to her mouth as it parted against his own. Her hands were cold against his cheeks, which made the warmth of her lips even more of a contrast. And those impressive breasts were pressing up against his chest, right where his arms were crossed.

He'd been so startled that he hadn't been able to respond at first, and she took his lack of response as some sort of challenge, he guessed, because she gently sucked on his lower lip, coaxing his mouth open. "Lips," she reminded him in a whisper.

He parted for her, and her tongue slipped into his mouth, dancing against his own. Delicate but determined, she stroked against his lips with the tip of her tongue, outlining the seam of his mouth before sliding the tip inside and rubbing it against his tongue.

Goddamn, Audrey's mouth was amazing. He was shocked that the prim woman could kiss. More than that, she kissed like a demon. Like she knew she was in charge and she was putting him in his place.

Her tongue stroked against his once more, boldly, and then retreated. "Tongue," she whispered.

"Mmm," he groaned when she gave a small sigh of pleasure and began to stroke her tongue into his mouth again. He slid his tongue along hers. She gave a little start when he began to respond, but then she yielded against him, and their mouths began to meld in a sensual interplay.

The kiss was incredible. Her soft tongue dancing along his, her sweet mouth parted, her lips joined to his. She tasted delicious, too—warm and like honey. Reese needed more of her. He let his arms fall to his sides and then his hands moved to her hips, close to her ass but not quite touching it. He knew if he grabbed at her, she'd flee, and he wanted more of this.

This sexy, confident Audrey that kissed like a fiend was at total odds with the sour, too-proper woman with the stiff back who he had such fun teasing, and fuck if it wasn't making him hard as all get-out. It was a surprise and a turn on all in one. His hands anchored at her waist, holding her against him. His cock had stirred at the wet thrust of her kiss, and within moments he was as hard as a rock. The press of those full breasts against his chest were almost as distracting as the slide of her tongue into his mouth.

After a moment, she pulled away with a small whimper, her mouth gleaming wet in the moonlight. She looked up at him with dazed eyes. "Pretty sure that was two minutes."

He groaned, leaning in toward her mouth again. "Fuck the two minutes."

She leaned just as far away from him, her nose wrinkling as if displeased. "Two minutes was the agreement."

And he was . . . a bit stumped. Wasn't she enjoying the kiss as much as he was? She'd sighed with pleasure. Her lips and tongue had been enthusiastic against his own. She'd pressed against him. And now that she'd gotten him all worked up . . . she was done? He growled low in his throat. "We can keep going if you want."

"I don't want," she said, and slid out of his grasp, taking a step backward. "This was just because you blackmailed me."

Somehow he doubted that. Reese hadn't missed that little jolt she'd made when he'd begun to tongue her back, or the little groan of response she'd made. But if she wanted to play games with him, that was fine. She'd learn that he was the king of playing flirty games, and they were just about to get started. "Whatever you say," he forced out in a casual voice. "You going back to the house now?"

"Yes," she said in a prim voice. "I am."

And she whirled and bolted for the house, her steps hurried.

Reese rubbed his lips, still feeling the slick warmth from their kiss, and grinned. Audrey might claim to be unaffected, but he'd bet money that it was a lie. There was a lot more underneath the surface than that girl let on.

And damn it all if he wasn't interested in finding out more. Now he needed to think of more ways to get that impulsive, fierce little hothead to show up once more.

Dear, sweet Lord, she was in way over her head.

Audrey raced back to the house, clutching the borrowed jacket to her shoulders. Her breath was coming fast and her legs felt wobbly and weak. It didn't make her stop, though—she raced up the wooden steps to the lodge and flung open the door, crashing into the house.

Cade glanced out of the bathroom doorway, seated on a small wooden stool he'd pulled into the bathroom. The sounds of retching continued, and Audrey knew her twin was still in there. "Everything okay?"

His beloved face looked so concerned, so beautiful . . . and she didn't want to see him at the moment. Not after she'd been kissing another man. Shame rocketed through her.

"Just fine," Audrey barked out, her voice a little more high-pitched than she would have preferred. A hot flush began to form on her cheeks, and she took a step toward the bathroom out of concern for her twin. "Is she okay?"

Cade nodded. "I'll stay with her. Keep her company."

From inside the bathroom, Daphne mumbled something that Audrey couldn't hear, and for a moment she was oddly thankful that Cade was the one volunteering to sit with

Daphne. She didn't think she could at the moment, not with the way her mind and body were racing. She gestured at the stairs. "I'm, um, just going to go upstairs."

"Okay." He turned back to Daphne and began to murmur something.

Audrey raced up the wooden stairs to the second floor of the lodge, where the bedrooms were. Daphne's shoes were kicked off in front of the last door on the end, so she guessed that was their room. She headed inside and frowned. The room stank of cigarettes and stale smoke. Heading toward the window on the far side of the room, Audrey opened the shutters and then cracked the window to air out the room. A rush of cold air came in, and she pulled the jacket closer to her.

It smelled like Reese. For a moment, she wanted to fling it off her body, but she glanced around the room instead. It was dark, and the only light coming in was from the full moon outside. No one would know she was up here. So she cautiously pulled the jacket closer and gave it another sniff.

If she had to admit it to herself, the scent was . . . wonderful. Reese smelled like soap and warmth and the outdoors and that spicy, musky scent she was starting to identify as pure Reese. Inhaling his scent made her think back to the kiss on the dock, and her gaze automatically went to the window, looking outside for a familiar form.

He was still there where she'd left him minutes ago. Slouched against the wooden railing of the dock, his stance casual and easy. His hand was lifted to his mouth and, as she watched, she could have sworn he was rubbing his lips.

It made a quiver erupt deep in her belly. Had he been affected by their kiss, too?

He glanced up at the lodge and, as soon as he did, she yelped and bolted away from the window, hiding behind the wall. She immediately chided herself for the foolish move. He wouldn't have been able to see her watching him, sniffing his jacket and basking in his scent.

Still.

Audrey put her back to the wall and slid down to the floor, pulling her knees close and wrapping the jacket around her body.

Cade was here tonight.

Cade was here, and she'd gone outside and kissed another man. What was *wrong* with her?

She'd been dreaming of spending a quiet weekend alone with Cade for years. Fantasized about the two of them spending time together, rekindling the old, comfortable friendship they'd had, and—in her eyes—maybe turning it into something more.

She hadn't factored in a sick junkie sister who would eat up Cade's free time. She certainly hadn't factored in Cade's buddy who would drive her insane in the space of mere seconds.

She could handle Daphne, though. Cade adored Daphne also, and her sister was such a mess that she wasn't really competition for Cade. Not on a romantic level, anyhow.

But she'd never factored in Reese. Reese, who'd been making out with a gorgeous, naked blonde when they'd arrived. Reese, who crawled under her skin and infuriated her with every word and smug smile on his handsome brute face. Reese, who'd blackmailed her into kissing him. She should have told him no. She should have told him to go ahead and tell Cade. What was the worst that would happen?

But instead, she'd gone outside to kiss Reese, even though she couldn't stand him and his arrogant ways. And she'd negotiated with him about where and how long the kiss should be. And even though she'd despised him for holding her to the bet, she'd had a wild, sick little butterfly of excitement in her stomach.

It had been so incredibly naughty. It was something that the good twin would never do . . . unless forced. And somehow because the control had been out of her hands, she'd wanted to do it. Not only that, but she'd wanted to prove to Reese that he wasn't the only one who could take someone by surprise. So she'd taken the plunge and kissed him.

She knew she was a good kisser. She'd had plenty of boyfriends despite her torch for Cade, but she'd only slept with a few of them. She didn't give it up easily, preferring the long weeks—and sometimes months—of endless petting and kissing to the actual consummation. And she'd had lots of experience with kissing, and she knew what would make a man sit up and notice. And she'd used every dirty trick in the book to rock his world and wipe that smug smile off his too-handsome face. She'd wanted to shake him up a little.

She hadn't counted on enjoying the kiss that much herself. But she had. Oh, she had. That butterfly of excitement returned, low in her belly, and she pressed her thighs together tightly. His lips had been soft and full, and he'd tasted so good. And he knew how to kiss, too. When his tongue had begun to stroke back against her own, she'd forgotten all about teaching him a lesson and had simply enjoyed the kiss for the kiss's sake.

It was because it was forbidden, she told herself. Nothing more. She wasn't supposed to be out on a dock in the middle of the night, kissing a cocky stranger. She should have been in the house, at her twin's side, showing Cade how good and devoted of a sister she was.

Showing him that she was the good, sweet twin and was so right for a man as kind and devoted and handsome as himself.

And instead she'd been tonguing Reese Durham.

And she'd *liked* it.

Mortified, Audrey buried her head in her hands. Unfortunately, that only made the scent of Reese waft more closely around her, thanks to the jacket.

He'd liked the kiss, too. She could tell that her aggressiveness had startled him in the beginning, and then he'd appreciated it. It had stroked her ego, to have this big, confident man taken down a peg by her kiss. But then she'd gotten lost in it. And then he'd offered to continue the kiss.

And she'd told him no. Put on the stiff poker face of the Audrey Who Meant Business.

But she'd really, really wanted to say yes. Oh, she'd wanted to say yes. For a brief moment in time, she'd wanted to be the bad twin, the wild twin, the twin who would sink down to the floor of the dock and make love to a man she barely knew just because he excited the part of her that she tried so hard to wrestle into control.

But Audrey was determined to be the good twin at all costs. Cade was a good, kind man with a virtuous heart. He wouldn't fall for someone who had a wild and impetuous side. He needed someone trustworthy and honorable, like himself.

And since all she'd ever wanted for herself was Cade's love, she'd pulled away.

So why was she regretting it, all alone up here in the dark?

It didn't make sense. And she kind of hated herself for it, even as she rubbed her own lips in memory.

Audrey woke up the next morning, curled on her side of the king bed. She'd slept on top of the covers and left the window open. The room was frigid and smelled of pine trees and ice, and the jacket she was cuddled in no longer smelled of the man she'd kissed last night. Just as well.

She'd slept on top of the covers, fully dressed, and vaguely remembered dozing off while waiting for her twin to return. The other side of the bed hadn't been touched, though, and Audrey rubbed her face, then changed into a new set of clothes for the day—a plain gray long-sleeved shirt and her favorite jeans. She splashed a bit of water on her face, then used her wet hands to smooth her wild hair into her typical no-nonsense bun. Then, she headed downstairs.

The lodge was silent, and Audrey crept down the hall, wondering where everyone was. Was she the first one awake? She supposed she should make breakfast if that was the case. Surely she couldn't mess up toast.

She crept into the living room area and paused. On the sofa directly across from the now-dark fireplace, Daphne was sprawled out, facedown. Her twin looked like hell; her skin was pasty, her features were haggard, and her hair was sweaty and plastered against her pale skin. Her face rested on a cushion in Cade's lap as he slept upright, his head tilted backward, his blond hair mussed. His mouth was open, a hint of a snore echoing from him. A plastic bucket rested between his feet, clearly for Daphne's use.

They both looked exhausted. Audrey felt a twinge of dismay at the sight. She should have been the one helping her twin through the night. Instead, she'd been wrapped up in her own turbulent thoughts. Cade, being the gentleman that he was, had taken over the task. She watched him sleep for a moment, admiring his clean, handsome features. There was a dark shadow of facial hair along his jaw, chin, and upper lip, and it was the first time she'd ever seen him look even slightly rumpled. It was a bit odd to see. Even his dress shirt was wrinkled, the sleeves rolled up at his elbows. He seemed oddly vulnerable, and she smiled to herself at the sight.

She was glad he was here, though. Not only was he helping with Daphne, but this would give her time to spend with him, too. She'd been dreaming of the day they would finally reunite, and though she hadn't planned it quite like this, she couldn't be sorry for it. Today, she resolved, she was going to spend at her sister's side.

And if Cade was there, too, even better.

She'd let them sleep for now, though, and she'd make breakfast. Audrey passed through the living room on silent, careful feet, and then headed through the swinging door into the kitchen.

The sight that greeted her there made her stop in her tracks.

His massive back was turned to her, muscles rippling and shoulders moving as Reese reached for something in one of the cabinets. The sleep pants he wore were hideously checkered, but they were also incredibly tight across his firm ass and low enough that they showed the indent of his lower back . . . and the fact that he wasn't wearing underwear. His feet were bare.

He turned and glanced at her as she stood in the doorway, petrified, and he gave her another one of those lazy, smug smiles. "Good morning," he whispered. His gaze seemed to pause at her mouth, then took in her tightly bound-up hair, and the smile grew amused. "Armoring up for battle?"

"Don't be ridiculous," she whispered back. "I came in here to make breakfast. I didn't realize anyone else was in here. What are you doing in here?"

"You," he told her with a point of the potato peeler in his hand, "are not getting anywhere near this food. Not after last night's debacle."

She padded to his side, crossing her arms over her chest, and studied the counter space in front of him. There was a bowl of beaten eggs, another bowl full of pancake batter, and he had a stack of washed potatoes in front of him. "What's all this? Don't tell me you've decided to cook?"

"Someone's got to do it," he said with a lopsided grin. "And those two in the living room look like they had a rough night."

"They do," she admitted. "I feel bad that it's not me out there."

"I don't," he told her. "You were busy keeping me occupied."

She smacked his arm and picked up one of the potatoes. "You want me to peel these?"

"I don't know." He leaned against the counter and gazed down at her. "Think you'll mess it up?"

She glared at him. "I have some skill, you know."

"Oh, I know that," he drawled, and it made a blush creep up her cheeks. She bit her lip when that crazy flutter began in her belly again. "But I was talking about potatoes."

She rolled her eyes and took the peeler from him, then grabbed a few potatoes and headed over to the garbage can. "I'll peel while you cook."

"Suit yourself," he told her, handing her the rest of the potatoes. He pulled out a skillet and set it on the stove top, then began to flip a few of the dials with the casual expertise of someone who had cooked plenty of meals. He whistled quietly under his breath and headed to the refrigerator, then bent over, his pants nearly splitting at the movement.

Audrey froze at the sight of his ass in the air, the pants pulled impossibly tight against his skin. She could practically run a ruler down the cleft of his ass. And it was a rather fine ass. She gaped at it a moment more, then forced herself to focus on the potatoes when he straightened and turned around with a package of bacon in his hand. She gave one of the potatoes a few awkward scrapes.

"Were you checking out my ass, Audrey?"

She sighed heavily. "You were sticking it in the air, Reese. It's hard not to."

"Did you like what you saw?"

"No," she said in her best prissy voice. "You have cellulite."

He laughed softly at that. "You're such a liar. Your face is all red."

She glared at him and scraped the potato a little harder.

He pulled out a knife from a nearby block and gestured at her. "Try and leave a little of the potato there for the actual pan."

She glanced down at the potato in her hand and noticed she was gouging half of it away with her angry scrapes. *Damn it.* She finished peeling it and tossed it on the counter with an irritated look at him, then grabbed the next one. "So you're leaving today?"

"Nah." He laid a couple of strips of bacon in the pan. "I needed a vacation, and that hasn't changed even though Camilla left."

She began to scrape the next potato angrily. "You weren't invited."

"Actually," he said in a lazy voice, "I was." He finished

laying bacon in the pan and then closed it up, returning it to the fridge. "Just because you didn't invite me doesn't mean I'm not welcome here."

"My sister's trying to get clean. She doesn't need someone like you disturbing her."

"Have I disturbed her at all? Has she indicated to you that I'm making her unhappy? Oh, that's right. You wouldn't know that because you've been too busy mooning after Cade and spending time with me to bother with her."

Audrey's wild scrapes took on a furious edge. "That's not it at all. I—ouch!" A sharp burst of pain blossomed in her finger and blood welled. She'd missed the potato and scraped her finger.

Reese gave a sigh and plucked the potato from her hand, tossing it in the sink. "Did you have to go and hurt yourself?"

Before she could protest, he grabbed her by the waist and hauled her onto the counter next to the sink, as if she weighed nothing. Her jaw dropped. Daphne was the lightweight. Audrey was . . . well, Audrey was solid in the most flattering of terms. But he'd picked her up like she was nothing. When he tugged her hand free from the fist she'd clenched it in, she allowed him to examine her wound, staring at him in dazed confusion.

He calmly turned on the water and ran her finger under the tap, fingers on her wrist. With his free hand, he pulled open a drawer and grabbed a box of Band-Aids, tugging one out. "This is why I'm not letting you cook, Audrey," he said, his voice teasing. "You have a nasty temper and you don't concentrate when you're mad." He glanced up at her through surprisingly thick lashes. "And around me, you seem to always be mad."

"Am not," she said in a soft voice, but he did have a point. She worked so hard to be controlled and efficient in all areas of her life, but this man seemed to undo all her efforts in the blink of an eye.

He turned off the water. Another drop of blood welled up on her finger even as he grabbed the Band-Aid from the counter. "It's still bleeding," she pointed out.

Reese leaned in and swiped his tongue over the small wound, licking it clean, and then slid the Band-Aid over it while she sat, frozen and in shock. Heat pulsed low in her belly at that small, impulsive gesture. She squeezed her thighs tight again.

"You shouldn't have done that," she breathed, surprised at how husky her voice was.

He glanced over at her, his gaze moving to her mouth, then back to her eyes. "Why is that?"

"I could have a disease."

That cocky grin spread across his face again. "You? Miss Proper? Miss Not a Hair Out of Place? I imagine you'd be Ms. Safety in the bedroom."

He made her sound so boring. For some reason, it bothered her. "You don't know what I'm like in the bedroom," she blurted. A split second later, she was horrified that those words had come out of her mouth.

"I'd like to learn," Reese told her, leaning close. His warm, musky scent filled her nostrils and her breathing started to speed up as he moved in. She thought for a moment he was going to kiss her, or touch her, or something, and that fluttering in her belly went wild with need, her pulse pounding at a spot between her legs that made her entire body ache.

But all he did was offer her a hand to help her down

from the counter. She took it, hopped down, and then looked up at him in confusion.

"Bacon's burning," was all he said, turning back to the stove. "Why don't you set the table? Less chance to injure yourself."

And when he gave her his back—and that tight butt—she found she wanted to kick him all over again. Preferably in that tight butt.

Breakfast was incredible. By the time Audrey had finished setting the table, Reese had arrived out of the kitchen with a plate full of perfectly cooked bacon—burning, her ass—a stack of fluffy pancakes, and the most perfectly cooked scrambled eggs she'd ever seen. There was a plate of dry toast and a pot of coffee on a potholder, and everything looked and smelled amazing. Audrey was impressed. How did such an arrogant, good-looking jerk turn out to be such a domestic when it came to the kitchen? He put her attempts to shame. She'd have to find out; there was more going on beneath the surface than she'd realized when it came to Reese Durham.

She forgot all of that, however, when Daphne and Cade appeared in the doorway. Her twin looked greenish beneath her pale skin and her hair was a tangled mess. Daphne's mouth was pressed tight, and without the thick fake lashes and heavy eye makeup, she looked wan and tired and far too old for her age. Audrey immediately rushed to her side, wrapping an arm around her waist. "How are you feeling?"

Daphne pushed her away irritably. "I'm fine. Leave me alone. Christ, you're hovering."

Hurt, Audrey took a step backward and glanced at

Cade, who seemed tired but gave her a gentle smile. "Thanks for cooking breakfast, Audrey. You really outdid yourself."

"Oh, I—"

Before she could finish her protest, Reese came up behind her and smacked her on the shoulder. "She did a terrific job, didn't she? I woke up this morning and there she was, hard at work, slaving over the stove."

Audrey cast him a withering look, but he only grinned down at her. Now what was he up to?

Daphne slumped into the nearest seat, then pressed a hand to her mouth. "I can't eat any of this. It's making my stomach turn."

"You should eat something," Audrey protested, anxiousness stirring through her. Daphne did look rather ill.

"I'll eat once I get my next pill," Daphne said, and gave Cade a hopeful look.

He checked his watch, then shook his head. "Not for another twelve hours. Sorry."

Daphne's mouth twisted and she pushed the plate in front of her away. "I'll eat in twelve hours, then."

"Daphne," Audrey began.

"You're not my mother, Aud. Shut up already."

Reese stepped forward and, to Audrey's surprise, he plunked down a mug in front of Daphne and filled it with black coffee. He tossed two pieces of dry toast onto her plate and pointed at it. "I'm not your mother, either, but you're going to eat that." He pointed at the coffee. "And you're going to drink that. And you're going to shut up about it."

Silence filled the room, and then Cade cleared his throat. "Well, the rest of us can eat, at least." He pulled out the chair next to Daphne.

Reese patted the chair next to where Audrey hovered,

on the opposite side of her twin. "Why don't you sit here next to Audrey, Cade? She'd probably like that."

Audrey glared at Reese. *God.* Why not be totally obvious about her crush?

Cade grinned at her. "I was thinking she'd probably want to sit next to you, Reese."

Oh, my God. Surely he didn't think she was interested in Reese. That was her worst nightmare come to life. "I can assure you that sitting next to Reese is the last thing I want."

"In that case," Cade said, pulling out Audrey's chair for her. She sat and gave him a radiant smile. He was such a wonderful man.

Daphne snorted and picked up one of the wedges of dry toast, nibbling on the corner and giving Reese a hateful look as he sat down next to her.

And that was how their first meal together at the cabin proceeded. Daphne picking at her food, Cade seated next to Audrey and keeping up the bulk of the conversation, expertly involving all parties so no one would feel left out, and Reese sitting across from her and giving her smug smiles as she ate the delicious breakfast he'd cooked and claimed she was responsible for.

It was a rather messy dynamic, Audrey thought to herself. And she imagined it was only going to get messier.

Out of guilt, Audrey stuck close to Daphne's side all day. She helped her twin take a shower since Daphne felt too weak to stand up on her own, and when Daphne took a nap and then threw up on their shared blankets, Audrey immediately changed the bed and did the laundry without a word of protest. Daphne, on the other hand, was surly and unpleasant to Audrey at all times, which only made Audrey want to try harder to please Daphne. She knew this was hard on Daphne, and she was there to help her get through it.

So she picked up after Daphne, and made her twin toast when she needed it, and read a book in the room while Daphne was sleeping. When Daphne was awake and throwing up, Audrey changed out her bucket, wiped her brow, and unpacked their things, keeping busy.

In a word, she hovered.

It wasn't that she thought Daphne would appreciate it. She didn't. It wasn't that Daphne needed her. She didn't, really. It was guilt, pure and simple, that kept her glued to Daphne's side.

She felt guilty about a lot of things. She felt guilty that Daphne was so sick and she'd pawned her off on Cade last night. She felt guilty that Daphne resented her. She felt guilty that she should have been concentrating on getting her twin better instead of her crush on Cade.

And she really, really felt guilty about last night's kiss with Reese. Or this morning, when he'd lifted her onto the counter and then licked her finger. She felt horribly guilty about how turned on those two simple things had made her.

She was in love with Cade. She was here for Daphne.

So why was she so utterly focused on Reese Durham? She didn't even like the man. He was a jerk and a player—two things that she despised. He was her opposite in every way. He'd blackmailed her into kissing him, for Pete's sake.

But . . . when he was around, she felt alive. And a bit wild and carefree. And incredibly, incredibly aroused.

And all of that was bad. She was the good twin. She was here for her sister. She was here because Daphne needed her, and Audrey was here because she wanted time with Cade.

Reese did not play into any of that.

So she hovered and mothered Daphne until her twin was slapping her hand away every time Audrey tried to put a damp towel on her forehead. And she continued to try to be helpful until Daphne screamed for her to fuck off. Cade arrived a moment later, pill and glass of water in hand, and Daphne had melted like putty in his hands.

And that just made Audrey feel worse. So she'd gone downstairs with her book, intending to spend a little time away from her twin. She'd automatically looked around the lodge to talk to Reese, but he'd been out taking a walk, and she told herself that the disappointment she felt was stupid.

She'd laid down on the couch in front of the fireplace and started to read, but had quickly drifted off to sleep. When she woke up later, it was dark, the fire out, and someone had put her book on the ground and covered her with a blanket. Tucking the blanket around her, Audrey headed back up the stairs and into the room she shared with Daphne. Her twin was huddled under the blankets, her barf bucket close at hand, and sweat covered her brow. The sheets were soaked with it.

Maybe the couch hadn't been such a bad idea after all. She returned to it and curled up with the blanket, imagining that Cade had seen her sleeping and lovingly tucked it around her. But for some reason, she kept seeing Cade's face with a smirky, un-Cade-like smile framed by a wicked goatee, and in her mind, the blanket smelled like Reese.

The next morning, she woke up to the quiet clank of pots and pans in the kitchen. Audrey yawned and rubbed her eyes, then crawled out from under the blankets and headed for the kitchen.

Sure enough, there was Reese, stirring a large pot on the stove, the smell of fresh-brewed coffee in the air. She appreciated the sight of his tight buns for a moment, then cleared her throat to announce her presence.

He turned and gave her a lazy smile. "Morning, sunshine."

For some reason, that look of frank appreciation in his eyes made her feel warm and fuzzy. Ugh. *Hormones, nothing more.* She was just thrilled someone had said something to her that didn't involve cursing and begging for pills. She leaned over the stove and peered into the pot. "What am I cooking for breakfast this morning?"

"You decided to make a big batch of oatmeal since it'll be easy on your sister's stomach," he said easily, sprinkling some brown sugar on top of the thick mix. "Good call."

"I'm an amazing cook," she said dryly. "Care to tell why you told everyone it was me?"

"You're trying to snag yourself a man," he said easily. "Wouldn't hurt to let Cade think you're a domestic goddess. He likes traditional women."

"Does he?" She filed that bit of information away. "Thanks, I guess."

He shrugged and glanced at her hair. "Rough night?"

Her brows drew together. "What makes you say that?"

"Your bun is askew."

Audrey's fingers flew to her hair. Sure enough, it was lopsided and puffy on one side. "Damn it."

Reese set down the spoon and turned to her, reaching for her hair. "Here, I'll fix it for you."

She frowned but stood still, dropping her hands. "That's very domestic of you."

"Nah. I mostly wanted to see what this looks like when

it's not in a grandma style." And he reached forward and snipped the band with a pair of scissors.

She yelped, pulling away even as he ran his fingers through her hair, making it puff out into a halo around her head. "You asshole!"

"Look at that! All that loose, untamed hair!" he teased, even as he tried to run his fingers through it again. "It's like you're a wild woman. What will people think?"

She gave him a light punch in the gut, trying to get him away from her. "I hate you so much!"

"All that red, luscious hair," he teased, massaging her scalp, undeterred by her declarations of hatred. "You want to get a man, you need to wear it down instead of dressing like a spinster schoolmarm."

"I am not a spinster schoolmarm," she huffed, twisting away and slapping at his hands when he reached for her hair again. "You're just saying that because you have a secret fetish for schoolmarm hair."

"You think so?"

"I think that's why you wanted me to kiss you so bad," she snapped. "I—"

"Hey, Cade," Reese said quickly, staring over her shoulder.

She gasped and whirled around to see.

No one was there.

That jerk. Audrey turned and smacked Reese's arm with her open palm, ignoring his mischievous grin. "You are such an asshole."

"And you are totally transparent." He gave her hair one last look of approval and then picked up his wooden spoon again, stirring the oatmeal. "Why not just tell the man you're in love with him? He's going to figure it out the way you keep fawning over him."

"I do not fawn over him," she said in a curt tone, pouring herself a cup of coffee.

"You do," he said. "Any man can tell that you've got the hots for him. What's it about him that jerks your chain? Is it the white knight thing? Blond hair? The money?"

She snorted, not bothering to dignify that with a real response.

"It's the money," he said smugly. "I knew it."

"Not the money," she gritted between her teeth. "Cade's different than most men, that's all."

"Different how? Because he's not trying to look up your skirt?" He gave her another appreciative look, his gaze lingering on her wild hair. *Was that . . . attraction in his eyes? God, he was such a pig.* And God, why did it make her want to preen a little? She was just as bad as he was.

"Cade's a gentleman," she said. "I don't know why I have to explain to you why I like Cade, but it's everything about him. It's the way he puts others before his own needs. It's the way he's always been so protective of us. It's the way he's friendly and polite to everyone. He's smart and successful without compromising his integrity. I've met few men like that." She cast him a sideways look and blew on her coffee a moment before adding, "Most men seem willing to use people just to push themselves ahead."

"You mean like me with the heiress in the hot tub? You can come right out and say it. It won't hurt my feelings."

"I mean exactly like that," she told him in a crisp tone. "It's not something that a man like Cade would do."

"Yeah," he agreed, and then turned to face her. He didn't look offended. If anything, Reese had that challenging gleam in his eyes as he studied her. "You want to know the difference between me and a man like Cade, though? I'll actually get what I want. Cade's too polite to admit what he wants, and he's going to end up unhappy. Me? I go after what I want and fuck it all if people don't like it. You can't live your life trying to please everyone but yourself, because you're going to end up the only person unhappy."

"And how do you know what Cade wants?"

"I'm his friend. It's obvious to me."

"And I'm not his friend?"

He shrugged. "I think your feelings for him—or what you think your feelings are for him—get in the way of what you really want."

She rolled her eyes. "I know what my feelings are for Cade, thank you. I don't need you telling me otherwise."

"Oh, I'm not. So how good of a kisser is he?"

Her mouth opened, and then closed immediately. "That's private information."

"You're blushing and you've got that prissy tone in your voice again. You haven't kissed him, have you?"

"He's kissed me before," she said blandly, thinking of the time he'd kissed her cheek when she was younger.

"On the cheek doesn't count," Reese said, as if reading her mind.

She was silent.

"Huh."

Okay, now that was irritating. "What's that little 'huh' supposed to mean?" she asked Reese.

"Nothing."

"It's not nothing."

"I was just curious how you haven't kissed the man you're in love with, but you'll kiss me just because I dared you."

"There's a difference between a dare and blackmail, thank you. I would never have taken a dare like that."

"Too chicken?"

Audrey gritted her teeth. "I'm not a chicken."

"You're too chicken to kiss Cade, it seems. How would I know if you're too chicken to do a dare? Seems to me like Little Miss Perfect isn't up for it. Too daring for her blood."

For some reason, his joke about her being "Little Miss Perfect" really bothered her. He made it sound like it was a bad thing to be a good person. "I'd kiss Cade if I wanted to. I just don't want him to know that I'm in love with him just yet."

"Chicken."

"I'm *not* a chicken."

"Then prove it." Reese's eyes gleamed. "You up for a little dare?"

She felt cornered. Cornered, and yet that butterfly was back in her belly. It felt like it was thundering when Reese gave her that sly look, too. "What sort of dare?"

"If you kiss Cade by sunset, I'll leave."

Her eyes widened. "That sounds almost too good to be true. Kiss Cade and get rid of the biggest thorn in my side? Where do I sign up?"

He clutched a hand to his chest. "You wound me, Audrey. You wouldn't miss me?"

"Not in the slightest," she said tartly, but that butterfly in her stomach begged to differ. "So all I need to do is kiss Cade and you'll pack up and leave? Challenge accepted."

"Hang on there," he said, putting down the spoon and turning off the stove. He moved the oatmeal to a back burner and then turned to face her. "Not so fast. You have to kiss Cade in front of me, where I can see it. None of this 'oh, I kissed him' and have it be a bullshit story you're making up just to get rid of me. I need to see it."

"Fine."

"On the mouth, tongue and all. Shouldn't be too hard since you're in love with the man." His grin widened. "Just kiss him like you did me last night."

Hot fire scorched her cheeks. "Fine. You might as well pack your bags, then."

"Oh, I'm not packing up so soon," he said, studying her. "I don't think you'll go through with it. And if you don't . . ."

She raised an eyebrow, anticipating what he'd say next. More kissing? Heat curled in her stomach at the thought. Strangely, she wouldn't be averse to more kissing when it came to Reese, which was dirty and wrong.

"We go skinny-dipping. Tonight."

Audrey's jaw dropped. "Excuse me?"

He moved across the kitchen and loomed over her, planting a hand on each side of the counter. "Did I stutter?" he asked with a grin. "You. Me. Naked. In the lake. Tonight. But that's only if you don't go through with this. If you do, well . . ." He shrugged. "I'll be gone by dawn. Promise."

She paused, contemplating this. It was a wild, ridiculous bet. She totally wanted to do it. If she won this stupid dare, she'd win big in all ways. Reese would be gone, his irritating presence would be removed from the cozy lodge, and she could devote her time to Cade . . . and her twin. Plus, *hello*, kissing Cade. That was a reward all on its own. Audrey drummed her fingers against her lower lip, thinking.

But kissing Cade would have to be initiated by her, unless he showed more interest than he had in the past.

She knew that with him she was still stuck in the safe "friend" or "little sister" zone. He'd never initiate a kiss—with tongue!—on his own. She'd have to be the one to come on to him, grab him and kiss him just like she'd done to Reese. It would require a bit of nerve.

Okay, a lot of nerve.

But if she won . . .

And yet, if she lost she'd be going skinny-dipping with this smirky, cocky oaf standing in front of her. She'd already kissed the goon, and now she was agreeing to get naked with him if she didn't follow through?

But he'd leave if she kissed Cade. And wasn't that what she wanted? Kill two birds with one stone. She glanced up at him. The grin on his face told her that he very much anticipated going skinny-dipping with her tonight.

He didn't think she could do it.

Audrey held out her hand, her pulse racing. "You're on. If I win, you leave. If you win, we go skinny-dipping."

Reese clasped his hand in hers and they shook on it.

Damn it, she was going to lose. This was not fair.

Of all days for this bet to happen, today was by far the worst. Daphne woke up early that morning, sullen and dizzy. Audrey had lingered around her for a time, bringing blankets and drinks when needed. She didn't mind helping, though she was curious why Reese moved in and out of the cabin and there was no sign of Cade, who normally was attentive when Daphne was awake.

When lunch had rolled around and Cade hadn't made an appearance, Audrey innocently asked, "Is Cade sleeping in?"

"Oh, he went to town for some more supplies," Daphne

said. "He left super early this morning. I needed more cigarettes and Reese suggested more groceries."

Audrey's eyes narrowed. She glanced over at Reese. "Did he now?"

"Huh," was all Reese said, but that know-it-all grin was on his mouth. He kicked his feet up on the coffee table and wiggled his eyebrows at Audrey.

That jerk. He'd known all along that Cade wasn't around, and he'd still made that stinking bet with her. She hated him. She really and truly hated him.

He'd planned this simply to get her to go skinny-dipping with him. "When will Cade be back?" she asked, keeping her voice as casual as she could.

Daphne shrugged, giving her a cross look. "Why do you care?"

Not for the first time, Audrey wished that her beloved twin wasn't going through the cranky-pants portion of withdrawal. "I'm sure he'll be back in time for your pill," Audrey told her. Considering that Daphne took it around dinnertime each night, it made sense.

Daphne rubbed her face, groaning. "Can't get here fast enough."

In that, they were in perfect agreement.

The afternoon passed in a whirlwind of tension for Audrey. She read her book, finished it, then paced the living room as Daphne napped fitfully upstairs. She'd have gone with Daphne except that Daphne had finally been irritated enough with Audrey's fussing to kick her out of the room and lock the door. Well, that suited Audrey just fine, she thought. *She can clean up her own vomit.* She read one of her books instead, sat on the back porch, and watched the sun sink far too close to the horizon for her own tastes.

Reese, meanwhile, chopped wood. He'd removed his shirt and, despite the fact that it was winter and somewhat brisk outside, he was covered in sweat as he placed a log on a stump and then sliced it neatly in half with the axe.

She told herself that the light on the porch was the best, and that was why she was out there. It wasn't because Reese was half naked and his muscles gleamed with sweat. Certainly not.

But when he tired of chopping wood and went upstairs to shower, Audrey was left alone to her own devices. She headed into the bathroom downstairs and studied her reflection thoughtfully. She'd have a limited window of time in which to kiss Cade when he got back. She had to make it happen. Had to. She was *not* skinny-dipping. Maybe she needed to put on some makeup and fix her hair in something other than a tight bun.

She pulled the tie out of her hair and let it fall around her shoulders. Reese had seemed to appreciate her hair soft and loose. And while she didn't care what Reese thought about how she looked, he seemed to be a good judge of what men found attractive. Hell, he dated all kinds of women. If Reese thought she was sexy with her hair down, Cade surely would, right?

Audrey ran the brush through her hair, finger-combing the loose curls and waves that her bun had made. Her hair was shiny and soft, the natural red a pale but pleasant orangey gold. Would he find her attractive? She retrieved her purse from the living room and pulled out her cosmetics bag. Nude lipstick, nude eyeshadow, and concealer for her under-eye circles. Nothing to make her into a gorgeous woman who needed to be kissed. With a sigh, she tossed the makeup back into her purse . . . and glanced at Daphne's battered makeup bag.

A short time later, she wore false eyelashes, her eyes were lined and smoky with kohl, and her lips were glossy with a slick, kissable gloss that made her lips look plump and juicy. Her freckles were toned down by a bit of powder, and the waves of her hair made her look soft and touchable.

Not bad. She didn't look much like the normal Audrey, but Cade tended to ignore the normal Audrey. He saw her as a bland but beloved friend. She fluttered her lashes at the mirror. With those on, she had to admit that she looked a bit more like her twin—albeit a fat, freckled version of the wispy, frail Daphne.

Maybe this wasn't such a good idea after all. Audrey hesitated, staring at her reflection.

The front door banged shut and she gasped. Cade was back. She turned and whirled out of the bathroom, shutting the door behind her.

He arrived with a few bags of groceries in his arms, looking a bit exhausted himself. Cade smiled at the sight of her and gestured at the groceries. "Hey, Aud. Help me bring these in?"

"Of course." She fluttered her eyelashes at him and smiled. "I'm so glad you're back."

Cade gave her a smile in return. "Me, too. It's good to see your lovely face."

Well, if that wasn't encouraging, she didn't know what was. Blushing with pleasure at the compliment, Audrey headed down the stairs to Cade's car and began to help him bring in the groceries. Their arms piled high with bags, Audrey was distracted and almost ran into Reese as she entered the cabin again.

Reese took the bags from her hands and then stopped at the sight of her.

"Is there a problem?" she whispered, keeping the smile on her face as Cade glanced over at them.

His face darkened into a bit of a scowl as he studied her hair and then her face. "Pulling out the big guns, I see."

"That's right," she said sweetly. "And the sun's not down yet. So even though you cheated, I still intend on winning. Get ready to leave."

Reese grunted and said nothing.

They put away the groceries in silence. Reese seemed to be stewing over the fact that she'd done her makeup and hair. Cade seemed preoccupied, and Audrey, well, Audrey was trying to figure out the best way to seduce her oldest friend in the space of an hour.

For some reason, it made her nervous. And reluctant. Loving Cade from afar was safe. No one's feelings were hurt when the other party didn't know you were interested. Her confession to him would change everything.

But it was either that, or skinny-dip with his best friend.

"How's Daphne doing?" Cade asked quietly. "Is she sleeping?"

"She's very cranky," Audrey said with a soft smile. "But she's going to be okay, I think."

"She's had a rough week," Cade said, concern in his voice. He seemed distracted and oddly enough, exhausted, as if he'd spent the last few nights up with Daphne at the sacrifice of his own sleep.

Which, Audrey supposed, he had. He was such a good friend to their family. Was it any wonder that she loved him? Audrey reached out and clasped his hand, squeezing it. "Thank you for being here for us."

Cade looked surprised at her touch, and then he squeezed her hand back, the gentle smile crossing his face.

"Of course. I said I'd always be here for Daphne, and I am. She knows she can count on me."

"We both can," Audrey told him, smiling up at his gorgeous, classically handsome features. He didn't look like Reese. Reese, whose face was handsome through sheer force of his personality. Reese, who looked like he'd be more comfortable at home in a boxing ring than in a business suit. Cade was beautiful like a statue. Reese was sexy like a force of nature.

"Move it or lose it," Reese said in her ear, shoving past to get to the fridge with the last of the groceries. Startled at Reese's callousness, Audrey almost scowled. He shot her a black look and indicated that she should let him past.

Audrey brushed up against Cade, letting her breasts push against his chest. To her surprise—and chagrin—Cade automatically moved back, ever the gentleman.

"Cade, can I talk to you privately for a minute?" Audrey pitched her voice to a husky, sexy timbre.

"I thought I would go check on Daphne," Cade said, gesturing at the stairs.

"This won't take long," she told him, touching his arm. "Please? It's important. I'd like to talk to you . . . somewhere where we can be alone." She turned and gave Reese a dirty look.

"Of course." Cade gestured courteously toward the door. "Is the porch all right?"

"The porch is terrific," she told him, heading in that direction. She cast a triumphant look at Reese, who seemed to be scowling at her. He hadn't thought she could do it, she thought smugly. She was about to prove him wrong. *Just you wait, Reese Durham. The player's about to be played.*

Audrey stepped out onto the porch and waited for Cade

to join her. He did a moment later, brows knitting together with concern as he shut the door behind him. “Is everything all right?”

She nodded and walked to the railing, gazing out over the beautiful scene before her. There was no snow despite the chilly weather, and the mountains were purple in the distance, the trees like green velvet against the orange and purple sky.

It was sunset, so she didn’t have much time to waste. Audrey automatically glanced back at the lodge and noticed Reese gazing out the window in the kitchen at her. All right then. She just had to push through and make this happen.

Cade was watching her with a curious look. “Did you want to talk about something, Audrey?”

She turned, resting her bottom against the railing of the porch, and clung to one of the wood posts. “Come here, Cade.” When he looked hesitant, she added, “I’d like to keep our voices down so as not to disturb the others.”

He nodded, his hands going to his pockets as he strolled toward her. When he was within grabbing distance, he tilted his head and studied her. “Good enough?”

“Good enough,” she agreed.

“So what’s this about?” His expression looked bleak for a moment. “It’s Daphne, isn’t it?”

“No, no,” she told him hastily. “Nothing as bad as that.”

“I’m worried about her,” he told Audrey. “She’s recovering but she’s not happy about it. This is something she has to want for herself. It’s not enough for us to want it for her. It’s like she doesn’t care.”

“I’m sure she cares,” Audrey said, trying not to feel impatient. If he was going to talk about her twin and her health issues, she'd never wrangle that kiss out of him. "That wasn't why I called you out here."

"Oh?" Cade ran a hand over his jaw, and she noticed that he still hadn't shaved. He seemed distracted, too. This was the most not together she'd ever seen Cade, and it threw her. Was he truly that concerned for Daphne? She was doing fine. She was throwing up less today and was able to keep some dry toast down. Give it another week or so and she'd be just fine. "What is it, then?"

Audrey's tongue suddenly felt glued to the roof of her mouth. This was her moment. This was the time that she put aside all childhood longings and secret crushes and confessed just how she felt about this man. How she'd felt for as far back as she could remember. How she'd always loved him. How he meant everything to her and she wanted to take this love she had for him and turn it from one-sided into something she could share with him.

His expression was gentle as he waited patiently for her to speak, and it encouraged her.

"I . . ." She swallowed hard. "I wanted to talk to you about . . . how much it means to me that you're here." God, this was harder than she thought, especially since he was waiting on her with that patient look in his eyes. "You and I, we go way back."

"We do," he said with a grin. "I remember when the neighborhood kids used to steal you and Daphne's trikes and I had to go and steal them back for you."

"You always were our hero," she said softly.

"I always will be," he said solemnly. "Anytime you or your sister need me, you know I'll be there."

"I know. Just like this weekend." Audrey reached out for his hand and clasped it. It was warm against her own, and he gave it another friendly squeeze. Like he would a little sister who needed encouragement. "I . . ."

"Yes?"

She leaned in a little, letting her hair fall forward on her cheek and fluttered her false eyelashes at him. If it gave any sort of effect like it did to Daphne, her eyes were big and bold with the fake lashes. She hoped she looked soft and vulnerable to him. Alluring, maybe. "I just wanted you to know how much I value that we can lean on you. You're so important in my life."

"You're important in mine, too," he assured her.

This was turning into a pat-on-the-back conversation more than anything else. *Just come right out with it*, she told herself. *Tell him you love him. Grab him by the collar and kiss him like you did Reese.*

Except this was Cade, and she couldn't be all impulsive with him. She remembered back on the docks, back when she was thirteen. The disappointed look he'd given her when she'd shoved Daphne into the water. Like she'd turned out to be someone he didn't want and didn't like. She never wanted to see that expression on his face again.

And looking at him now, with a touch of impatience in his eyes as he waited for her to say what was so important, she realized . . . he'd be looking at her like that again if she confessed how she felt.

Because she knew, she just *knew*, that it was one-sided.

And the words glued in her throat for good.

"Cade?" Daphne's voice called out from the house. "Cade, are you back? Do you have my pill?"

Cade touched Audrey's arm, then glanced back at the lodge. "I need to go, Audrey. We'll finish this later?"

"Sure," she said with a small disappointed sigh. "Later."

He gave her another small smile, then headed back into the house, gently closing the door behind him.

Audrey stared out into the woods at the hateful sunset.

She could have taken matters into her own hands. Planted a kiss on Cade whether he'd wanted it or not, just to get Reese out of the house and win the bet. But that would have felt wrong on so many levels that she wouldn't have been able to handle it. She was frustrated with Cade for not giving her the perfect opening, but more than that, she was frustrated with herself.

After all, she'd been the one to accept the stinking bet.

The door creaked open and she didn't look over. She knew exactly who it was. It was Reese coming to gloat about how he'd won their little dare. This was two in a row that he'd more or less forced her to walk right into. She should be incredibly pissed.

Instead, that butterfly of excitement was back in her stomach, making her pulse race.

"Ahem."

She glanced over at Reese. He stood on the porch, arms crossed over an old gym T-shirt borrowed from Cade, a pleased smile on his face. "You get cold feet in the last moment, Miss Prim and Proper?"

"Something like that," she said, then shrugged. "Of course, it's impossible to win when someone deliberately stacks the deck against you."

"Who would do such an outrageous thing?"

"Someone who was up at dawn with Cade and knew he wasn't in the house when the bet was made," she said dryly.

He gestured at himself in mock surprise, then flashed her a naughty—oh so naughty—grin. "I told you I'd do whatever it takes when it comes down to winning."

"You certainly proved that today," she told him, forcing her voice to be utterly bland. "Way to go. You won yourself a skinny-dip with Daphne Petty's unattractive twin sister. Congratulations."

He gave her an odd look. "You're making it rather hard to gloat."

"What's there to gloat over?"

"The fact that I won a hot night of skinny-dipping with a lush, sexy redhead?"

She snorted. "You're just gloating because you won. No more, no less. You don't have to lay it on so thick."

"Suit yourself," Reese said, then glanced out at the pond. "You want to go now?"

"In broad daylight?" She looked scandalized.

"An hour from now?"

She considered it, then shook her head. "Daph and Cade will still be awake. I don't want them knowing about this little bet of ours."

"Heaven forbid anyone have fun while at this cabin," Reese said dryly.

Fun for you, she thought with a dark frown. "Midnight."

"You chickening out on me, Petty?"

"Don't be ridiculous. I just don't want everyone knowing our business."

"Midnight it is, then," he conceded. "But if you try to bail on me—"

"I'm not going to bail!" God, he was irritating. God, she wished that flutter in her belly would go away.

"Good." After a moment of silence, he turned and walked back into the house.

Apparently she now had a midnight date for skinny-dipping. *Hell.* Audrey sighed. Why was it that when she'd pictured this cozy weekend in the cabin with Cade, she'd imagined snuggling up with him by firelight while Daphne slept and they got to know each other all over again? Instead, the bad twin had the undivided attention of the hero and the good twin seemed to be making all kinds of crazy, ridiculous bets with the local miscreant.

Wasn't the good twin supposed to be the one who was rewarded at the end of the day? Somehow it didn't feel like it.

FIVE

The hours ticked past agonizingly slow. Dinner was awkward, with Daphne refusing to eat again. Reese made burgers for Audrey and Cade, and when he'd claimed it was her recipe for the delicious burgers, she'd done the dishes as a thank-you. He was still pulling his weight when it came to this charade, after all. Now if he'd only quit giving her such knowing looks, she'd possibly quit blushing.

Citing exhaustion, Audrey went to bed early that night. She dug through her clothing, looking for a bra and panty set that would be as close as possible to a swimsuit. No dice. Unlike all the romance heroines she read about, she didn't wear pretty, sexy underwear just because she could. Audrey liked function and utility in all her clothing, right down to her undergarments. Her serviceable nude-colored bra and matching bikini panties would have to do.

And then she laid down and tried to sleep for a few hours, but that was impossible. The butterflies in her stomach had somehow turned into something the size of ponies, and her pulse was pounding so loud in her ears that she was surprised the crashing wasn't bringing the others running.

She was . . . nervous. This wasn't something that sensible Audrey Petty, good twin extraordinaire, did. Daphne might, but Daphne also liked mind-altering drugs and booze.

When her twin came in a few hours later, Audrey feigned sleep. It didn't matter. Daphne immediately dropped onto her side of the bed, adjusted her pillows, and was sound asleep within moments. Audrey waited a few minutes more anyhow, then glanced over at the clock on the bedside.

Eleven thirty. *Damn.* Another half hour to go.

She lay in bed waiting, stiff with anticipation, watching the clock tick down toward midnight. She prayed Cade was fast asleep and she wouldn't wake him up when she snuck out. How utterly mortifying would that be?

All too soon, it was time. She swung her legs over the side of the bed and paused, waiting for Daphne to stir. Her twin was sound asleep, though, and after a moment's hesitation, she got out of bed entirely.

No response. *Well, that was good.*

Audrey pulled on a pair of jeans over her sleep shirt and then dragged her hair into its usual tight bun. She padded down the hall, wincing with every creak the floorboards made.

Reese was waiting by the back door of the lodge, leaning against it and checking his watch. He was dressed in those sleep pants he seemed to live in and another one of Cade's too-tight T-shirts. He grinned at the sight of her, his gaze moving back to her tight bun. "All armored up, I see."

"Just shut up and let's do this already," she told him in a hushed voice.

"Wait here a second," he told her, and disappeared into the hall. He returned a minute later with a pair of fluffy towels.

For some reason, the sight of those towels made her stomach drop. *Oh, God.* She was really, really going to do this. Panic flashed through her, and she forced it down. She'd get this over with as quickly as possible and head back to bed. No one needed to know about it. No big deal. Guys like Reese probably went skinny-dipping with women all the time.

She plucked a towel from his hand and opened the back door, stepping outside.

The night air was brisk. No, more than that. It was chilly. She gave a small shiver as she stepped out, feeling the wind cut through the thin fabric of her clothing. "Can't we do this some other night when it's not this cold?"

"Would you rather use the hot tub?"

Visions of Reese naked in the hot tub with the heiress flashed through her mind, and she frowned at the reminder. "Absolutely not."

He chuckled, his hand going to the small of her back. "Come on, then."

The walk down to the shore of the lake seemed to take forever. Reese was murmuring something but she wasn't paying attention. The butterfly in her stomach seemed to have taken up permanent residence, and she walked in a fog, the only thing soaking through her mind the strong, warm hand at the small of her back. For some reason, she liked that hand.

And then they were at the end of the dock. Audrey stared down at the dark water lapping against the wood and then looked dubiously at Reese. "I just want you to know that I hate you."

Reese chuckled, setting his towel down on the dock a safe distance away and then putting his hands on his hips. "So, you ready?"

"Of course not." She tossed her towel down on top of his. "I'm not going in first, either."

"Yeah, you are. You're the one who lost the bet."

"Am not," she told him. "How do I know you won't just run back to the house once I jump in the water?"

"Because I'm a man of my word?" He gave her a playful leer. "Plus, I relish the thought of seeing you naked."

"The feeling's not mutual," she said in a prim voice, though his words sent excitement coursing through her veins. *Oh, Lord.* She was going to see Reese naked again. She hadn't been paying attention to how he'd looked that first day that she'd caught him in nothing but a Speedo in the hot tub. Now, her mind was flashing vivid pictures over and over again, trying to pull together the full package of his, ahem, package.

She had to admit she was curious to see that. Not that she would ever tell him such a thing. Never.

"Fine, if you're going to be a chicken, I'll go first." Reese casually reached for the hem of his shirt and pulled it over his head. She watched his muscles flex in a gorgeous fashion as he stripped the shirt off, all lovely, gleaming skin and perfect muscle. Then, he turned and winked at her, as if knowing that she watched him.

It made her blush . . . but she didn't look away.

He tossed the shirt onto his towel, and then his hands went to the waist of his pants. In a flash, they were down around his ankles and she was staring at naked hips, the curve of perfect, naked ass, and a cock that was already swelling with excitement.

Her mouth went dry. He was gorgeous. She wanted to reach out and run her fingers along that smooth skin, feel the curve of his ass. Touch the cock nestled in the hair at his groin. Kiss him all over again and see how his body responded to her touch. But she didn't. She stood there, frozen, as he tossed the pants onto the discarded pile of his clothing. Then he stretched his arms over his head, casually, as if about to head into a swim meet.

Her eyes narrowed at him. "You're enjoying this, aren't you?"

"Immensely." He grinned at her and then stepped off the dock.

There was a small splash of water and then a small intake of breath that made her freeze up. "Cold?"

"Not too bad," he admitted. She was sad to see that he was entirely covered up by the water. Only his shoulders and his head were above the ripples of the lake. "Now your turn."

She hesitated.

"You gonna go all scaredy cat on me, Miss Goody Two Shoes?"

Audrey scowled at him, walking to the end of the dock next to him. The fire in her belly had returned, somewhat stoked by the sight of him so naked and gorgeous. She refused to think about how her pasty white skin and too-full figure would look in comparison to his. He'd asked for this, and she'd give it to him. With that fire encouraging her on, Audrey pulled her own sleep shirt off and then unzipped her jeans, letting them pool at her feet as she daintily stepped out of them. Now she was just in her plain bra and panties.

"Take your hair down," he called out.

"Not hardly," she told him, reaching for the clasp on the back of her bra. She hesitated a moment, her bravado slipping away a bit under the heat of his gaze. He was watching her, waiting for her to strip naked. Could she do this? Not that she had much of a choice. Biting her lip, Audrey closed her eyes, took a deep breath, and unclasped her bra, letting it fall to the ground. Without opening her eyes to see his reaction, she shimmied out of her panties, kicked them aside, and then took that last step off the dock before she could second guess herself.

The water was like ice.

As soon as it hit her skin, it sucked all the air out of her lungs and she let out a yelp of surprise. Her eyes had been closed and she hadn't judged how deep the water was, and the next moment, her head went under. She'd never felt anything so cold. She bobbed back to the surface, her eyes flying open. Immediately, her teeth began to chatter. "Oh, my God! C-c-cold!"

He grinned at her, then raised a finger to his lips to indicate that she should be silent.

She splashed water at him. "Don't you sh-sh-shush me. I'm fucking freezing! You should have told me!" He'd been so casual about the water. *It's not too bad.*

He was such a liar.

"If I had told you, you wouldn't have jumped in and you'd have deprived me of my sweet win and a chance to see you naked." He grinned, and she noticed that his lips were a little blue.

"You suck!"

"Audrey, hush or you're going to wake everyone up," he told her in a low voice, swimming a little closer. His hand grasped her arm.

She gasped at how warm his hand felt against her skin even in the cold water. Automatically, she reached for him and pressed her naked body up against his, wrapping her arms around his neck. She moaned at how warm he felt against her. It was like she was in a vat of ice and holding on to a space heater. "God, you feel good."

His arms went around her, his hand sliding to her ass and tugging her closer. A small groan escaped his throat. "Ditto."

Audrey shivered against him, her body plastered to his. One of her legs went around his hips, drawing him closer to her. It was an intimate, slick embrace but all she cared about was warmth. "Exactly how long do we have to stay in here?"

"I don't feel like moving," he told her, and squeezed one of her ass cheeks in response. His voice had gone low and husky.

She was about to protest that she did and she wanted to move ASAP, but her face was pressed against his cheek, her breasts pushed on his chest. He wasn't mauling her, either. He was just more or less standing there and letting her climb all over him—well, except for the hand squeezing her ass. And as she clung to his warmth, she realized that his body felt good against hers. All hard planes and delicious muscle and skin. Her mouth was exceedingly close to his ear, and he twitched every time she breathed out.

And the impulsive, fiery Audrey she tried so hard to clamp down came to the forefront. She leaned in and nibbled gently at his earlobe, taking it between her teeth.

Reese groaned and his hands clenched against her, and his other arm locked around her back, pushing her against him, hard.

She liked that response. So she took his earlobe in her mouth and began to gently suck on it.

His hips worked against her own, bucking a little. That hand clenched against her ass clenched all over again, as if he was trying to control himself and failing mightily. "Ah fuck, Audrey. That feels incredible."

She nipped at his ear again, and then moved to his jaw, sliding her lips along his mouth. He turned his head and his mouth moved to capture hers, even as he hauled her other leg around his hip.

Audrey moaned, clinging to him as his tongue began to thrust into her mouth, her hips bearing down against his cock. He slid between her legs, pressing hard against her sex, and then held there. No penetration, just the sheer pleasure of skin against skin. She tightened her legs around him and deepened the kiss, clutching at his shoulders.

It was not a soft, easy exploration of mouths like before. This kiss was hard, furious, and deep. It was uncontrolled and wild, and her teeth were chattering, lips shivering, and neither of them cared. Teeth clashed and tongues thrust with abandon.

His hand slid along her side in the icy water, a spot of warmth in the chill. When he slid between them and cupped her breast, she whimpered. He felt so good against her. He growled low in his throat at her response, his thumb grazing over her nipple, stroking the already tight peak over and over again. "Been wanting to touch these since the first day I saw you," he panted into her mouth.

"Liar," she said with a soft moan, her teeth tugging at his lower lip. She enjoyed his groan of response.

"Not lying," he told her, pinching the nipple between two fingers and rolling it, his gaze on her to see her response.

"Knew that underneath all that proper do-gooder Audrey there was the fiery girl. Fucking love bringing her out to play."

She moaned, burying her face against his neck as sensation coiled through her. "God, your fingers."

"You like that, firecracker?" His hand slipped away from her breast and she whimpered a protest. It slid between their bodies and she felt him brush against the curls of her sex under the water. "Like it when I use my fingers on you?"

Her fingernails dug into his skin, unable to respond. Instead, she just licked at his neck and bit at his collarbone, trying to show him how much she liked his touch after all. This was wild and wicked and she was out here with a man who was all wrong for her.

And she was loving every damn minute of it.

His hot fingers slipped between her folds and she cried out as he brushed her clit, biting down on his shoulder. Reese chuckled low, the sound almost guttural with need. "There's my fiery girl," he groaned, circling a finger around her clit, making her body shiver with need. "Want me to make you come?"

She buried her face against his skin, her mouth pressing hot and sucking at his flesh. Her hips bounced against his fingers, working against him, and letting that speak for her. She sucked on his skin, and then moved to another patch of skin, biting and licking and nibbling and sucking again, unable to help herself. All the while, she moved her hips against his fingers. She needed this so bad.

"Say my name, fiery girl," he murmured as her movements became more frantic, water splashing between the two of them. When she didn't respond, his fingers stopped their torturous circles.

"Reese," she growled low against his skin, and then bit him.

"Ah, fuck, that's right," he told her in a low breath. "Say it again and I'll make you come so good."

God, she needed to come, too. Her hips kept circling against his, and she clung to him. "Reese," she said between bites of his skin, then moved back to his neck and bit and licked at the cords of muscle. "Reese. I'm so close."

"Are you?" he breathed. His fingers against her clit changed their pattern, moving from tormenting circles to slow, delicious strokes from her core back up to her clit. "Are you—"

"Yes," she panted, clinging to him. "Please. Please, Reese—"

A light clicked onto their faces. "Reese? That you?"

Audrey froze. Reese froze. His hands moved off her body and he automatically sank deeper into the water, then shoved her behind him, covering his face with a hand.

A hand that had just recently been between her legs. Audrey huddled behind him, clinging to his back.

"Who's there?" Reese called.

A laugh. "Damn, buddy. Who else would be here?" The light clicked off. "I thought I heard some noise and came out to investigate. Uh, hi, Audrey."

Oh, God. It was Cade. Horror and mortification swept over her. She'd been bouncing on Reese—his best friend Reese! She was trying to come while the man she'd been in love with since grade school had caught them.

This was truly the worst night of her life. Hot tears of agony began to seep out from her lashes and a little sob caught in her throat. "Hi," she managed, but it came out rough.

Reese's hand brushed over her arm as if to comfort her.

"Hey, Cade, do you mind going back inside?" Reese said loudly. "You're shriveling my boner."

"Sorry. I didn't mean to interrupt." The light clicked on again and turned away. "You two carry on."

He didn't even sound mortified at catching them. At finding Audrey with Reese. He sounded . . . amused. And that hurt. It hurt a lot. If he'd even cared a bit about her in any way other than as friends, he'd have been upset or jealous. Instead, he was just amused at catching them.

Reese continued to rub her arm, protectively hiding her behind him. After a long minute, he murmured, "He's gone."

Audrey flung him away, gulping down the tears of shame in her throat. She swam away from Reese, heading for the shore. Half of her expected him to argue, but he didn't and simply swam after her. When she made it to the shore, she ran for her towel and wrapped it around her body, grabbing her clothes and running for the house.

"Audrey, wait!" Reese called after her. "Do you want to talk about this?"

"No!" she said, and ran before he could say anything else.

Well, damn. He could kill Cade for having such shitty timing.

Reese wrapped the towel around his hips and picked up his clothes, heading back toward the house. Audrey had run away moments ago, and he was pretty sure she was crying. And Reese was pretty sure that bothered him on levels he hadn't expected it to bother him on.

Cade didn't love her. If she ever got over her blind infatuation with the man and stopped to use her eyes, she'd realize it. But she only saw what she wanted to see, and it frustrated him.

Audrey was gorgeous. Not in the flashy way of the women he normally dated. Those women were perfectly tanned, perfectly toned, and had nothing going on between their ears except for when their next nail salon appointment would be. Those women bored him. Audrey, meanwhile, seemed to constantly keep him on his toes. He liked that she was unafraid to snipe back at him. He liked that she was constantly thinking, even if her thoughts did seem to be focused on either Cade or her sister.

And he really liked that fiery girl he kept coaxing to the surface. There was a lot of hidden spark inside of Audrey, and he had no idea why she worked so hard to clamp it down, hiding behind dull clothes and a skin-tight bun of hair. It was why he kept pushing at her. He wanted to see the woman break through the rigid surface.

And that Audrey? She was an animal. He grinned and rubbed his earlobe as he headed to the house, thinking of the way she'd come on to him. No coaxing from him this time. She'd made out with his ear and then kissed him back with a ferocious intensity. She'd wrapped her legs around him and bounced against his cock with fearless abandon, pressing those big breasts against his chest. And God, if that hadn't been the sexiest thing he'd seen in a long damn time. She'd been close to coming—he could tell in the way she'd bitten and licked at his skin like she wanted to crawl inside him.

Except Cade and his shitty, shitty timing had ruined it. Reese re-entered the lodge and shut the door quietly behind him. The living room was silent, and all parties were likely in their rooms and pretending to be asleep once more. Reese headed up to his room and discarded the towel as soon as he shut the door behind him. He was a bit chilled but it could wait. Instead, he walked up to the large mirror on the wall and turned on the lamp on the nearby dresser.

And grinned. His shoulder was covered in red welts from where her mouth had left hickies on him. He flexed and turned, glancing at his back. There were dozens of red scores from her nails.

Audrey was a little demon, wasn't she? He liked that. He turned the lamp off and slid into bed, under the covers.

His cock was hard and aching, and his hand absently stroked it as he thought of Audrey on the dock, her pearly skin gleaming in the moonlight. Her body was fuller than most women he'd dated, her hips thick. But she'd been soft and delicious in his arms, and those curvy hips tapered into an hourglass waist before curving back out again for that wonderful pair of large breasts she had. He was a breast man, and she had a magnificent set—full and heavy, tipped with tight pink nipples. She clearly didn't find herself attractive but, God, she was gorgeous. Sexier than Camilla. Definitely sexier than Audrey's sickly, famous sister that Cade seemed so infatuated with.

Maybe it was a good thing that Cade had caught them. Maybe she'd wake up and realize that Cade had zero interest in her . . . and she'd move on to someone like, say, Reese.

He'd be happy to have that lush redhead clinging to him in bed. Just thinking about that made his hand pump faster on his cock. She deserved better than Cade. No, scratch that, he thought with a frown. Cade was the best guy that Reese knew. He was kind and generous and always thinking of others. But Audrey was so contained and careful around him. That Audrey didn't need to be around twenty-four seven. She needed someone who would make the fiery girl come out. Someone like him.

Running a hand over his shoulder again, he grinned and thought of the hickies on his skin. Tomorrow he'd have to wear a wife-beater to show off the marks. He couldn't wait to see the angry flush on her cheeks at the sight. He continued to stroke himself, his hand tighter and moving faster on his cock, imagining Audrey's flushed cheeks, lush breasts, and that tight bun that never even let a tendril of hair escape. How she kept everything so tightly wound and neat that when she exploded, it was like a volcano.

His orgasm took him by surprise. He grunted, still working his cock as he spilled over his hand. *Great.* He'd just come imagining a woman's prissy bun coming undone. And for some reason, Reese couldn't stop grinning.

Audrey trembled in bed, bundled in a new set of pajamas, alternating between fury and shame.

Fury because she wondered if Reese had set up the skinny-dipping rendezvous deliberately so Cade would catch them. He knew how she felt about Cade. Knew she loved him, and he had nothing but derision for her feelings. He'd made that very clear. She wouldn't put it past him to have set up the situation with Cade.

Except she knew Cade wouldn't go along with something like that just to humiliate her. Cade was too . . . well, Cade was too nice.

And she was the one who had started it when she'd kissed Reese.

Horror coiled through her and she wanted to hide under the blankets and never come out. She'd come on to Reese Durham. She'd been unable to resist pressing up against him and she was the one who had attacked him like a starving woman. He'd simply been following her lead.

Why was she so attracted to the man? She should have been focused entirely on Cade, but instead she was hyper-aware of Reese's every motion, right down to the way his ass flexed when he bent over.

It bothered her that this was the opportunity she'd been waiting for—some alone time with Cade. And she was spending it all bickering with Reese and groping him every time Cade's back was turned.

And Cade had caught them tonight. And he'd thought nothing of the two of them making out together. No jealousy, nothing.

And she should be utterly devastated. She should be. But she was embarrassed and ashamed. Her hand slid between her legs and she sighed. And she was still a little horny, which sucked.

The next morning at dawn, Reese dressed in a wife-beater and a pair of sweatpants he found in one of Cade's drawers and made a pot of coffee before heading out to chop more wood. Audrey seemed to like a fire going all day and he liked pleasing her with something that simple.

He'd chopped two logs before the back door opened and Cade slipped out in a warm sweater and jeans, carrying two mugs of coffee. He moved down the steps and approached Reese, then offered one to him. "Can we talk for a minute?"

"This about last night?" Reese asked, taking the mug.

"Naturally."

Reese grunted and moved to sit on the chopping log.

Cade sat nearby on the steps, cradling the mug of coffee in his hands. He studied it for a minute and then glanced over at Reese, squinting into the rising sun. "So. You and Audrey. You want to tell me what that's all about?"

"Just a little bit of harmless flirtation," Reese said easily. "Why do you want to know? You're not interested in her, are you?"

Cade gave him an impatient look. "You know she's like a sister to me. I don't want to see her get hurt by you."

"I'm not going to hurt her. Jesus, Cade. When did you turn into my dad?"

"You two were naked in the water last night. Wrapped around each other. It's normal for me to have concerns. We both know you're a player, Reese."

So he was. They each had their different strengths. Logan was a leader of men. Cade's strength was his generosity of heart and open-minded thinking. Reese's strength lay in people—specifically using them for his own needs. He didn't do it out of meanness; most women knew what they were getting when they got together with him. His tabloid moniker of "Playboy Billionaire" was well earned.

But for some reason, it irritated him that Cade automatically assumed he was using Audrey. "I'm not going to hurt her, Cade. We're just having a bit of fun. Lay off."

"The girls said you were here with someone else when I arrived. Camilla, was it?"

Reese sighed. "Camilla's a good girl, but she's just business. Her dad owns the hotel chain that's thinking about investing in the cruise line."

"And so you're going to sleep with her?"

Reese shrugged. "We were just having fun, too."

"That's your problem, Reese. You don't take anything seriously when it comes to women. Audrey's not a girl you can use and discard." Cade's brows pulled together and for a moment he looked rather unhappy. "She deserves better."

"Better than me? You're wounding me, man."

"I know you're just bored—"

"Oh, fuck off with that," Reese interrupted, his temper coming to the front. "I'm not fucking around with her because I'm bored. Now you're insulting me and her."

"I just want to know if you really like her, Reese. That's all. She's not your normal type." Cade's voice smoothed out. "I wasn't trying to piss you off."

"I know. She's like a sister to you." Reese rubbed at his forehead and then chugged the coffee before tossing the rest of the mug's contents to the ground. "I get that. I just . . . I don't know. She's different. I like making her get all fiery and pissed off, because then she comes at me like a tigress."

Cade chuckled and grimaced. "It's weird to hear that about Audrey. I've known her since we were children and I don't think anyone's ever described her as a tigress."

"She's not bland or boring," Reese said, feeling the need to defend her. "She just wants everyone to think that. It's all an act she puts on so people will appreciate her or some shit."

"I never said she was bland or boring." Cade looked surprised at the thought. "I've known the twins since grade school. They're both too smart for their own good. That's why I had to ask you what your intentions were."

"And if I said I was going to fuck her and have a good time and not think about it when I leave?"

"It'd strain our friendship," Cade said.

He'd guessed as much. Cade took responsibility so seriously, and he felt responsible for the Petty twins. "Yeah, well, you don't have to worry too much." It was on the tip of his tongue to tell Cade that Audrey was in love with *him*, not Reese, but for some reason, the words wouldn't come out. He couldn't lash out at Cade simply because his ego was wounded a bit.

And hell, Cade was right to wonder. If Audrey indicated that she wanted in Reese's bed? He'd have her there and on her back in no time at all. He closed his eyes and rubbed his face, remembering the way she'd clung to him in the water and bucked against his hand. Fuck, that had been hot.

Even knowing she was in love with Cade didn't stop him. Audrey was a firecracker under that prim demeanor, and he liked having it come to the surface. More than that, he liked being the one to experience it. Someone like Cade wouldn't know how to bring out the best in her.

She needed someone like Reese to unlock the passion inside her.

It'd just be wasted on nice, polite Cade. She needed a bastard like Reese. Someone who'd push her until she lashed back.

He grinned, rubbing his shoulder. And he had the marks to prove it.

"Why do you say that?" Cade asked, interrupting Reese's thoughts.

"Huh?" He'd forgotten what they were talking about, lost in thoughts of Audrey underneath him, scratching up his back, demanding more.

"You said I don't have to worry too much. Why is that?"

"Oh." Reese thought for a minute, then walked over and handed Cade his empty coffee mug. "Because I don't plan on breaking her heart. Trust me when I say she's got it well guarded."

"Something's bothering you."

Audrey looked up from her bowl of oatmeal at Daphne

and her face automatically colored bright red. "I don't know what you mean."

Daphne rolled her eyes and stabbed her spoon into the bowl repeatedly. "It's just the two of us. You don't have to pretend with me."

She was right, Audrey had to acknowledge. The two men were out getting firewood and had left them alone for breakfast. There had been coffee made and oatmeal on the stove, though Daphne had claimed to not be hungry. Audrey'd fixed her a bowl anyhow, since her too-thin twin needed to eat rather desperately.

And now Daphne was staring at her like she'd grown another head. "So you're not going to tell me?"

"Tell you what?" Audrey said innocently. "You should eat, you know. I worked hard on making breakfast."

Daphne snorted and pulled out a pack of cigarettes. "I know you didn't make the food, Aud. I've tasted your cooking before, remember? I don't know why we're all keeping up the charade, but you can't fool me."

As Daphne lit a cigarette and took a long drag, Audrey wrinkled her nose. "Do you have to smoke that right here? It stinks."

"It does, doesn't it?" Daphne glanced down at the cigarette between her bony fingers. "I don't even like the taste, really."

"Then why smoke it?"

"Because you took away my crack pipe," Daphne said with a coy grin. When Audrey didn't smile, she sighed. "That was a joke, sis."

"Not funny."

Daphne took another pull on the cigarette and then flicked the ashes in her oatmeal bowl. "So, you going to tell me what's going on or am I going to have to guess?"

When Audrey hesitated again, a hurt look crossed Daphne's face. "You don't ever talk to me anymore, you know. I wish you would."

A burst of longing swelled in Audrey's chest. Back before Daphne had gone to LA to pursue her career in music, the twins had been incredibly close. Ever since they'd parted, though, Audrey felt as if she'd lost her other half. It hurt, and she desperately wanted her sister back. But that would take effort on both sides, she supposed. So she sighed and stirred her oatmeal, not really eating it, either. "I'm just a little mixed up at the moment."

"Oh?" Daphne's black-dyed brows went up. "Man trouble?"

Audrey blushed.

"Man trouble," Daphne agreed without a word being said from Audrey. "So tell me the scoop. Is it the big hunk?"

"Big hunk?" Audrey repeated.

Daphne waved her cigarette in the air. "You know. Cade's friend. What's his name. I can't remember. Was too busy puking my guts out. The one who's constantly looking at you. Hot tub Romeo."

Did Reese look at her all the time? Audrey hadn't realized. "His name's Reese Durham. He's one of Cade's billionaire friends."

"Yuck. Men with money are nothing but trouble." For a moment, Daphne looked sad, then shook it off, taking another puff of her cigarette. "So are you having sex with him?"

"Not yet." Audrey bit her lip. "But I really want to."

"So have sex with him."

She shook her head. "Not that simple, Daph. I kind of have a thing for Cade." Understatement of the year.

"Mmm. Love troubles." Daphne's eyes sparked with

interest, and she looked less tired for the first time in days. "So glad that they're someone else's for a change."

"Have you had love troubles?" Audrey asked. Daphne never shared any of the details of her relationships, though her songs were always teasing about men and breakups.

Daphne flicked her fingers, as if brushing the comment away. "Bygones. We're talking about you right now, sis. So you want the big hunk but you're afraid that it might interfere with your crush on Cade? Is he aware of how you feel?"

Audrey thought for a moment, wondering what to tell her sister. "He knows I exist, but it's definitely one-sided."

Daphne grinned. "So here's what you do. Nail the hot tub hottie until you're bored of him, and then go back to moping about Cade."

Audrey stood up, her shoulders squaring defensively. "Now you're just making fun of me. Not cool, Daph. I thought we were having a real discussion."

"Wait," Daphne said, reaching for Audrey's arm. "I was serious. What's wrong with hitting it until you quit it?"

Audrey stared at her twin. "Are you kidding? This is me we're talking about. I'm not the kind to sleep with a man just for sex's sake."

"You're not in a relationship, Audrey. Like you said, Cade doesn't even know you have feelings for him. Why not have a little fun? Play the field a bit? It's just physical. Have a little fling. Cade can't be mad that you hooked up with someone if you aren't with him."

Audrey bit her lip, considering. "I don't know."

"You're not old and married. Act your age. God. You make me feel old just being around you."

That hurt. "Gee, thanks Daph."

"I'm serious. Don't you ever have fun? You always look

so serious and unhappy, like you're doing your best to be the most vanilla, boring person you can imagine. That's no way to live." Daphne stubbed her cigarette out in the oatmeal bowl. "I was hoping you were having a turnaround this week. You just seemed so lively. A bit irritated, but still lively. I liked seeing that in you. At least then you had some spark, instead of just gray and bland all the time."

Knew that underneath all that proper do-gooder Audrey there was the fiery girl. Fucking love bringing her out to play.

Audrey thought for a long moment, staring at her oatmeal bowl. How much should she tell Daphne about what was truly going on? Could she count on Daphne to be discreet? She glanced over at her twin, who was pulling a new cigarette out of her pack, her hands trembling slightly. And then Audrey decided to trust Daphne just a little.

"I went skinny-dipping with Reese last night."

The new cigarette Daphne had just placed between her lips automatically fell out. She snagged it then pulled out her lighter. "Get out. You did? I'm proud of you."

For some reason, her twin's approval was . . . appealing. Even if it was over something as naughty as skinny-dipping. "Cade caught us, too."

Daphne grimaced. "You want to talk about someone who's no fun. Cade's picture's next to *serious* in the dictionary. So he caught you, huh? What did you do?"

"Hmm. Scream and ran for the house with a towel around me?"

"How did I sleep through this?" Daphne murmured, grinning. She gave her head a little shake. "So you going to go catch up where you left off tonight?"

"I don't know," Audrey admitted. The idea was taking root in her mind and it had a strange amount of appeal.

Use Reese like he used women? Sleep with him just for sex's sake? Was it such a terrible idea? "I wouldn't know what to tell Cade about what's going on."

"It's none of Cade's business," Daphne said in a pert tone. "He has zero claim on you at the moment. The only people it's between are you, that big hunk, and your twin sister who gets to hear all the secrets." She grinned at Audrey. "You'll have to tell me how it is."

"You're assuming I'm going to go through with it," Audrey said in a crisp tone.

"Don't get all proper with me, Aud. I know you. And I encourage this act of liberation. I say go for it."

"I'm glad I have your approval," Audrey teased, but the idea was now in her head and it wouldn't go away. What would it be like to sleep with a man, no strings attached? A man as sexy as Reese who drove her as crazy as he did?

She knew anything with him wouldn't be permanent. Not a bit. He used women like Camilla in the hot tub. They were diversions, and she was the current one.

But wouldn't it be fun—just for a little while—to be the diversion?

SIX

With that morning's conversation she'd had with Daphne still going through her mind, Audrey cleaned up the kitchen, straightened the living room, and then went upstairs to check her appearance.

Shirt: plain black and long sleeved. Jeans: serviceable. Hair: tight bun. Skin: fresh scrubbed and freckled. It'd have to do. Audrey smoothed a hand over her bun and then headed outside, looking for Reese.

He wasn't hard to find—the sound of chopping wood rang in her ears even from inside the house. Sure enough, he stood up in a small clearing near a pile of wood, axe in hand. He was wearing a muscle shirt, his corded arms bare and gleaming with sweat. He'd obviously been at things for some time.

"Reese?" She shielded her eyes from the sun and stood a decent distance away. "Can we talk for a moment?"

He turned to her and tossed the axe down to the ground. "Sure, what's up?"

She glanced around. "Where's Cade?"

"Out for a morning walk. He wanted to clear his head. That what you wanted to talk about?" He wiped at his brow, then picked up a water bottle from nearby.

As he straightened, she noticed a series of reddish purple marks on his skin. She leaned in, trying to figure out what they were. Then she gasped as she realized just what it was, her memory flicking back to last night. She recalled her mouth on his skin, biting and sucking at his tight muscles.

Good God, she'd covered him with hickies. "Your shoulder!"

Reese grinned, looking rather pleased with himself. He plucked at his shirt. "Thought I'd show them off."

Her jaw ground. "Did Cade see those?"

"He did."

"Annnnd you wore that shirt on purpose."

"I might have." He winked at her, then took a swig from his water bottle. "So what's on your mind?"

She stared at the markings on his shoulder, feeling heat creeping through her body at the sight. She'd done that to him? She'd been wild and out of control last night.

She wanted to do it again.

But she'd mess with him a little first. Audrey grabbed a handful of his shirt. "We need to talk."

"Someone's the voice of authority," he said, amused. But he followed her lead.

She dragged him through the muddy yard, around to the far side of the lodge, then under the wraparound porch. The cord of wood that the men worked to constantly replenish was stored underneath, next to the cellar doors.

Anyone standing underneath the porch was shielded from all eyes, the windows above only giving a view to the trees and lake below. It was perfect for what she wanted to do.

When he followed her under the porch, ducking his head to ensure he didn't crack his skull, he gave her an odd look. "Why are we heading under here?"

Audrey tugged at his shirt, dragging him closer. "Because we didn't finish what we started last night," she told him in a low voice.

Then her hand went to his cock, and she rubbed.

The breath hissed out of his throat. Reese stared down at her for a moment, incredulous, and then a slow smile spread over his face. "Mercenary little thing, aren't you? I like that."

"Do you now?" She leaned in and nipped at his chin, feeling the scrape of stubble. Odd how that excited the hell out of her. "Why don't you show me?"

"Exactly what business did we leave unfinished the other night?" Reese murmured, pushing her backward a step until her back was up against the woodpile. Rough bits of wood clung to her clothing and scraped at her flesh through the fabric, but she didn't care.

"I'm sure you can guess."

"Well, last I recall, I had my hand between your legs and you were riding me."

Heat pooled between her legs and her breathing sped up. "That sounds about right."

"You want to fuck right here on the woodpile?"

Her hand rubbed along the hardening length in his pants, enjoying the sensation of him under her fingers . . . and the heady feeling of power she had at manhandling him. "I was thinking more like a bit of heavy petting here in the woodpile," she said, and let her lips graze against his mouth. "Then maybe a nice, dirty fuck later."

Reese groaned, thrusting against her hand. His slid to the waistband of her pants. "You want me to make you come?"

"That's what I had in mind, yeah." She licked her lips and glanced up at him through her lashes. "I was thinking that maybe we could make each other come."

"Mmm," he breathed, watching her with intense blue eyes. "I think I can agree to that . . . on one condition."

She looked up at him, curious. "Condition?"

To her surprise, he reached for the tight knot of her hair and pulled at the hair band. "This needs to come free. I want the wild Audrey, not the uptight one."

She snorted, half tempted to punch him in the gut for calling her uptight . . . but there was too much heat pumping through her veins to even think of something like that. She simply stood still while he tugged her hair free and let it fall around her shoulders in a bright red sweep.

"That's better," he murmured. "Sexy, dirty little Audrey. It's like that wild side of yours is the best kept secret around."

Her fingers curled around the stiff length of him tenting the front of his pants. "And your wild side is the worst kept secret."

Reese chuckled low, pulling her against him and letting his hands slide to her ass. "Flattery will get you everywhere."

"It wasn't intended to be flattery," she told him, even as she lightly stroked her hand up and down his length. "You're not my type."

"Then why are you stroking my cock?" His hand played

with the waistband of her panties again, except this time he slid his fingers inside her.

"I told you," she whispered. "You need to finish what you started."

And she reached for the laces of his sleep pants, tugging at the string until the knot came loose and the fabric pooled loosely around his waist. He wasn't wearing underwear—again—and she caught a glimpse of the large head of his cock, flushed with his own excitement, a droplet of precum glistening on the head.

The sight of him made a tremor rush through her body, and that tremor intensified when she felt his fingertips sweep over her mound, brushing against the curls there.

He groaned at the feel of her, the sound soft against her messy hair. "Wet already, Audrey? You just that excited or you been thinking about coming out here and grabbing me all morning?"

Her hand moved into his pants, cupping his hot, bare flesh. "Maybe a little bit of both?" She leaned in and licked a drop of sweat from his hickey-flushed shoulder. His cock in her hand was scorching, so hot against her that it was like touching fire.

Reese's fingertips grazed against her clit, seeking it out. At her shuddering response to his touch, he stopped there and rubbed lightly, brushing back and forth against the sensitized bud with the pads of his fingers. "That's the spot."

Audrey whimpered, her fingers curling around his cock and stroking him with a jerky motion.

"Shhh, shhh," he told her, murmuring low in her ear, his breath tickling her hair. "Go slow, sugar. I've got control of you now." His hand brushed against her nape, and then he grabbed a handful of her hair, tilting her head back and exposing her neck. His lips moved against her jawline, teeth scraping at her skin. "Sexy little spitfire. My naughty little firecracker."

As he murmured the words against her skin, his fingers kept stroking at her wet heat, rubbing through the slick folds as she clung to him. He'd stroke down to the well of her sex, circle her sensitive skin there, and then glide up to her clit, and repeat that maddening circle. His movements were slow and unhurried—deliberately, she assumed, to make her force him to speed up somehow.

He was causing her to get distracted, too, her mouth working silently as every brush of his talented fingers made her body shudder anew. She was having a hard time concentrating on stroking his cock, her fingers lightly dancing along the head and brushing at the pre-cum there. She rolled the wetness along the head, exploring him with her touch. Reese was definitely well formed, the crown large and thick, the length of his shaft smooth and long. She moved down to his sac, and felt him, heavy and hot, in her grip.

Reese groaned and licked at her jaw. "Talented with those hands, aren't you?"

"I could say the same for you," she told him, and rocked her hips against his fingers when he stroked her clit.

"Ah, that's it, sugar. You going to ride my palm?" He pressed the heel of his palm against her clit, his fingers grazing at her core, and stopped moving.

She whimpered, clutching at the length of him with her one hand, the other fisted into his shirt.

"That's right," he told her, his mouth sliding over her lips. He brushed against hers in the lightest of kisses, a mere flirtation. "Rock against me again, Audrey. Let me feel you move."

She followed his lead, moaning when her movements

forced the heel of his palm hard against her clit. The sensation was incredible, and she repeated it, her hips jerking against him.

"Do it again," he commanded in a low voice. "Ride me, Audrey." He kissed down her neck, his tongue flicking at her skin.

She did, bucking against him. Then, she couldn't seem to stop herself. She rubbed up against him, over and over, like a wanton. Wild with the need he was building in her, Audrey leaned back against the woodpile, her hips moving harder and faster as she forced her sex against his palm. She was so wet that his entire hand was coated with her juices, though from his own soft encouragements, he liked the sight of that.

He continued to murmur at her, encouraging her to ride him, even as his mouth slid a little lower, brushing at the valley between her breasts and licking the skin exposed by her collar. But when he nuzzled at her breast through her clothing and slid his hand to cup one of her breasts, arching it to his mouth? When he bit the hard, aching tip through her clothing?

She shattered. A low, guttural groan erupted from her throat and she clenched her hand around his hard cock, still dripping with pre-cum, as her own orgasm rushed through her.

"Shhh," he warned, moving up to cover her mouth with his. She heard the low chuckle he swallowed just before his lips covered hers, his tongue thrusting into her mouth as he ground the heel of his hand against her clit in a circular motion, extending the ripples of her orgasm until she was whimpering against him, her knees weak. "That's my girl," he told her when they finally parted, Audrey limp from the force of her orgasm.

Dazed, she struggled to reorient to her surroundings. She was shoved up against the woodpile. His hand was in her now-soaked panties. His other hand still cupped her breast, occasionally grazing his thumb over the nipple he'd bitten.

And she was still clinging to the length of his hard, erect cock as it jutted out from his pants.

Reese leaned in and kissed her again, with a bit more urgency behind it. "You going to do me the honors, firecracker?"

She clenched her hand slightly around his length, enjoying the tremor of response that shot through him. "Actually, I thought I was done here. I'm sure you can handle yourself."

He laughed, seemingly delighted in her prickliness. "You tease." He nibbled at her lips. "I can handle it myself, all right. But your hands are far more pleasant than mine. Less callus."

Her lips curled with amusement. She had to admit, he was rather fun to play with. He wasn't begging for her to give him head. He was letting her know it was okay with him if she wanted to stop, but he wouldn't turn her down if she wanted to continue.

Oh, she definitely wanted to continue. That wicked streak she fought so hard to clamp down was humming like a freight train inside of her. What did it matter if she was a little bad with just one man? Like Daphne had said—she could use him, play with him a bit, and then walk away unscathed. She wasn't in a relationship, after all.

She was just having fun.

And so she gave him a naughty smile and wiggled out of his grip, then dropped to her knees in front of him.

He groaned at the sight. "Fuck, look at you. Gorgeous."

Audrey grinned up at him, then parted her lips and leaned forward, just a little. She didn't move to take his cock in her mouth. She simply sat there, a few inches away, her lips parted with anticipation.

And she looked up at him, waiting.

"Damn, that's hot." Reese's hand slid into her hair, stroking through the tangled locks and caressing her scalp. He didn't surge forward like she'd expected. Instead, he stared down at her, considering for a long moment. Then those strong fingers curled at the base of her head and gently forced her forward.

Her lips went around the head of his cock, her hands sliding to his ass to anchor herself. Audrey let the wet head of him graze over her lips, back and forth in a light motion for a moment, before taking him into her mouth and sucking hard enough to form hollows in her cheeks.

Above her, Reese grunted approval, but didn't move, didn't begin to fuck her face. It was as if he were enjoying the sight of her as much as the feel, and wanted to savor it.

She could appreciate that. It made her feel incredibly sexy, knowing that he was enjoying looking at her going down on him. And it made her excited all over again. She dug her fingers into the tight muscles of his ass, appreciating their rock-hard firmness. God, he had a nice ass. She squeezed it and then released the head of his cock with an audible pop, then rubbed her mouth along the head again. Pre-cum slicked her lips and she licked them clean with her tongue, then let it flick out and swipe over the crown of his cock.

"Just like that," he told her in a husky voice, his fingers tightening on the base of her head. "That's beautiful, Audrey. Take me in your mouth again."

She leaned in, but instead of sinking down on him, she

formed her tongue into a hard point and trailed it along his cock, exploring him. She circled the head with the tip of her tongue, licking at his glans, then the ridge of the crown. There was a thick vein along the underside, and she ran her tongue along it, too, then lightly tongued the base of him before moving back to the crown again.

"Mmm," he told her, and she looked up to see his eyes closed for a moment in ecstasy. "I have to admit, I never imagined that prim, proper little Audrey would be so good with my cock."

She slid a hand to the base of his cock and gave him a little pump as she slicked her tongue over the head again. "What, did you think I was a sweet little virgin?"

He chuckled, his fingers tight in her hair. Not pushing, just holding her there. "The thought did cross my mind."

"Not virginal in the slightest," she told him softly. "Maybe I just like making a man work for it." She licked the underside of the crown. "And then I make it worth his while."

"Goddamn, you sure do."

She grinned and then took him deep again, sucking deep and sliding her mouth down until she met the hand clenched around his base, then slid back, then took him deep again, feeling him butt against the back of her throat. She loosened her jaw and began to work him deeper.

"Ah, fuck. That feels amazing." He began to work her head, just a little. "Definitely not virginal. Definitely not."

She let him lead her, sucking him deep with each small thrust of his hips, riding the pressure of his hand. His arousal was turning her on all over again, his pure enjoyment of her working him so intensely pleasurable. Most men just expected a blow job, but Reese made it seem like she was blowing his mind along with his cock.

Well, she definitely knew her way around a good blow job. And she had another trick up her sleeve. She slid back and wrapped both hands around his cock, as if she were holding a baseball bat, and ignored the pressure he put on the back of her head for her to return to deep throating him. Instead, she took the head of him and sucked, running her tongue along him.

And then she began to hum.

She felt him jerk in surprise, but she held on to him and kept humming. Not a song, just a low, wordless tune that made her throat vibrate. She increased the intensity of her humming, rolling the head of him on her tongue.

"Oh, fuck. That's . . . God, that's good." His hand clenched her hair tight. "Just like that. Keep humming."

So she did. Louder and harder. Her hands pumped the base of him in time to her humming.

"Damn," he bit out, and then he began to buck his hips in response, then stilled. "Audrey, I'm going to come if you don't stop—"

She hummed louder and pumped him again.

"Ah, damn." Reese thrust into her mouth again, taking control. She tried to keep humming but he began to thrust into her mouth, and then he stiffened. Her mouth flooded with his cum, the tangy burst of him filling her mouth. She swallowed as he pulled out of her mouth, shuddering, and leaned back, wiping at her lips as he leaned against the woodpile, breathing hard.

When he was able to catch his breath, he looked back over at her and that cocky grin slid across his face. "Damn. I need you out here every morning when I'm chopping wood. That'd make this a lot less monotonous."

Audrey got to her feet and delicately wiped the corners of her mouth. "You're welcome," she said in a prim voice.

He smirked at her, then moved forward and grabbed her by the back of her head again. To her surprise, he leaned in and gave her a hard, rough kiss. "Thank you."

And she was already turned on again. Giving him a blow job and then kissing him? Wasn't exactly killing her libido. If anything, it felt more ramped up than ever. "So," she breathed. "Tonight?"

His gaze was hot on her face. "Name the time and place."

"Midnight," she told him. "We'll meet at the dock and head out into the woods. Bring condoms."

"You bring a blanket," he told her. "I'll bring the wood."

She groaned. "That was a terrible joke."

"Yeah, I get corny after sex. Sorry about that." He leaned in and kissed the tip of her nose in a surprisingly tender gesture. "Now you know my big secret."

"I promise to blackmail you with it at every opportunity," she told him lightly, then ran her fingers through her hair, trying to comb it into a semblance of normalcy.

He stopped her hand. "Leave it down for me. I like it a bit mussed and wild."

Heat bloomed in her cheeks again, but she dropped her hand. "Down it is."

"Down tonight, too."

She nodded, and that butterfly in her belly went wild at the thought. *Tonight.*

It was going to be a very long day.

The day passed with excruciating slowness for Audrey. She did her best to stay calm, cool, and collected. All the while, her thoughts raged like an inferno.

She was going to have sex. With Reese. Tonight. In the woods. Secret, dirty sex with a man who used women like they were Kleenex. And she was excited as hell.

Still, she had to act like nothing was going on, or Cade and Daphne would figure out that something was up. So she cleaned house, since she knew that wouldn't strike Daphne as out of the ordinary. Audrey loved things in their neat, orderly place, and her apartment was always spotless. So she organized the cabin to keep her mind busy, knowing that Daphne certainly wouldn't volunteer. She scrubbed the kitchen and mopped the floors. She straightened up the room she shared with messy Daphne. She cleaned the bathrooms and did laundry, since the cabin also boasted a tiny washing machine and dryer.

She folded clothes and dusted, and all the while Daphne and Cade played cards in the living room while Reese napped on one of the couches. She made sure to saunter past Reese's couch and gave it a nice kick just to wake him up. She had to make it seem like he irritated her, of course.

In truth, her faux irritation at him was quickly turning into a turn on. She couldn't stop thinking about their interlude in the woodpile. The way he'd gripped her tangled hair and drove into her mouth while she clenched her hands against his tight ass. The way his lips had grazed over her own as his fingers stroked up and down the slippery wetness between her thighs, moving over her clit and driving her wild.

No wonder Reese was so popular—he was a rather attentive lover. He seemed to be fascinated with what would turn her on as well as getting his own. She liked that. She'd had a fair amount of lovers in the past, and only a few had been truly interested in driving her crazy. Most men were more interested in what they could do to get into her panties and, once there, didn't care all that much about if she came. So she'd learned to be a bit more aggressive in bed because she knew that was the only way she'd get what she wanted out of things. It worked well for her, most times. Reese seemed to like it, too.

When she was out of laundry to wash, she did the sheets and blankets next, stripping each bed and keeping herself busy. Daphne rolled her eyes at Audrey's industriousness, a cigarette hanging from her lips as she studied her cards.

She could have sworn that Reese was smiling to himself when she passed by with a blanket, though, and had to hurry out of the room before that blush threatened to turn her face cherry red. She was so freaking obvious sometimes.

After the laundry was done, she made sandwiches for dinner (since she was still having to pretend that she was the master chef in their little domicile) and then headed upstairs for a long, leisurely shower. She wanted to smell clean and delicious for their meeting tonight. Audrey borrowed Daphne's expensive soaps and shampoos, and then took her time shaving. She considered the mound of her pubic hair for a moment. Would she shock Reese by going bare? She stared at her razor, thinking, then changed her mind. She wasn't going to change who she was to impress a man. So she simply tidied things up and then headed into the room she shared with Daphne, lounging on the bed as she read one of her romance novels and painted her toenails and fingernails a pale nude.

The blanket she'd promised to bring that night? Audrey stashed it under the bed in preparation, and then dressed in her matching bra and underwear, wishing she'd brought something sexy. Heck, that she *owned* something sexy.

Eventually, day passed into night and everyone retired sometime around ten. Daphne chatted with Audrey as they readied for bed, her twin seemingly more animated than she had been in days. The horrible shakes were going away, as was the constant vomiting. She was pale but no longer that sickly seeming greenish shade that had worried Audrey. And if she smoked like a chimney? Well, that was all right. Smoking was a bit easier to quit than coke and Xanax, after all. She was down to a half a pill a night, thanks to Cade's careful planning and repeated consultations with his on-call doctor, and soon she'd be off the Xanax for sure. Her progress made Audrey happy, though she was concerned that Daphne would backslide as soon as they turned around. What would happen when she returned to LA and the fast-paced lifestyle she was accustomed to? Her twin didn't seem like a changed person.

But she couldn't worry about that right now.

They went to bed and Audrey lay next to her sister, trying to make her breathing seem slow and regular. In reality, her pulse was racing, her mind wide awake. She was going to have sex with Reese Durham. That thought alone was enough to keep her body wound up to a fever pitch of anticipation. Hell, she was pretty sure she was wet simply thinking about how the evening would go. She'd mentally pictured it at least a dozen times already that day. Reese pushing her up against a tree and fucking her. Reese laying her down on the blanket and making exquisitely slow love to her. Reese flipping her over for doggy-style sex. Laying atop of Reese for sixty-nine.

Okay, this wasn't helping her pulse slow down any. Audrey locked her fingers over her chest and pretended to sleep, exquisitely aware of her twin in bed next to her. It took seemingly forever for Daphne's breathing to slow down and become even, small snores escaping her throat. She lay there, still, waiting for her to slide into deep slumber. And all the while, she'd peek over and glance at the alarm clock, waiting for midnight.

Ten thirty.

Eleven.

Eleven fifteen.

Eleven twenty.

Good Lord. Audrey was practically fidgeting as she stared at the clock. Time seemed to slow, and then speed up again.

Eleven fifty-five.

Eleven fifty-nine.

Twelve.

It was twelve. Time to go. She swallowed hard, suddenly nervous, and turned to glance at sleeping Daphne. Her twin was huddled on the edge of the bed, wrapped in the blankets, clutching her pillow. Her sleep was peaceful, her breathing regular. Good.

With exquisite slowness, Audrey slid out from under the covers, and then carefully rolled out of bed, one twitching, screaming muscle at a time. Then, she carefully pulled out the quilt she'd put aside for that night and zipped up a hoodie over her pajamas. Blanket in hand, she tiptoed out of the room, feeling very much like a naughty teenager on her way to sneak out and meet her boyfriend for illicit sex.

Except she'd never done that as a teenager. She'd always covered for Daphne.

This wasn't naughtiness, she assured herself as she shut the door to their shared room and then crept down the stairs. No one was awake or in the living room, so she headed outside, carefully shutting the door behind her like she was an old pro at sneaking out to meet men. Audrey headed down to the dock, the evening quiet and brisk around her. It was still. Almost too still. And that meant her thoughts were loud in her own head.

Not naughtiness, she told herself again. It was more like . . . scratching an itch. No one would ever know that she'd had sex with Reese, she'd get him out of her system, and then she'd go back to her sad, endless crush on Cade.

Strange how she hadn't given him that much thought while she'd been here at the cabin with him. She frowned, smoothing a hand over the blanket. She was just too distracted, she decided. First by the fact that her twin was here and in trouble, and then with Reese constantly flirting and challenging her. She didn't have as much time to spend with Cade as she'd hoped. Still, this was a reunion of sorts, and she imagined they'd be closer than they were before when everyone returned to their regular lives. That would be a good thing.

Except at that point, she'd have slept with his best friend. And he'd caught them skinny-dipping together. He wasn't likely to forget that. A sick pit formed in her stomach. Was her fling with Reese going to torpedo her chances with Cade forevermore? Did she want to do this? She hesitated, glancing around the silent, dark dock as she waited for Reese. The playboy. The user of women. The one who was totally and completely wrong for her in every way that Cade was so very right for her.

Maybe this was a mistake after all. She should turn right around and head back up to bed. Leave him hanging and pretend like this never happened.

She had almost made her mind up to do exactly that when one of the boards creaked behind her, and then a warm back pressed against her own. One hand circled around to her front, cupping one of her heavy breasts, his thumb stroking over the nipple through the fabric. "Hello, sexy," Reese murmured in her ear, and then his tongue lightly traced the shell of it as his thumb rubbed a circle over her now-hard nipple. "Am I glad to see you."

And there went her resolve. Audrey weakened, leaning against him, a tiny whimper escaping her throat as heat flooded her body. God, he knew just how to touch her to make all of her bones turn to mush. She turned to look at him, noticed he was wearing the same thing he always did—a cheesy workout T-shirt and a pair of sleep pants. Didn't Cade have anything decent in this house he could borrow?

"Let's get out of here," he whispered against her hair, lips brushing her ear, "and find somewhere private, shall we?"

She nodded, all thoughts of his wardrobe disappearing from her mind, and his hand went to the small of her back as he led her down the dock. She was going to do this. She was really going to do this. Damn the consequences. She needed this night with Reese to get him out of her system. He was like a burr under her skin, always there, an itch she couldn't scratch. Driving her mad and distracting her. This would take care of it.

She hoped.

His hand on her back was like a brand against her skin, her body acutely aware of that small, polite touch. He led her through the thickening trees and into the woods, far from the cabin. They left the lake behind and headed even deeper, until she couldn't see the night skies overhead because the trees had grown so thick, and it grew steadily darker.

"Do you know where you're going?" she had to ask at one point.

"I do," he said. "The perfect little spot. It's not much farther."

"Is it safe to be out here? What about bears and wildcats and things?" Audrey hadn't been thinking of such things when she'd suggested the woods, but she was thinking about them now that it was so incredibly dark and the trees so thick.

She heard his chuckle. "We'll be making too much noise. Don't worry about it. You don't want Cade to find us again, do you?"

"God, no," she breathed, annoyed at his small snort of derision. What was *that* supposed to mean? But she didn't have the chance to ask.

"Here we are," Reese said, gesturing at the area in front of him.

She had to admit, to her night-blind eyes, it didn't look like much. There was a pair of trees growing close together, forming a bit of a cradle between the roots in the ground, but that was about it. "Should I be impressed? What am I looking for?"

"These trees are perfect for us, my scowly little firecracker. They'll keep us shielded from the wind and the branches are low enough to climb if anything decides to check us out."

She froze. "I thought you said we were safe?"

"I know, but my ass is spectacular when it's naked, and you never know." She caught a glimpse of his white smile flashing in the darkness. "Plus, I hid a few things out here earlier."

"Did you?" She hadn't realized he'd left the house. "Things like what?"

He took the blanket out of her hands and began to unfold it. "You'll see."

"Things like what?" she repeated. "I can't say I'm into whips and things, if that's what you have in mind. I'm not that kind of girl." Plus, the thought of Reese having whips at hand at all times—and probably to use on Camilla—bothered the hell out of her. The bolt of jealousy that slammed through her was humiliating.

"Calm down, Audrey," Reese said in a slightly annoyed voice, spreading the blanket between the cradle of the tree roots. "Nothing weird, Miss Prim. Condoms. Bottles of water. Things like that. Jesus."

"Oh." Well, now she felt stupid. "Don't call me Miss Prim."

"Miss Prim," he teased in that irritating voice, turning to face her. His arms crossed over his chest, as if daring her to do something about it. "You are Miss Prim. Your hair's up again, even. Didn't I ask you to wear it down?"

So she'd pulled it into a ponytail for tonight. Like that was supposed to be weird? It didn't give him leave to insult her. She gave his chest a slight shove out of irritation. "Stop it, Reese. You're being a dick."

"And you're being Little Miss Goody Two Shoes all over again. I have to say, I'm not a fan. What happened to that wild redhead who molested me by the woodpile earlier this morning?"

Her mouth tightened. "I'm not your Barbie doll. I'm not going to put my hair a certain way just because it makes your dick hard."

"Gee, and I thought you wanted my dick hard. You certainly seemed to this morning. Remember that? You had your mouth open, just waiting for me to shove it in—"

Fury blossomed through her and she grabbed the front of his shirt, wanting to shake him for being such a douchebag. Why was he being like this? It was like he was deliberately trying to piss her off. And he just kept talking, which made her angrier, so she did the only thing she could think of to shut him up.

She planted her mouth on his in a furious kiss.

That worked. The stream of irritating conversation coming from him immediately dried up as her lips mashed on his in that furious lip lock. Suddenly his hands were on her shoulders and he was clenching her against him, the kiss growing hotter and wilder. Their lips ground together without any regard for coordination, all teeth and lips and furious, frantic kissing. It was punishment and wildness all rolled into one, and her body practically vibrated with emotion as his tongue swept against her own.

She captured his tongue with her lips and sucked on the tip, then flicked her own tongue against it, rewarded with his groan of pleasure. All that anger had turned, somehow, into a competitive sort of spirit, and she suddenly wanted to drive him wild. To make him as mindless and crazy as he made her. So Audrey became more aggressive with the kiss, continuing to suck at his tongue, then let him slide away from her. Then she tugged his lower lip into her mouth and lightly bit down on it as she raked her fingernails down the front of his shirt in an aggressive mood.

Reese groaned again, louder, and she felt his fingers clench on her shoulders. He wasn't moving, either; he was letting her take the lead.

Well, she'd show him just how much she could do with the lead, she decided. Her hands went to his shirt and she jerked at it, trying to tear it off him without breaking the locked, tongue-tangling kiss they were sharing. She took the advantage on the kiss, her tongue moving against his in an aggressive pace, letting out all the emotion she'd built up for the day. She'd pictured their coming together a dozen times earlier that day; each one had involved slow, sweet, romantic sex. A leisurely exploring of bodies. The reality was nothing like that—she needed this, and she needed it rough and hard and right away, and she was going to demonstrate to him exactly what she needed.

Reese raised his arms so she could jerk the shirt over his head, but it was too tight and not moving nearly fast enough for her liking. The sound of fabric tearing made her pause for a moment, breaking the kiss as she stared down at the jagged hole she'd torn through the collar of his shirt. Then she ripped that tear, suddenly aroused by the thought of tearing the shirt off this man, and the fabric came apart in her hands.

He groaned, reaching for her ponytail, and pulled her hair free. "You ripping all my clothes off, sexy?"

"Hush, Reese," she told him, shoving the fabric of the destroyed shirt aside. "No talking." She slid her hands over the flat planes of his stomach, admiring the way his muscles felt under her fingers. God, that was good. His nipples were flat and hard, and when her exploring fingertips scraped over them, he hissed in response.

So she leaned in and bit one.

He made a surprised sound, and then his hands went to her hair, holding her head against him, as if he wanted her to bite him again. So she did, taking the hard little nub of his nipple between her teeth and giving it a small, sharp bite, then flicking away the pain with her teeth. All the while, her hands went to his sleep pants and she jerked at the knot holding them there. It came free and she slammed his pants down his thighs, freeing his cock.

No underwear, again. She wondered if Reese even wore the things. Then she decided she didn't care.

She pressed a kiss on his abdomen, her mouth urgent, and then slid the pants all the way down his legs. "Lie down," she commanded him.

He did so without a word of protest, moving onto the blanket. She tugged at her own pajama pants, frantic with the need to get them off, and as she stripped them from her legs and divested herself of her panties, she heard the crinkle of a condom. She turned to look at him, and he patted the blanket next to him. As if she was going to lie next to him and let him take over.

Fat chance. She was still burning with an angry mix of rage and desire, and that meant that she was taking control. Ignoring the rest of her clothing, she moved, her bottom half bare, to the blankets and shoved at his shoulder until he lay on his back. Then, she straddled him and lay on his stomach, enjoying the way his eyes widened in the darkness.

"You going to ride me, firecracker?" His voice was a husky, pleased whisper.

Audrey didn't answer him. She simply rolled her hips against his belly and enjoyed his muffled sound of pleasure. His hands went to her bare thighs, holding her against him. She leaned in and gave him another punishing kiss, this one all furious lips and pent-up desire, and when they were both panting with need, she raised her hips, grasped his cock, and guided him inside her, lowering until she was seated on his length.

And then she gave a small sigh of pleasure at that.

"Ah, fuck, Audrey. Damn, you feel good." His hands clenched on her thighs. "I think I like it when you get all bossy and pissed."

He wanted to see bossy and pissed, did he? She let her nails scrape over one of his nipples again, and then she bucked her hips, just a little. The resulting sensation that rippled through her nearly drove her mad, though. He was so big, so full inside her that it hit all of her nerve endings just right, soothing the ache that had made her crazed with need all day. That itch needed to be scratched, and it needed it right now.

So she began to rock, adjusting a little here and there to find a rhythm. It was surprisingly easy to find one despite the fact that she was almost never the one on top when she had sex. She was normally too self-conscious of her large breasts and how they jiggled. But they weren't bare right now and she was too fired up to even care, so she began to bounce on top of him, her hips rising and slamming back down on the full length of him. He responded, flicking his hips up with quick, short thrusts to match her movements and to give them more power.

Soon enough, they were driving against each other, each thrust progressively rougher and wilder. A low ache began to burn inside her with each wild thrust, and she recognized it as her oncoming orgasm. It was an elusive, flighty thing without oral, though, so she closed her eyes, braced her hands on his chest, and concentrated her movements on making it happen. She was barely aware of him, lost in the chase of her own pleasure as she rode him, the roughness exciting her body and making her become even more wild, more abandoned on top of him. Each body-rocking slam brought her that much closer.

And then it was there, blossoming through her body and making her clench. She cried out in surprise at just how good it felt, her pussy spasming with the sheer pleasure, her thighs locking. She lost her rhythm, but it didn't matter. Reese had her, and his movements underneath her took on a furious edge. He pounded into her, grunting with every hard, bracing thrust as she lost herself in the spiral of her orgasm.

Then he cussed, his body stiffening against hers, and she realized he was coming, too. His hips jerked one more time, and she felt the tremor that rolled through him.

And she collapsed on his chest, breathing hard and utterly pleased with herself.

She'd just used a man. And it was awesome.

Well, damn. That had worked out better than he'd hoped.

Reese ran a hand along the back of the woman collapsed on top of him and tried not to smile. Audrey was naked from the waist down, her pants discarded somewhere in the bushes nearby. She straddled him, laying over his chest, and still wore the zipped hoodie and shirt she'd started with.

She'd been in such a rush to climb on top of him that she hadn't realized she was still half dressed. Either that, or she simply hadn't cared. Either one was a turn on.

He'd realized, when Audrey had been jumpy earlier, that she was having second thoughts. Lots of second thoughts. And that was disappointing to him. He'd been watching her all day as she cleaned the cabin from top to bottom, keeping busy. The seductive, wild Audrey he loved to coax out to play had disappeared entirely behind industrious, do-gooder Audrey, and that drove him batty.

Though he had to admit, the sight of that tight little bun she wore was starting to be a turn on for him. Maybe it was because he knew that underneath that perfect, no-nonsense exterior, she was a demon waiting to be unleashed.

He'd wanted that demon crawling all over him tonight, too. But when she'd been hesitant and snippy, he figured he had one chance to make her forget all about what was bothering her.

So he'd irritated her.

It had worked, too. She'd more or less pounced on him with bruising kisses and then torn the shirt right off his back. She'd commanded him to lay down, straddled him, and then rode him with an intense look on her face that told him that it was all about her in that moment, not him.

He'd felt a little used. And more than a little aroused. She'd gone after what she'd wanted and she'd made it happen. Reese had been worried for a moment that he'd have to deal with hesitant, cold Audrey, to whittle down her defenses until she'd been moaning under his hands.

He shouldn't have worried. His Audrey was fierce and even though she was a bit of a dictator between the sheets, he had to admit he'd enjoyed every moment of it.

Then he frowned at himself. *His* Audrey? What the hell was he thinking? Then again, it did seem like there were two parts to Audrey Petty—one part efficient, buttoned-up assistant who didn't know how to have fun if it bit her in the ass, and one part sexual glutton.

It was an enticing combination.

His hand slid over her ass, enjoying the feel of the naked, plump cheek under his fingers. Now that she was sated, he could enjoy leisurely exploring her. Seeing her naked. He'd gotten a good look at her lush figure on the dock when they'd been skinny-dipping, but touching and seeing were two different things, and he wanted to touch everything, explore with his hands.

So he reached behind him and felt around until he found the small bag he'd stashed in the roots of the nearby tree.

He pulled out the small camping lantern and set it at his head, then clicked it on.

She squinted, sitting upright on his chest. The look on her face was half sated, half confused. "What's that for?"

"That's so I can get a good look at that delicious body of yours," Reese told her, reaching for the zipper on the hoodie she still wore and easing it down. "Unless you're not done using me."

She flushed, the sight evident now that they had a bit of light. "You liked being used," she told him stubbornly.

"Oh, no complaints here," he said with a grin. "But the night's young and I'm without a shirt, so I figured we might as well stay out here a bit longer." And he eased the zipper down, not entirely surprised to see a matching dark blue nightshirt underneath. "Can I get you naked?"

She rolled off him and sat next to him on the blanket, curling her plump legs delicately underneath her. "I'm just warning you, I don't look like a supermodel. I'm not your type."

"I'm well aware of that," Reese told her. He pulled off the used condom and tossed it into the trash bag he'd brought for such purposes. "You're not a supermodel," he agreed, moving forward and ignoring her warnings and beginning to unbutton her pajama top. "Ask me if I care."

"I'm not going to ask," she told him.

"Good. Then neither of us is going to care," he said, and leaned in to kiss her lightly again. "Every time I've touched you, it's been dark. I want to see if there are freckles on those pretty breasts."

She responded to his soft, coaxing kiss, making a little mewing noise in the back of her throat that made his cock jump in response. "There might be," she whispered.

"Then lay back and let me count them."

Audrey did, and the sight of her laying back on the blanket, her passion-glazed gaze on him as he undid her buttons, was causing his cock to harden all over again. It was like she'd let all of her defenses go in one big, fiery orgasm and now she was soft and pleasing and delicious in his arms. God, he liked that. She was like a present he got to unwrap every time he touched her, and this hadn't gotten old yet. Not in the slightest. Her red hair haloed out around her head, gleaming in the light of the lantern and making the rest of her skin seem porcelain-pale in contrast.

Her gaze was on him as he slowly undid each button, until he finished the last one. Then he pushed the nightshirt apart, brushing it and the unzipped jacket to the side, exposing her torso.

And he drank in the sight of her.

He knew Audrey wasn't reed thin. That didn't bother him, and it didn't seem to bother her for the most part, which he appreciated. Her body was a marked contrast from the women he normally took to bed, though, and he ran an appreciative eye over her. She had breasts, for one. Most of the models and starlets he dated seemed to run extremely flat, which was a shame, because he loved a gorgeous pair of breasts. And damn if Audrey's weren't two of the most magnificent breasts he'd ever laid his eyes upon. They were real, for starters, and very full due to the lushness of her figure. He reached out and cupped one, feeling the weight of it in his hand with appreciation. They were heavy with their own fullness, plump and tipped with a pale pink, tiny nipple that was utterly delightful. Her pale skin was dotted with a few freckles in the valley between her breasts, and then that milk pale, creamy color on the undersides of each breast.

"Gorgeous," he told her truthfully. "I've seen a lot of breasts and these might be the most beautiful ones I've ever seen." He ran the back of an appreciative finger over one nipple, enjoying the way her body jerked in response, setting that deliciously full breast to quivering.

He let his fingers slide into the valley between her breasts, then traced down her belly. Most of the women he'd had in his bed recently were Hollywood thin, with visible ribs under the skin and concave bellies. Audrey was not. Her belly was smooth and slightly rounded just below her belly button, her waist dipping in and then flaring out at the hips again. Not his normal, but again, perfect. He found that he liked her softer curves quite a bit. His thumb grazed her belly button and then he moved lower, sliding that finger down to the triangle of her sex and the damp dark red curls there. A natural redhead. He'd known that, but he still found it fascinating and more than a bit erotic.

She moaned at his touch, raising a finger to her mouth and then biting down on it, as if she didn't want to interrupt his exploration.

"You have an amazing figure, Audrey." His finger stroked the wet seam of her pussy, appreciating the feel of her. He knew she wanted him to slide deeper, to seek out her clit and begin to arouse her again, but Reese was a fan of the tease as well as sex, and he knew the small brush of his finger over that enticing seam would drive her wild. So he repeated the motion, over and over, watching her face as the little shudders of pleasure and anticipation began to rip through her. "Do you like it when I look at you? Touch you?"

Still biting down on that knuckle, she nodded, her eyes wide and soft with need.

"Is it okay if I play with you a little?"

Again, she nodded, and he felt her nudge her thighs apart a little, as if coaxing his hand to touch her in the places she ached.

But he didn't. Instead, he let his hand trail down her soft—so soft—plump thigh, then her knee, and then down her calf. She was pale all over, though there were more freckles on her legs, which he found adorable. Every moment that he looked at her, he seemed to find something new and enjoyable to focus on. Lovely. Just lovely. He could stare at her all night and never get enough.

But he wanted to play with her, too. So he took her hand and helped her sit up, and they pulled the last of her clothing off her and tossed it aside. Now she was as naked as he was. When she lay back down on the blanket, he settled back down next to her, on his side, and continued to leisurely trace his hand over her body. His hands were drawn back to her breasts. He was definitely a breast man, and hers were lovely. He reached out and cupped one again, plumping it in his hand. The nipple poked upright, the tip of it hard and practically begging for his tongue. *Such a sweet little bud.* He leaned over and licked it, gauging Audrey's response, and was gratified when she sucked in a sharp breath. He rolled the nipple against his lips, then tongued it again. When she made no response, he began to gently suck on the tip, teasing it with his teeth and then alternately flicking it again.

She whimpered, and he glanced up to see that knuckle back in her mouth, as if she was trying to bite back her responses. That wouldn't do at all. He wanted his firecracker to be noisy, to gratify him with her moans and to shake the woods with her response. So he reached up and pulled that hand away from her mouth, kissing the bite marks on her skin. "Why are you determined to be quiet?"

"What if someone hears us?"

"No one will," he said. "You're not going to make me bring rope next time, are you? To tie your hands?"

Her eyes simmered with that. "Fat chance." But she let her hands fall to her sides, her gaze on him. "Better?"

"Much." And he leaned down and bit that tiny nipple again, his fingers kneading the plump weight of her breast. She moaned a little, but it was enough to prompt him to keep going. He continued to suck and tease at the nipple in his mouth, and his hand moved to her other breast. His fingers teased and coaxed the other nipple, and that brought a response from her.

She cried out, her back arching, and then her fingers were in his hair, holding his head against her as he teased. "Please, Reese."

"Please what?" he asked, brushing his lips over one tight nipple. He was fascinated by her pretty breasts. "I could spend all day nibbling on these. Don't you want me to?"

A low groan of need escaped her and she clung to him. "I think you just like torturing me."

"Oh, undoubtedly," he said, and licked the stiff point just as his thumb swiped over the other, teasing it. "You're a pleasure to touch, I have to admit. Soft and lush and gorgeous."

The fingers in his hair stroked and kneaded, caressing him as he continued to tongue her nipple. But he was enjoying her reactions. He wanted more of them. So his other hand slid down her ribcage and stroked over her belly, enjoying the way her hips rose in response to him. Audrey might be cool to him in a conversation, but she loved his touch.

His hand continued down her rounded stomach, then slid down to her pussy once more. He rested his hand there, enjoying the small whimpers that escaped her and the way her hands tightened in his hair, as if unconsciously encouraging him. He ignored it, though, continuing to lick and tease that delicious little peak against his lips, and his hand remained in place at her pussy, feeling the warmth and wetness of her against him.

When he didn't make a move forward, she arched against his palm, her breath quickening. "Reese."

"What do you want, Audrey?" He breathed the words on her nipple and then blew on the wet tip, appreciating the shiver that rippled through her. "Do you want to tell me?"

"I hate you," she moaned, her fingers tightening in his hair until she was practically pulling it. "You want me to beg you, don't you?"

"Mmm, I do love a fine round of begging," he admitted, then nipped her breast to get her to moan again. "And I admit that I'd love to hear you begging me. Do you want me to slide my fingers through your pussy and find your clit?"

Her sharp intake of breath was gratifying. "Oh, yes. Do that."

"Why don't you tell me to?" His hand pressed down, ever so slightly, on her pussy.

She whimpered again and raised her hips, grinding against his hand. "Fuck you."

"I think I'll have you beg for that, too," he said musingly.

She groaned in frustration. Her hands pushed at his head, trying to get him to travel down her body, but he resisted. "Ugh. You suck."

"Another thing you'll have to beg for," he told her in a coaxing voice. "Though I'm told I suck amazingly." And he licked the nipple and grinned up at her.

To his delight, Audrey squirmed in his arms—*squirmed*—and moaned. "You . . . you . . . tease."

"Mmm," he said, and nuzzled the nipple again.

"Please," she exploded. "Please give me more."

"More what?"

"Your mouth," she breathed. "I need it."

"Mmm. Need it where?" He flicked the nipple with his tongue in a leisurely fashion. "I'm afraid I lack specifics."

"My pussy," she said in a low voice, her teeth gritted as if the words were being ripped from her throat.

Ah, his sweet little control freak. Reese chuckled and moved his fingers against her pussy. "You don't want me to start with my hands? Impatient, aren't we?"

"Hands are good, too," she panted.

"You want to ask me for my hands?"

"No?"

"Shame," he said, enjoying her flustered breaths. "I've a mind to use them right about now." And he dipped a finger into her hot, slick well.

She arched up, almost coming off the blanket. "Ah! Reese!" Her cry echoed in the woods and she clapped a horrified hand over her mouth.

"Now that sounded sweet," he chuckled. "I think you deserve a reward." And his finger brushed through her wetness, sliding back and forth in a teasing pattern, heading for her clit. She was soaking wet, her pussy and thighs damp with her juices. He circled the hard bud of her clit. "Does that feel better, sexy?"

She cried out, her eyes closed with ecstasy, and her legs parted even more for him.

Audrey was glorious in her need. He ran his finger along her clit again, then slid down deeper, circling her opening. He slid his first finger inside her, and when she whimpered, added a second finger, stroking her. She was so slick with her own juices that her body was making soft sucking noises, as if greedy for his fingers. And with every stroke of his fingers into her warmth, he'd reach up and brush her clit with his thumb.

Her cries grew more frantic, more frequent, and her hips began to roll against his fingers, adding to her own pleasure. He drove his fingers into her over and over, fucking her with his hand, watching her responses. She was gorgeous. Her head was thrown back, the white column of her throat gleaming in the lantern light, her breasts jiggling and bouncing with every roll of her hips. He loved that she went after her own need with a single-minded intensity. Some women he'd been with pretended to be enjoying things, but then would fake a tepid orgasm.

Audrey, on the other hand, would mount a man and use him until she got what she needed. He liked that. And he drove harder into that soft well, curving his fingers when he was deep inside her, wanting to give her as much pleasure as possible.

A spasm clenched around his hand, and then Audrey was coming, hard and rough, her small, wordless cries keening in the night air. Her pussy clenched over and over around his hand, her muscles contracting, and she gasped as if she'd just run a marathon, breathing hard.

"Now that was pretty," Reese told her in a husky voice. "It's impossible to look away when you come, Audrey. The look on your face is incredible."

She opened her eyes and gazed at him, her expression soft, her lips plump as if she'd been biting them. She looked so incredibly fuckable that it made his cock ache with need, but he forced himself to ignore it, intent on teasing the hell out of this luscious woman spread out before him.

Reese lifted his hand and licked his fingers, shining with her juices. "Taste beautiful, too."

Her eyes widened and she inhaled sharply, watching him.

Her taste was indeed delicious, sweet and salty all at once. He wanted more of that enticing flavor. He moved and bent between her legs, pushing her knees until they were up in the air. That exposed her smooth bottom to him as well as her wet, gleaming folds. "I'm going to lick you until you come again, Audrey."

She trembled, and he could feel it in the arm he had bracing her legs in the air. "I just came twice."

"I don't care," he told her, moving down between her legs. "That's not going to stop me. That just makes you juicier for my tongue. Like a peach." He felt her quiver again and braced his hands on the backs of her thighs, keeping her legs spread in the air. Then he leaned in and gave her a long, slow lick. She was so fucking wet that she coated his tongue with her juices. Delicious.

Audrey gave a low, keening moan at the sweep of his tongue, and the trembles in her legs grew. "Reese," she panted. "Please. I'm so sensitive—"

"Then that makes this more of a pleasure," he told her, and buried his face in her folds.

He was gratified at her cry of delight and swept his tongue against her sex, tasting her, exploring her. He lapped at her core, enjoying the continual trembles of her body. But when he moved back to her clit and began to lap at it with his tongue, she jerked and moaned his name again.

“Oh, God, Reese, I’m coming again.”

“Then keep coming.” He continued to tease her clit with his tongue, then sucked and nibbled at it. All the while, she rocked her hips against his mouth in little motions, strangled moans escaping her throat as she came. And when the moans continued, he wondered if she was still coming, but didn’t stop to check. He just kept licking and sucking at that small nub of pleasure. He slid two fingers deep into her pussy and began to thrust in time with his tongue against her clit. Her pussy was quivering, muscles clenching spasmodically against his hand, and her cries were growing wilder.

Audrey gave a sharp cry and a burst of wetness hit his tongue. *Ah fuck, that was hot.* Suddenly, he wanted to sink inside her and feel her clenching all around him. He sat up in a rush and grabbed another condom from his stash, tearing open the packet and shoving it on as quick as he could. He wanted her to keep coming, to feel that hot, tight pussy clasping him as her entire body trembled.

When he had the condom on, he turned back to her and noticed that her legs were back on the blanket, her breasts heaving with her gasps of air.

“Naughty Audrey,” he murmured, moving back to her and thrusting her legs into the air again. “Who told you I was done?” He bent to continue licking at her, wanting to drive her into that fever pitch once more.

She made a choked sound, and then she was moaning all over again. “Oh, fuck, Reese . . . oh, God. Oh, God! I can’t take it!”

He bet she could, though. So he continued to work her sensitive clit with his tongue, and when her moans became keening again, he slid a finger deep inside her and felt her pussy quivering all around him.

Ah, perfect. He sat up on his knees, put his hands on her calves and guided them to his shoulders, and then leaned in, burying his cock inside her.

Audrey gasped, her entire body jerking. He felt her clenching around him, the ripples continuous. It was like she was coming over and over again, and it felt incredible. He thrust hard into her, rolling her forward with the force of his hips.

She cried out as he sank deep and began to pump, her breasts quivering and swaying with every rough thrust deep inside of her. She was like a tight glove around his cock that kept clenching and getting tighter, and fuck all if he wasn't going to last very long. He continued to pump into her, determined to make this last until he wrung a few more of those keening cries out of her.

"You coming, Audrey?" he gritted, though he knew the answer.

Her soft moan seemed to shoot directly to his balls, her eyes closed, head thrown back with pleasure. "Can't. Stop. Coming. Reese. Oh, God, Reese."

"Good girl," he told her, thrusting hard and sinking deeper with every movement. Ah fuck, she was so good to sink into, those soft thighs bouncing against him, her big breasts moving with the force of his thrusts. "Tell me you want me to come, Audrey."

She whimpered, her head thrashing on the blanket, nearly insensible.

"Tell me . . . you want me . . . to come . . . Audrey," he gritted out, punctuating each pause with a rough thrust.

"Oh, fuck," she panted, and then her lips parted and a wordless keening escaped her again. He felt the ripples in her pussy clenching around him anew. "Reese!" she finally panted, her words breathless. "Come. *Please.*"

That need in her voice broke his control, made his orgasm explode to the forefront. His cock surged and then he was coming with a groan, his own body losing control. He stroked into her again, once, twice, letting the aftershocks of pleasure ride through him.

And then he released her and rolled to the side, flipping to his back and trying to catch his breath.

They both panted in the silence, neither one saying a thing for a long time. Reese stared up at the tree branches overhead, pleased with himself. Sex was normally his favorite hobby, but Audrey seemed to enjoy taking it to new heights. He decided there was an intense pleasure in being conquered and then turning right back around and conquering her. Their familiar push-pull relationship continued in the bedroom as well.

Strange how much he enjoyed that.

With an idle hand, he tugged the condom off and tossed it back into the plastic bag, then rolled over to pull her against him. Her body was damp with a fine sheen of sweat, but she was curvy and warm and delicious to touch, so he pulled her close.

A small whimper escaped her. "No more. My vagina surrenders."

Reese chuckled and pressed a kiss to her shoulder. "It needs to build up some stamina, I think."

"It had stamina," she protested. "You destroyed it." She snuggled down against him, hugging the arm he wrapped around her waist. "Oh, my God. I don't think I've ever come so much in my life."

"Yeah," he mused, unable to resist teasing her. "I'm pretty good at that sort of thing."

Audrey's disgusted little snort made him laugh. He pressed another kiss to her shoulder and couldn't resist reaching out to idly play with one of her breasts. "Admit it. I was the best you ever had."

"I will admit no such thing," she told him in a pleased, sleepy voice, but she gave another soft sound of pleasure when he tweaked her nipple again.

That was okay. He was pretty sure he knew the answer anyhow. Reese grinned.

SEVEN

Are you going to sleep all day?" Daphne prodded her shoulder.

Audrey rolled over in bed and pulled the pillow over her face, snuggling down into the blankets. "Yes," she murmured sleepily. "Go away."

"Get up," Daphne told her again. "I need breakfast."

"Cook your own damn breakfast," Audrey retorted, hiding her face in the pillows.

"Nope," Daphne said, a bit too cheerful. "You're supposed to be taking care of me, remember?"

Audrey groaned and rolled over, staring at her twin. She frowned up at her, a smile cracking her face when Daphne wiggled her eyebrows. For a moment, she seemed just like Audrey's old twin again—mischievous and demanding—and her heart melted. "Fine, I'm getting up. But just for you."

"Perfect," Daphne said with a grin.

Audrey rolled out of bed and was unable to resist a groan

as her muscles protested. She felt sore on several levels, her breasts sensitive, her inner thighs sensitive . . . among other things. Stretching to shake out some of the kinks, she yawned and glanced back at Daphne.

Her twin hadn't moved from the bed. Her head was tilted to one side, and she watched Audrey with narrow, suspicious eyes.

"What?" Audrey asked defensively.

"Why are you walking so stiff?" Daphne's eyes widened. "Did you nail hot tub Romeo?"

"Oh, my God, shut up, Daphne." She rushed back to her twin's side and clamped a hand over her mouth. "Do you have to be so loud?"

Daphne wrestled out from behind Audrey's hand and shook out her messy hair. "I'm serious," she hissed. "Did you nail him? Last night? You little slut you!"

Audrey felt her face turning bright red. "Just be quiet, Daph. And don't say a word to anyone."

"Who would I tell? Cade?" She snorted. "What happened to your crush on him?"

Audrey shrugged, feeling a little guilty—but not a lot. She felt too good at the moment. "You told me that I could use a man, remember? Use him for my own needs and then not worry about it? Reese is the perfect no-strings-attached playmate. We both know it's not going anywhere, so why not have a little fun while we're together?"

Daphne shook her head. "Well, yeah, but why do you listen to me? I'm the twin with bad judgment, remember? Why would anyone take my advice? You can't sleep with one man and be crushing on the other while under the same roof. That's not cool."

Audrey's jaw dropped. "You told me yesterday that I should go for it. What's with the turnabout?"

Daphne shrugged. “I just don’t want Cade to get hurt in this, that’s all.”

“Yeah, well, what about your twin? Don’t my feelings count more than his?”

Daphne just gave her an exasperated look.

Audrey said nothing. If she wanted to be honest, she could have told her twin that she hadn’t given much thought to Cade lately at all. She’d been too distracted with constant thoughts of Reese. Reese and his playful smiles, his playboy attitude, the way he loved to get under her skin and make her explode . . . and then the way he’d make her get all fired up just so he could reap the benefits. Her lips twitched with amusement at that. He seemed to be the only person who liked seeing her naughty half come to the surface. Most everyone would rather have competent, ultra-composed Audrey.

It was nice to not have to be so perfect sometimes.

“Let’s just go eat breakfast, all right?” Audrey slid back off the bed and headed to the closet to get dressed.

The sisters dressed and headed down the stairs. Audrey had expected to see Reese in the kitchen, or hovering in the area, but he was nowhere to be found. There was a note on the fridge and Daphne grabbed it, reading it. “Gone to town to find a fax machine. Back soon. Cade.” She shrugged and glanced at the empty stove top. “No oatmeal today, huh? Guess he got tired of cooking for us. Or maybe you wore him out.” She gave Audrey a sly look.

Audrey ignored it and headed for the cabinet, pulling out a box of cereal. “Here. Breakfast is served.”

“Wow, nice to see the gourmet is in the house,” Daphne said sarcastically, but she took the box and headed to the table while Audrey got bowls.

They ate in companionable silence, Daphne smoking

her first cigarette of the day and Audrey stifling yawns behind her hand. Despite her tiredness, she felt good. Really good. Incredibly good. So good that she was pretty sure it'd be obvious to anyone who saw her.

She and Reese had made love for hours in the woods last night. After that first mind-blowing round, he'd turned the tables on her and had licked and teased her until she seemed to be in a constant state of orgasm. She'd never experienced anything quite like that before, and by the end of it, she'd been totally wrung out. Reese, however, had quite a bit more stamina than her, and after a few rounds of cuddling, he'd rolled her onto her back and then made long, slow, languid love to her. And then he'd done so again a few hours later. And just before dawn, when they were about to head back to the lodge to crawl into bed, he'd pushed her back down on the blankets and given her a rough and dirty fucking that had left her breathless.

She'd been staggering with exhaustion by the time they made it back to the lodge, but sated. And she'd fallen into bed and slept for hours.

And she couldn't stop thinking about it.

As if on cue, Reese descended down the stairs, scratching his bare chest. He yawned, wearing a pair of Cade's sleep pants that were about three inches too short for him, and headed for the twins in the kitchen area, grinning. "Ladies. How are we this morning?" He snagged the box from between them and headed to one of the cabinets to get a bowl.

"Well," Daphne said brightly, examining her cigarette. "One of us is fine, and one of us is walking bowlegged. I'll let you determine which one is which."

He paused, then glanced over at Audrey, who shot her sister a mortified look.

"I see someone's feeling better," Reese said.

"Yeah, she's back in fighting form all right," Audrey said, grateful for the distraction.

"Good thing. I like my women a little fiery," Reese said, and when she glared at him, he winked. *Oh, they were going to be like that this morning, were they?*

"I thought you liked them breathing," Audrey said in her best prim voice.

"Actually, I prefer it when they can hold their breath," Reese said, returning to the table with a bowl. He dumped a ton of cereal into it and then reached for the milk when Daphne handed it his way. "Or humming. I like it when they hum. You know any good songs, Audrey?"

She nearly choked on her mouthful of cereal and gave him a heated look.

"No? Just a one note kind of girl?"

Damn it, now she was going to blush. She thought of the woodpile and the way she'd hummed a long, single note while she'd had him in her mouth. Clearly he was thinking of that, too.

"Okay, I'm officially out of this weird-ass conversation," Daphne said with a glance at Audrey. "You two carry on. I'm going to call Cade and tell him to bring some more cigarettes."

"You do that," Audrey said quietly. As soon as Daphne left the dining area, Audrey scooped a bit of cereal onto her spoon and launched it at Reese. "Oh, my God, could you be more obvious?"

"Me?" He laughed, batting away the bits of cereal with a grin, clearly enjoying himself. "You're the one walking all bowlegged."

"That's because someone was a little too enthusiastic last night!"

His face sobered. "Seriously. Are you okay? You're not hurting, are you?"

She rolled her eyes at him. "Will you be quiet? I'm fine. My muscles are just . . . sore."

Reese gave her an interested look. "You sure do blush easily, too. You know when you blush, it goes all the way to your nipples?"

Oh, God, she could feel that blushing even now. "You're going to kill me before this day is out, aren't you?"

"I might. Does this mean if you get angry enough, we might have to meet by the woodpile again?" His voice took on a husky note.

That butterfly fluttered low in her belly again, warmth flooding through her body, and Audrey found herself imagining meeting him there again, tearing at each other with abandon. "Maybe," she hedged. Though who was she kidding? All he had to do was crook his finger and she'd practically jump on him, eager for a second round.

Of course, she was pretty sure it was mutual, given the looks he was shooting her way. A peculiar sense of pleasure slid through her. To think that she, Audrey Petty, the boring twin, had one of the world's most famous playboys ready to jump her at the mere sign that she was interested.

She had to admit, it was good for the ego.

There was a knock at the front door.

"Someone want to get that?" Daphne called from the living room. "I'm kind of hiding out here, remember?"

Audrey and Reese exchanged glances, and Audrey got up from the table, curious. Their cabin was in a remote location in the midst of nothing but the woods. This was private property. Who could possibly be coming out to visit?

She glanced at her twin, who was retreating to the kitchen, and then opened the door.

Camilla strolled in, tossing her long blonde hair over one shoulder. She wore an adorable fur-lined white winter coat, matched with a miniskirt and stockings over a pair of sky-high designer leather boots. Her makeup was perfect and her outfit sexy, and she looked right past Audrey as if she wasn't there. Her eyes scanned the room for Reese, her face lighting up at the sight of him in his pajamas. "Darling! You're still here after all."

Audrey's stomach clenched and she stood in the doorway like a statue as the beautiful heiress moved to Reese's side. She was tall and slender and her appearance was perfect in contrast to Audrey, who wore a pair of ratty pajamas, had her hair twisted into a messy bun, and not a shred of makeup. Oh, and she was walking bowlegged, unlike Camilla's perfect glide across the cabin floor.

And she watched through narrowed eyes as Camilla moved to Reese and wrapped her arm around his neck, leaning in and giving him a kiss on the mouth. She half expected him to push her away, or maybe look over at Audrey and give her an apologetic look.

But he didn't. He simply accepted Camilla's peck.

Anger flared through Audrey. Well, wasn't this lovely. No sooner did she sleep with the man than he forgot that she ever existed. She'd guessed as much, but it still stung her ego, just a bit.

Ah, fuck. Camilla had the shittiest timing ever. Reese wanted to put his hands around that slender throat and wring her pretty neck. Of course, Camilla had no idea why he was irritated, seeing as how she'd traipsed back to the cabin after abandoning him for days without a second thought.

Audrey, on the other hand, had stiffened up, her back going plank-straight and her entire body rigid. Gone was that soft teasing playfulness from this morning and the bright blushes. Instead, she was staring at him with something akin to loathing. That bothered him.

"Did you miss me?" Camilla asked, draping her lithe form all over him and kissing him repeatedly, as if they didn't have an audience. "I wasn't sure if you'd still be here, but when I heard you weren't at work, I decided to come out and see for myself." She gave him a pretty pout. "I figured it was either that or you were avoiding me."

He detangled her clinging arms from his shoulders, finding himself a bit annoyed at her coy actions. "How can I be avoiding you, sweetheart, when I'm right where you left me? Without clothes, I might add?"

She gave a lighthearted giggle and clung to his arm. "But you look so sexy without clothes, Reese baby."

Out of the corner of his eye, he saw Audrey roll her eyes and make a disgusted face, heading into the kitchen.

"That's nice," he told Camilla in a dismissive voice, pulling her clinging hands away from him. "I probably need to head back into the city at some point anyhow." Especially since the main reason why he'd stayed here had disappeared into the kitchen, no doubt to stick pins in a Reese-shaped voodoo doll of some kind.

"Don't bother," Camilla said, unzipping her coat. "I talked to Daddy for you about the cruise line. He says we can do whatever I want, as long as it makes me happy." She gave him a flirty smile. "I'm in charge of whether or not things fly."

That was exactly what Reese had been hoping for when he'd begun to court Camilla's attention. He knew her father was looking for a project to put the young heiress on to keep her busy and to test her business acumen. He also knew that Camilla liked nothing more than going on vacation and spending money. This was perfect for his plans.

But for some reason, he found himself annoyed with her and her timing. He wanted to go to Audrey and explain why he couldn't push Camilla away, and why he had to keep her focused attention on himself when all he really wanted to do was drag Audrey against him and kiss her again.

But his company needed the cash influx that Camilla's business could bring in, along with the prestige. Camilla herself was a media figure, and if she started to push the cruise line to all her celebrity friends, word would get around and their luxury cruises would soon be the premier vacation for the rich and famous, and those wanting to vacation with the rich and famous.

She just had shit timing was all.

So he clasped her hands and forced himself to put on his best flirty smile. "I'm staying here with friends this week, Camilla. Cade's here and he's the owner of the cabin, so we're going to have to share space. And I'm afraid all the rooms are taken."

"Oh, that's okay." She looked unconcerned. "I'll just stay in yours. You want to go get my suitcase out of the car?"

Daphne's eyebrows went to her forehead and she gave Reese a disgusted look that reminded him so much of Audrey that he did a double take. Of course it did; they were twins despite Daphne's wasted appearance.

Camilla noticed at that moment the new person who now stood in the doorway of the kitchen. Her jaw dropped. "Daphne Petty?"

Daphne gave a wan smile. "Hi."

"Oh, my God!" Camilla's hands flailed with excitement and she did a little hop, which was not an easy feat in her stiletto boots. "I am your biggest fan, for real! I love you!"

"Thank you," Daphne said, giving her sister a "help me" look.

"What are you doing here in the woods?" Camilla's eyes widened. "Oh, my gosh, are you writing your next album? I could totally help you with that! I'm really great with lyrics."

"Super," Daphne said, keeping that cheerful smile on her face through great effort. She looked over at the others in the room for help. "Reese?"

"Just a minute," he told her. "I need to check on something. Why don't you wait here in the kitchen with Daphne, Camilla?" He turned and gave Daphne his most brilliant smile.

Like a charm, Camilla turned and squealed with delight, clapping her hands. "I am just your biggest fan," she gushed, sounding like a schoolgirl. "You have no idea. I had front-row tickets when you were in Prague for the White Lightning concert tour, and—"

While Daphne shot him dirty looks, he slipped past the kitchen.

Audrey was now in the living room, straightening magazines and books on the coffee table and dusting with a small, checkered rag. The place was spotless, but she continued to go over the furniture as if cleaning would somehow ease the turmoil in her mind.

"Audrey, we need to talk," Reese began.

She gave him a scathing look. "What's there to talk about?"

"You and me. Camilla."

"You and me and Camilla are *not* an issue," she told him in a stiff voice. "You and I had no sort of agreement together, remember? It was just flirtation, nothing more. I just happened to forget that you flirt with everything that has tits."

He sighed. "Look. I don't want Camilla here, either, but I can't send her away. She's a big part of a crucial deal that I need for a potential business venture to succeed."

The look on her face turned even more wintry. "So you mean to tell me that you don't like the fact that a beautiful, wealthy socialite is draping herself all over you? Because I saw your face and it didn't exactly seem like much of a hardship, if you ask me."

"Audrey—"

"No, that's fine, Reese, honestly. My feelings are not hurt." She gave him a wide-eyed look that seemed calm despite the heated flush rising on her cheeks. "You and I had a bit of a fling in the woods. It's not a big deal. No one suggested any sort of commitment, least of all me. Remember, I'm in love with Cade. Seeing Camilla here just made me realize that I've been pursuing the wrong sort of thing with you here, but I'm glad that my head's on straight now." She gave him a little smile. "Last night was fun, though. I suppose I should say thank you."

Jesus. She made it sound like they'd had a tea party instead of blisteringly hot sex. "So is that all you're going to say to me?"

"What would you like for me to say, Reese? That I'm hurt and furious at you? The only reason we got involved was because you blackmailed me over my crush on Cade. I'll just focus on him now."

For some reason, the fact that she kept throwing Cade's name into the conversation grated on his nerves. "Is that so?"

She glanced up at him, leaning against the sofa. "What do you care? You have your heiress and you need to fuck her for your business deal, right? Go right ahead. I won't stop you." She gestured at the doorway of the kitchen. "I'll even cheer you on. It'll make it easier for me to focus on Cade."

"So you think your path is clear because another woman showed up?" Reese moved a little closer to her, until they were practically nose to nose. And she was vibrating with angry energy, which just made him even more aroused and drawn to her. "Is that why you keep bringing Cade's name up? Because you want to lash out at me?"

She stared up at him, the look on her face challenging. "Maybe I do. Or maybe I am thinking I should invite Cade to go skinny-dipping and see what I get out of this."

He scowled.

She scowled back.

And then she reached for him, and he reached for her, and suddenly their mouths were on each other, furiously kissing. He felt her teeth sink into his lower lip, heard his own groan of pleasure as her body pressed against his, and the kiss turned wilder and even more strangely erotic. Fuck, but the woman could do the best angry kiss in the world, and his body was practically jumping out of his skin at her touch. Audrey gave a soft whimper that was at odds with the furious kisses she was pressing on him, her tongue gliding into his mouth.

He sucked on it, determined to gentle her.

She melted against him, her breasts pressing against his chest. Her mouth fitted to his and their tongues met, slicking back and forth in a way that made the melding of their mouths seem somehow perfect together.

She just fit him. She fit him perfectly.

And he had to pull away. Reese took a step backward, gently detangling from Audrey, disappointed that he had to do so. "I'm sorry. It's not fair to you for us to do this. As much as I want to drag you up over this sofa and fuck you right here, it's not fair to you—or Camilla—if I do it."

Audrey considered him for a moment, a wry smile twisting her mouth. "That sounds stunningly admirable for a guy who's juggling two women."

He ran a hand down his face, exhausted at the thought. "It's not like that. I figured when Camilla ran out, we were done. How was I supposed to know she'd waltz back in here a few days later, pretending like I'm late for our next date?" God, the girl was exhausting him and she'd just shown up. He hadn't realized how glad he'd been that she was gone until she'd returned.

"So what's she mean to you?" Audrey's voice was quiet, serious. "Be honest with me, Reese. I can handle it."

"You want honesty?" He gave her a rueful look. "She's arm candy and a business deal that I want pretty badly. If I could get the business deal without Camilla I'd take it in a heartbeat. But because she's the strings attached to it, we were just playing around. I was flirting with her, showing her a bit of attention."

"Like a gigolo." Her voice was flat.

"Jesus, not like that."

"Really? Gigolos have sex for money. Isn't that what you're doing?"

"You think that girl out there wants a serious relationship?" He gestured to the doorway. "Hell no. She wants a fling with a sexy guy. Nothing more, nothing less. Something to gossip about to her friends. She doesn't give a shit about me or how I feel. Her expectations aren't the same as yours."

"I have no expectations," she said coolly. Then she ruined it by blurting, "So did you sleep with her?"

"Not yet." And he was suddenly fucking thankful for that. "You interrupted us in the hot tub, remember?"

"Oh." She considered him, then said, "Well, it's your fault we're in this situation."

"Me? Are you kidding?"

"No, I'm serious." She crossed her arms over her chest, drawing his gaze there. Damn, but she had a magnificent chest. It was hidden by the shapeless pajamas, but now that he knew what was underneath there? He couldn't stop thinking about those large, perfect globes bouncing as he stroked into her.

Ah, hell. Now he was thinking about her breasts again. He forced himself to focus.

"It's your fault that we slept together, because you dared me."

"I didn't dare you to sleep with me."

"No, but you dared me to kiss you, and then you dared me to go skinny-dipping with you." She gave a delicate shrug. "It was a natural event in the chain of things, but my point is that if you hadn't dared me, we wouldn't be in this situation."

"It takes two to tango, you know. You're not blameless in this."

"I never dared you once!"

"You're right," he said, throwing his hands up. "Let's just blame it all on me. It's all my fault."

"You want me to take a share of the blame, then?"

She was getting riled up, which just made him want her even more. *Damn.* He hadn't been kidding about tossing her over the couch and fucking her. He shifted his weight, determined not to reach into his pants and adjust himself. "It'd be nice."

"Fine then. How about a dare for you?" She gave him

a challenging look, then flicked her fingers at him. "Seal the deal with your heiress. That's the dare."

"*That's* the dare? Are you kidding? You want me to sleep with someone else?"

"That's the dare," she agreed. "You sleep with her, you win. I'll let you choose what you win. I—"

"Anal sex," he said immediately, waiting for her to freak out. Most women did as soon as anal was mentioned.

Her cheeks pinkened, but she continued. "Like I was saying, if you win, you choose. If I win, I get to choose something."

"And what do you choose?" He leaned close to her, so close that he was seconds away from kissing her soft mouth.

"I think you have to stay here and be my slave for a day."

It was his turn to smirk. What a childish sort of request. She wasn't very good at this game. "That's all you're going to ask for? You do realize that if I win, I get to fuck the heiress *and* you again? Don't you want to ask for something bigger than that?"

She gave him a sad look. "Reese, does it matter what I ask for? Honestly? We both know you're not going to lose." Audrey reached up, caressed his cheek, brushed her lips against his, and then left the room.

And he was left dumbfounded for a long moment, because he had no idea what to think. Audrey didn't expect to win their bet. She'd agreed to have sex with him—anal sex—if she lost, and she didn't expect to win. But he had a feeling that if he slept with Camilla, that bet would be the last time he'd see Audrey ever again.

It'd be a bittersweet victory. He'd have his business merger. He'd have Camilla.

And he'd lose Audrey. She'd go through with the bet—his firecracker didn't back down from a challenge—but after that? She'd be long gone.

And for some reason, that bothered him a hell of a lot more than the thought of losing the cruise line deal.

EIGHT

"You sure you're okay?" Daphne asked Audrey for the millionth time that day. "You seem kind of moody."

"I'm fine," Audrey repeated. She stuffed her hands in her coat pockets and watched her breath puff into the chilly forest air. "I just had to get out of the cabin for a bit, you know. It was . . . stifling."

"You mean because of the bimbo?" Daphne pulled out a cigarette as they paused on their walk. They were circling the edge of the lake, enjoying the afternoon sunshine and the crisp cold front that had settled in. There was no snow yet but they were assured it was on its way, and they decided to take a walk before things got too chilly.

Mostly, Audrey just wanted to get out of the house. With the addition of another person—a loud, gossipy person—it made the cozy house miserable. Camilla chewed gum as if it were trying to get away from her and texted on her phone constantly. She sucked up to Daphne as though she'd never met a star before, and then spent the rest of her time trying to sit in Reese's lap and cuddle with him.

To be fair to Reese, he seemed a bit . . . pained by Camilla's attentions. It looked as if he tolerated them, but just barely, and that made Audrey feel a little better.

But only a little.

"I can't believe he fucked you and then he's just going to let her crawl all over him like it's no big deal," Daphne said in a bitter voice, then lit her cigarette. She took a long drag, then pulled it from her lips and flicked the ashes to the ground. "And you're just sitting there and taking it. Aren't you mad?"

Oh, she was mad. But what could she do? "It's complicated," Audrey found herself saying in a calm voice. "I knew Reese was a fling when I met him, though."

"But you just slept with him last night—"

"Okay," Audrey exploded at her twin. "I'm fucking hurt, all right? Is that what you want to hear?"

"It beats that insipid 'It's complicated,'" she mimicked, making a face. "I mean hell, Audrey, it's all right to get mad sometimes, you know." When Audrey sent a nasty look her way, she shrugged. "I just wish I could help, that's all."

"Well, you can't," Audrey said, staring out at the lake glumly. "It'll either work itself out, or it won't."

"What about the thing with Cade?"

Audrey shot a look at her sister. "What do you mean?"

"Do you still have feelings for him? Maybe you should turn to him."

For some reason, that made Audrey feel weird. Turn to Cade after sleeping with his best friend? Confess that she'd been hurt by Reese and fall into Cade's arms? "No," she said after a moment. "I wouldn't feel right about it."

It wouldn't feel right on several levels—it'd be unfair to

Reese, and for all that he was letting Camilla fling herself all over him, she didn't feel like he was a bad guy. Too caught in his own web, maybe, but not a bad guy. And it wouldn't be fair to Cade, either. He'd pull his white knight act, determined to fix things somehow. And she hated to think how he could possibly fix a broken heart.

She stopped herself, then shook her head. Her heart wasn't broken. Her heart wasn't even involved.

"Cade's a good guy, you know," Daphne said quietly. "You two would be perfect together."

Audrey gave a faint smile. "I always thought the same thing." But for some reason, that didn't sound nearly as interesting to her anymore. She thought of Reese's roguish smile and the way he constantly strove to drive her absolutely up a wall. Maybe that was what she needed—someone to push her out of her neat, orderly life and make her spit a bit of fire. She had to admit that she felt more alive around him.

"Oh, well," Daphne said after a moment. She flicked her cigarette into the lake and pulled out her pack, frowning. "Damn it, that was the last one. I'm heading back to the house to get more. You want to come?"

"No thanks. I think I'll stay out here a bit longer," Audrey said, turning back to the lake. "Clear my head a bit more before returning. Camilla's perfume is killing me."

"Ha." Daphne snorted. "Someone should tell her it's gauche to bathe in her own line of perfume."

"Yeah, but someone won't, because she's rich and powerful." Audrey shared a smile with her twin, then waved her back toward the lodge. "Go. I'll be in in a few."

Daphne headed back up the path and Audrey circled the lake again, lost in her thoughts. She really didn't know what to make of the situation. Was she the other woman? Just a bit of a fling? What was Reese other than the best friend of the man she was supposed to be in love with but hadn't really thought about much since arriving? She didn't have answers.

After about a half hour of walking alone, she arrived back at the dock and turned to head back to the lodge. As she headed back up the path, she heard voices and paused.

It was a male and a female voice. Curious, Audrey sneaked along the side of the cabin, listening in. The two were standing by the woodpile, and as she got closer, she could hear Reese and Camilla talking.

A stab of jealousy gutted her, and Audrey stopped short, surprised at herself. Why was she jealous? Reese wasn't hers. Not really. There was nothing for her to be possessive about, but when she heard Camilla's voice, she couldn't stop her hands from clenching into fists. Unable to help herself, she slid forward along the lodge so she could listen in a bit more. After all, that wouldn't hurt things, would it?

"Camilla," Reese sighed. "Please. Don't make this harder for me than it already is. I'm not trying to hurt you. I'm just trying to make you understand. That's all."

"How am I supposed to understand? How did you change your mind so quickly?" There was a pause and a crunch of grass, as if someone was stepping. "A few days ago, we were in the hot tub, enjoying ourselves." Camilla's voice turned seductive, and Audrey pictured her leaning into Reese, her hands on his chest. "I don't see how things have changed that much in that little time," the heiress continued.

"Well, for starters, you left me behind," Reese replied. "No clothes, no phone, no nothing. I have to admit I wasn't a fan of that."

"I was nervous," Camilla said in a soft voice. "She was taking pictures with her phone. You know my father wouldn't be happy if I got caught in a hot tub with a strange man."

"Topless," Reese added.

"Topless," Camilla agreed in that slinky voice. "So you understand?"

"Oh, I understand. It doesn't mean that it doesn't annoy me."

"So is that why you're turning me down?" Her voice became petulant.

Turning her . . . down? Audrey cocked her head and took another step forward, suddenly intensely curious as to what the two were saying. The knot in her throat became dry as a bone.

"Don't make this more difficult than it is, Camilla." Reese's voice was calm and easy, but it sounded a little dead to Audrey's ears. As if he was saying the words but truly didn't care how Camilla felt. Was this how he was with other women? How did they not notice his utter boredom with them?

Was he ever like that with her? She made a mental note to pay attention the next time she talked to him in private.

"I don't see why this has to be difficult at all, Reese. You told me you wanted me." She gave another huffy sigh, and then asked, "Is there someone else?"

Audrey held her breath.

"I'm sleeping with someone, yeah."

"Do you love her?"

Audrey nearly swallowed her tongue.

Reese laughed. "Don't be ridiculous. This is me you're talking to."

And just like that, her heart plummeted back to reality.

For a moment, Audrey felt weirdly crushed. She mentally shook herself. Why did that bother her? Wasn't she just using the man for a mindless fling, too? Who cared if he was in love?

Certainly not her. She was supposed to be in love with someone else.

Camilla gasped. "Is it Daphne Petty? Ohmigod. You're sleeping with Daphne Petty? Reese!" For a moment there, Camilla sounded excited, and then she quieted. "Is it true that she's hooked on the hard stuff? She looks like a mess in there. Yuck."

"Camilla," Reese said in a warning tone.

"I won't tell anyone. But you have to get me backstage at her next concert. She has this really hot drummer and I—"

"Camilla, I'm not sleeping with Daphne Petty."

There was a long pause, and Audrey could practically hear the gears grinding to a halt in Camilla's pretty blonde head. Then, she snorted. "There's no one else here but the fat chick. Don't tell me you're riding that moped?"

Audrey bristled. *That little bitch.*

"Shut up, Camilla," Reese said in that same bored, dismissive voice. "I trust this won't affect business?"

"What are you talking about? Of course it affects business. You think I won't tell Daddy about this?"

"I rather hoped you wouldn't."

Audrey bit her lip. She was still annoyed about the fat comment, and now Camilla was going to hold the business deal over Reese's head? She supposed Reese deserved it for trying to use the heiress for his own means, but it bothered her to have him more or less held hostage by the spoiled blonde's whims.

"You know what they say," Reese said flatly. "Never mix business with pleasure."

"But, Reese—" Camilla's voice took on that whining tone. "You're not being fair to me. Sleep with the fat chick or Daphne Petty. I don't care. She can be your gimme." Her voice turned seductive in a flash, surprising Audrey. "But I don't see why that has to spoil our fun."

"Doesn't it?"

Audrey ducked behind the stairs when she heard footsteps. Sure enough, Camilla came stomping past in her adorable outfit, a pout on her pink, glossy lips. She paused at the steps, oblivious to Audrey hovering in the shadows behind them, and turned to give Reese one last look. "If you want that business deal, you know where I'll be." Her shoulders gave a slight shrug. "I think we can still have fun together, but that's up to you."

"I'll keep that in mind," Reese told her.

"So . . ." Camilla asked.

He sighed. "My answer is still no."

Audrey ducked farther back into the shadows as Camilla went up the stairs of the cabin and Reese turned to walk down to the lake. She watched his broad back as he left. Their little fling had come close to ruining Reese's business deal. It sounded like Camilla still wanted Reese, even though he didn't want her, and that was confusing to Audrey.

Why was he turning down the heiress? It didn't make sense. Because of their bet? Did he really want to be Audrey's slave for a day?

She almost snorted aloud. She doubted he wanted that more than the anal sex she'd agreed to.

It had been shocking to Audrey to hear him suggest

such a thing as part of their dare. She'd guessed from the challenging, almost playful look on Reese's face that he'd expected her to freeze up or flip out on him. He'd been trying to get a rise out of her.

Instead, she'd agreed to it. God only knew why. She'd never had anal sex, and she wasn't sure she wanted to sleep with a man—no matter how sexy he was—right after he rolled out of another woman's bed. But somehow, she'd found herself agreeing to it, knowing it was pretty much a sure thing that she was going to lose.

Reese coaxed her wild streak to the forefront, and she liked it. Just the thought of doing wild, dirty, forbidden sex with him sent a whole fleet of butterflies through her stomach.

Of course, his turning down Camilla had never really even been a consideration. It was downright strange. Not only was he losing guaranteed sex from two women—and according to Reese's reputation with ladies, he never turned down no-strings-attached sex—but he was in danger of losing his precious business deal.

And that made her feel weird.

She should have never dared him to seal the deal with Camilla. Maybe he hadn't liked that Audrey was trying to force him in one direction or another and that was why he'd gotten cold feet. Maybe he was just denying Camilla at the moment so she'd only want him more when he returned.

Or maybe there was a bit more there with the "fat chick" he was nailing? Audrey felt a heated blush creeping over her cheeks at the thought, and she pressed her palms to her face.

What a silly thought. She couldn't hold on to someone

like Reese any more than she could hold on to a handful of lake water. He was witty, sexy, urbane, and had women falling all over him. She was calm, efficient, and boring. Well, most of the time. When she was with him, she was . . . different.

She should confront Reese, she decided. Make him tell her what was going on behind his thought process so she could quit wondering about it. They were friends, after all. He'd tell her.

But for some reason, Audrey found herself slinking away so Reese wouldn't see her, wouldn't know she'd been listening in to their conversation. She'd give him the afternoon. That would allow him plenty of time to change his mind and see where he landed with this thing.

And maybe give her stomach time to calm down and quit acting all excited, like he'd just chosen her to take to the prom or something.

Audrey lurked in the house for the rest of the day, determined to act like nothing was wrong.

Like Camilla hadn't gotten into her car and driven away, tires screeching down the gravel road.

Like Reese hadn't gone upstairs and slammed his door as if he were annoyed at the world, and then spent the afternoon up there, avoiding the rest of them.

Like both Cade and Daphne weren't giving her curious looks and whispering to each other, trying to figure out what was going on.

Nope. Audrey acted as if nothing was going on. She popped a bowl of popcorn and settled down in front of the fire with her book and read, acting as if she didn't have a care in the world.

In all reality, she'd already finished the book. Twice. She was simply staring at the pages, lost in her own thoughts. Well, except for when it came to the love scenes. She read those at least twice more with great attention to detail. She might have also pictured herself in the place of the heroine, and Reese in the place of the hero. At least once. And then she felt weird about it and went back to staring at the page, turning over the conversation with Camilla in her mind.

She couldn't figure out Reese's motives as to why he'd turned down the heiress. The way she could see it, there were only a few possibilities as to why he'd refuse Camilla's blatant invitation: that he was truly interested in Audrey, that he was determined to make Camilla suffer for abandoning him, or that Camilla had some horrible sort of sexually transmitted disease and this was an easy out.

Oddly enough, the latter two were the most probable. *Especially the STD*, she thought, then chided herself for being unfair. Camilla's greatest crime was being interested in the same man who Audrey was.

Then again, the bitch did call her fat.

Feet thumped on the stairs and Audrey looked up from her book. Cade and Daphne had gone for a walk around the lake—they all usually took at least one turn around the lake with a partner daily since there wasn't a TV in the lodge and not much to do in the way of entertainment otherwise—so Audrey knew it must have been Reese heading down the stairs.

She resisted the urge to smooth a hand over her bun.

Sure enough, it was Reese, dressed in a dark burgundy open-collared shirt that actually fit him and a pair of jeans. She guessed Camilla must have returned with his clothing.

He looked sexy as hell in it, too. Audrey eyed his tight ass in his jeans appreciatively.

He gave her a black look as he passed by the couch, his foul mood clearly lingering, then headed into the kitchen. She put aside her romance novel and her empty popcorn bowl and sat up. That look he'd given her was a warning one. A "not right now" look. A "don't fuck with me today, I'm not in the mood" look. Too bad for him that he was alone in the cabin with the one woman immune to Reese Durham's black glare. He didn't scare her. Hell, he didn't even intimidate her, really. She just wanted to know why he was so cranky, and why he'd turned the heiress down.

She headed into the kitchen after him.

Reese was bent over, pulling something out of the fridge. When he straightened, he gave her a foul look and tossed the package of ground beef on the counter. "Go away, Audrey. I'm not in the mood."

"That's not like you," Audrey said in a deliberately light voice, moving a bit closer to him anyhow. "Rumor has it that you're always in the mood."

He ignored her, pulling a sauté pan out of the cabinet and thumping it on the stove with a bit of force. When she didn't move back, he glared at her again, reached past her, and grabbed a knife, then slit open the meat and dumped it in the pan.

"So you're not talking to me?" she asked.

"I thought I told you to go away."

"Are you mad that you chased your heiress away?"

That time, the glare he gave her was icy. Reese gestured at the pan. "Do you mind? I'm trying to make dinner so you can keep romancing Cade into thinking you're the perfect woman."

"Mmm," she said, eyeing him. For some reason, it was adorable seeing Reese all moody and blustery. Maybe it was because she was normally the one on the defensive and Reese the one on the offensive. Turning the tables? Kind of fun. "So what am I cooking?"

"Spaghetti." As if to prove the point, he grabbed a large pot and turned, thumping it into the sink with a crash, and then began to fill it with water.

"Wonderful. Cade loves spaghetti. That's rather thoughtful of me." She crossed her arms under her breasts and leaned up against the counter. "I don't suppose I thought of garlic bread, too?"

He glared at her hatefully, then turned a knob on the oven, preheating it. "You did. Happy now? Can you go?"

Audrey tilted her head, studying him. "I will after you tell me what's going through your head."

"It's none of your business."

"Really? You think it's none of my business?"

He ignored her, turning off the tap and then moving the pot of water to the stove top, as if she weren't speaking. That was fine. She'd break through that icy facade at some point, and then he'd snap. Kind of like she always did.

And for some reason, that started to turn her on.

Audrey tugged at her T-shirt, hoping her hardening nipples weren't visible through the fabric. She continued to watch him, then commented, "So why'd you turn Camilla away?"

"I didn't." The two syllables sounded gritted, as if spoken through clenched teeth.

"Really?" She pretended to pick a piece of lint off his sleeve, oh so casual. "That wasn't what I heard." And she waited for the inevitable blow-up.

Reese slowly turned, looking at her long and hard. "What did you hear?"

She gave a small shrug, but felt her panties get a little damp with arousal. "I overheard you talking to Camilla back by the woodpile. You're riding the moped, remember?" At his unmoving face, she continued on. "You know the joke. Fat chicks are like mopeds. Fun to ride but you never let your buddies see it—"

"I know what she meant, Audrey. And I never said you were fat."

"No, you didn't. Camilla did. You told her you were sleeping with me, though, and it torpedoed your big business deal. And I don't understand why you did that."

He gave her a scathing look, then grabbed a spatula and began to stir the ground beef that sizzled in the skillet. "I said we weren't talking about it."

"Did you decide that you didn't want the business deal?" she asked, knowing she was goading him. "Or maybe Camilla wasn't your type after all? She told you that she didn't care if you slept with me as long as you had fun with her. Was that the problem? You weren't having fun? Or maybe—"

He set the spatula down, his hands clenching. "Let it go, Audrey."

"Maybe you're chicken," she continued. "Maybe you felt like you couldn't back up your bet, so it was safer to lose to me. Not every guy's in the right sort of mindset for anal sex, after all—"

Reese turned away before she could finish. Audrey let her words trail off, curious and a little disappointed. All that ammo she'd been throwing at him and he wasn't even going to say anything to her? As she watched, he moved to the oven and turned off the knob. Then he did the same to the stove and gave her another glare. "You want to be in the kitchen so bad, you can cook dinner."

And he began to stalk away.

She reached out and grabbed his arm. "You want to know what I think?"

"No, but I'm sure you'll tell me." He tried to pull away.

Audrey ignored his attempts to lose her. He was well versed in pushing her out of her own comfort zone, and it was time someone turned the tables on him. "I think you're pouting."

That got his attention. His gaze snapped back to her and he gave her a black scowl. "Excuse me?"

"You heard me. You're pouting. You're sulking because you turned down a woman who holds the purse strings to a lucrative business deal and you're mad at yourself for doing it, because you don't understand why you did so. And you want to know something? I don't understand it, either."

The look in his eyes got darker. "Audrey . . ."

"I'm serious. If it's because you're sleeping with me, well then, that was a bit ridiculous, don't you think? I told you that we don't have anything going on between the two of us. You should have taken her deal." Her fingers might have stroked his arm through that dark sleeve, feeling the cords of his muscles. "That was a stupid move."

"I don't need a lecture from you," he said, his mood still black. But he wasn't pulling away any longer.

"We both know it was stupid, though," Audrey continued, her voice getting husky. "Stupid and very un-Reese Durham of you. Playboy Reese Durham would have slept with her and demanded the business deal, and then kicked her out of bed once you had it."

"That's right," he said with a bitter laugh. "The male gigolo."

That hadn't been what she'd meant. At least, not at the moment. So she simply stroked her hands up his arm, unable to stop herself from touching him. God, he was cute in Cade's awkwardly tight clothing, but in his own? He had this savage, predatory grace—a businessman out to break hearts and drop panties. And it was doing wicked, wicked things to her.

"Nothing but sex," she said lightly. And she meant for it to come out as some sort of rebuttal or clarification, but instead it sounded breathless and incredibly, wildly turned on.

One hard hand moved to her waist, and then in a flash, Reese was grabbing her and jerking her against him. Audrey's breath stole out of her lungs as his head bent to hers and then he gave her a crushing kiss, full of pent-up frustration and longing and laced with eroticism.

It seemed that she hadn't been the only one feeling the sparks between the two of them. Good. If she was crazy, at least they were crazy together. Audrey moaned, her arms going around his neck, and his mouth drove against her own, his tongue sliding into her mouth with a fierce intensity that promised all kinds of things that made her core ache.

He groaned low in his throat and then he pushed her back up against the counter, the kiss taking on a hot, wild edge. With his hips pinning hers against the counter, he thrust against her in a suggestive motion, letting her know exactly just how into this he was. And he was hard as a rock.

Just the feel of him against her made Audrey breathless with need. She whimpered and her hands went to his shirt, frantically plucking at the buttons. She needed skin, wanted to feel him against her.

He followed her lead and began to drag at the waist of

her jeans, then headed for her fly. The kisses he pressed to her mouth became quick and abrupt, as if he needed to pull away and couldn't seem to do it, continually heading back to her mouth for one more round, one more kiss, one more slick of tongue against her own. "You want to do this here?" he breathed against her mouth. "Where are Daphne and Cade?"

"Out for a walk," she told him, then leaned in and took his lower lip between her teeth, then sucked on it.

"To my room, then." Reese grabbed her by the hips and pulled her into his arms. Audrey squeaked in surprise, her arms flinging around his neck in fright at being lifted off the counter.

"Put me down!"

"Hell no," Reese said, and buried his face in her cleavage. "I like you just like this."

For some reason, that made her feel playful . . . and he didn't feel like he was straining to hold her. So Audrey relaxed a little and locked her legs around him, then rubbed her breasts against his chin as he carried her toward the stairs.

He gave a soft little groan when her hard nipples scraped against his jaw. "God, you have the most perfect breasts. I think I need them in my face more often."

"Get me into your bed and you can have them in your face in about thirty seconds," she said.

Reese carried her up the stairs and they headed down the hall to the last room, the one that Reese had been staying in. He flung open the door and strode inside, then tossed Audrey down on his bed with a bounce, his eyes watching her with avid interest.

She leaned up on her elbows, surveying his room. It was

kind of a disaster area—no neat freak here. Dirty laundry was strewn all over the floor and the bed wasn't made, which was a far cry from her own room. She liked seeing that. It only emphasized the differences between her and Reese, and she liked those differences a lot. They were what made him so much fun to be with, so different. So incredibly arousing.

He kicked the door shut and then strode over to the bed with a gleam in his eyes that made her breathless. She quivered when he loomed over her, and then he undid a few buttons on his shirt, then yanked the entire thing over his head, exposing his hard, delicious body and that fascinating tattoo on one arm. Her fingers itched to touch him, but she forced herself to continue laying in bed, propped up on her elbows, and simply enjoy the show.

As if for her benefit, Reese tugged at his belt with rapid jerks, zipping it through the belt loops and then flinging it against the wall. His jeans were down in a flash, and again he wasn't wearing anything underneath, his thick cock springing free and erect. "Do you ever wear underwear?"

"Too confining," Reese told her. "You should try it sometime."

"I don't think so."

For some reason, her distaste at the thought made him grin. "Damn, I love it when you talk all prim and proper to me."

She flushed. It felt a bit like an insult, even though she knew he didn't mean it that way. Time for her to change from prim and proper, then. She reached for her bun, intending to pull her hair down.

To her surprise, Reese stopped her. "Leave it up."

Audrey looked up at him. "Leave it up?"

"Yeah." He climbed over her on the bed, sliding between her legs as if he belonged there. "You must be getting to me, because seeing that tight little bun turns me on now."

"Oh?" Her voice came out with a bit of a wobble, the heat pooling between her legs at the feel of him pressing there.

"Maybe it's because I know that underneath that efficient, wholesome exterior, there's a wild woman just waiting to get out. And I know that I can coax her to come out and play." His hand stroked over the fullness of her breast, then plumped it, his gaze fascinated as he watched her.

She moaned, dropping her elbows and laying flat on the bed. She was his to touch, his to play with.

"I can feel your nipples through the fabric, Audrey," he told her, circling one through the layers of bra and T-shirt and driving her wild. "You know what that does to me when I see that?"

"The same thing my bun does?" she guessed.

He chuckled, and then his fingers were reaching for the zipper of her jeans, even as he leaned in and nipped at the tip of her breast, then buried his face in her cleavage again. "So fucking sexy."

She did feel sexy in his arms. Like her curves were an incredible turn on to him instead of a turn off. Like she wasn't the plain, boring Petty sister. She was uninhibited and delicious and just for him. And she loved it. She cupped her breasts and pushed them toward him, letting him nuzzle at the valley.

He tugged at her jeans again, and then groaned. "You need to take these off."

She lifted her hips slightly and began to reach for the buttons, but he stilled her hands. "I have a better idea."

"Oh?"

"Flip over for me." His eyes were hot on hers.

Her throat went dry. Anal? Now? She wasn't sure she was ready. "I—"

Reese's eyes widened and he chuckled, burying his face in her breasts again. "I lost that bet, remember?" His hand slid along the curve of her thigh in her jeans. "I just wanted to take you from behind."

Her face flamed with embarrassment. "Oh. Of course." She got up from the bed and undid her jeans, then let them pool to her feet and stepped out of them. Next went her cotton bikini panties, and then she stripped off her plain shirt and her bra. Reese watched her every move, his gaze caressing her.

When she was naked, she glanced at the bed and then slid into his arms. She wrapped hers around him and pulled his head back to her breasts.

"Mmm." He nuzzled at one of her nipples again, lightly licking the tip. "So lush and gorgeous. I love your big, heavy breasts. I could play with them for hours."

"But I ache so badly for you," Audrey told him, shivering when he grazed her nipple with his teeth. "I don't think I could last for hours."

"No?" Reese gave her a hot look, then ran a hand along her ass and lightly smacked it. "Get down on all fours, then."

A quiver ran through her body and she did as he commanded, feeling a bit exposed as she did so. He got up out of the bed and she glanced over her shoulder to see him at the nearby dresser, rolling a condom onto his cock. Reese moved back to the bed and she glanced away, staring at the headboard, waiting for his touch.

She didn't have to wait long. His hands slid over her ass again, feeling her smooth flesh, caressing her skin. "Look at all this beautiful ass," he murmured appreciatively. "Not a freckle on it. You've never gone sunbathing naked, have you?"

"No," she breathed, pushing back against him just a little. "I'm not brave enough."

"I'd make you brave," he told her in a low voice.

"I know you would." And he would. He made her a bolder person, and she loved it.

His hand continued to trail along her hip, caressing the indentation of her waist, then traveled to her spine and moved along it, stroking her like he would a kitten. "I could stare at you for hours."

She whimpered, letting him know just how much this was torturing her, and nudged back against him again.

"But I won't," he murmured, and then she felt the head of his cock at the well of her sex a mere instant before he pushed deep inside her in a single hard thrust.

Audrey's breath caught in her throat, and her muscles locked as she drank in the sensation of him seated deep inside her. He felt good. His cock seemed to be so big and thick that he rubbed inside her just perfectly. And there hadn't been a bit of pain when he'd sunk deep, which meant that she'd been incredibly wet and ready for him. She leaned forward on her elbows a bit, moaning with pleasure and lifting her ass for him.

"Ah, beautiful," he told her, and his hands gripped her waist. Then he slid out, almost all the way, leaving only the tip inside her, and pushed back in with one hard thrust. He repeated the motion, his hands clasping her waist and dragging her back against him.

Her breasts, now loose from her confining bra, swayed with every rough stroke, and Audrey moaned, pressing her cheek to the bedding as he continued to pump into her.

Faster and harder he stroked into her, and she could feel the build starting low in her pussy, need spiraling inside her. He continued to rock into her, rough and hard and demanding, and she leaned into each driving thrust with her hips.

"Touch yourself, sugar. I want to have you come with me."

She whimpered again, and her hand slid under her body to her lifted hips, and then to her pussy. She dipped her fingers delicately between her wet folds even as he continued to fuck her roughly from behind. Her fingertips lightly scored her clit, and erotic pleasure exploded through her body. "Reese," she said with a ragged breath, and began to circle her clit with her fingers with a rapid pace that wouldn't last long. "Oh, God, need you so bad. Oh, Reese."

"That's right," he gritted, and his thrusting took on an even harder, rougher edge. "You belong to me, don't you, Audrey?"

"Oh, God, yes." Her fingers circled faster and faster. The tension built in her legs and she curled her toes, feeling the clench of her building orgasm in her calf muscles.

"Tell me that, then. Tell me you don't want anyone but me. Tell me you won't let that fucking sexy little bun down for anyone but me."

She moaned, rubbing herself even faster. "No one but you, Reese. Don't want no one but you."

"Good," he growled, and the word was so animalistic and utterly satisfied that it took her by surprise. Not that it mattered, because then she was coming, her body launching into orgasm, and she gave a choked cry of his name, her muscles clenching and working around him even as he continued to stroke deep into her from behind.

And then he cried out her name, and she knew he came.

His strokes were growing jagged and wild and so rough that she could hear his balls slap against her skin, could feel him smacking against her pussy. And it made her quiver all over again, the orgasm continuing to rip through her for long, intense moments.

And then it slowed, as it always did, and she panted, cheek pressed to the sheets that smelled like Reese, and felt him peel out of her to dispose of the condom. She breathed heavily and sat up, considering her surroundings. She was in his room, an intruder. Should she get quietly dressed again and head into the shower? He hadn't wanted her around him earlier, at least not until he'd exploded and they'd more or less dragged each other to bed.

But she wasn't just a quickie fuck, so she grabbed his covers and slid underneath them, waiting for him to return to bed once he'd cleaned himself off. He'd have to deal with her and the conversation she wanted to have. If he didn't, well, that was too bad for him, because she was determined to talk.

Reese returned to the bed a few moments later and slid under the covers with her, then tugged her against him. He pulled her on her side and spooned her against his now-softening cock, snuggling close. His head buried against her neck and he began to nibble on her ear. "God, I love touching you."

She smiled at him and wrapped her arms around his. This felt so good. She felt warm and delicious and wanted in his arms.

Which meant he was probably trying to distract her. She wasn't fooled for a minute. "So tell me about the business deal."

"Not right now, Audrey."

"Right now is a perfect time," she pointed out. "You've just taken the edge off and you've already chased Camilla away, so you might as well tell me about it. It's not going to affect things anymore either way."

"Hmm," he said, and she could tell he was thinking it over. It was almost like he didn't want to ask for help. Not that she had much to give, but he seemed reluctant to open up about any of it, as if that might convey a weakness of some kind.

"Come on," she said with a nudge. "It might help you to bounce ideas off someone else."

He hesitated a moment more, then slid his hand over her hip, caressing her skin. "I made a bad investment last year." His fingers stroked her curves and she lay perfectly still beneath him, sensing he was about to open up and that it was difficult for him. "My company's private, so no one knows exactly how bad off we are except myself and my board. It was a gamble on medical technology. Cade told me not to invest, but I thought I knew more than him and took a risk." He shrugged. "Turned out he was right. It was a bloodbath and I lost a fortune. I was close to making my billion and now I'm at risk for losing everything."

Her throat locked. "Your . . . billion?"

"Mmmhmm." His fingers stroked down the inside of her thigh. "All of us have at least a billion, except me."

"All of who?"

He slid his fingers to the curve of her knee and played with the soft skin there. "It's not important." He leaned in and kissed her shoulder, then grazed his mouth over her skin. "I've had to fight for every dollar that came my way. If I'd been patient and listened to Cade's advice, I'd have made it by now. Instead, my company's drowning and I thought that pairing up with Camilla's father on a celebrity cruise line would be the way out."

"Except Camilla doesn't care about the business half as much as she cares about having fun with you," Audrey told him, leaning into his casual caresses.

"Something like that," he murmured. "So you see my problem."

"You're friends with billionaires," she pointed out, her breath catching when his hand moved abruptly to her nipple and began to tease it. "Why not ask Cade or Logan to help you out?"

"Pride," he told her bluntly. "Out of our group, only Cade and I came from nothing. I won't be the one who asks for a handout."

Our group? she wondered, but didn't ask. It was like she was only getting half of the story, and he was distracting her with caresses instead. Not that she minded the caresses, but she wanted to help him, prove that she was different from the women he normally dated.

And then she wondered to herself why it mattered, but somehow it did.

"So why not approach Camilla's father directly?" she asked him. "Tell him that his daughter's not taking things seriously and you want a real business investment. Camilla will be mad at you but if her father truly wants to invest with you, then maybe he'll understand."

"Mmm," he said again, his noncommittal response she was becoming all too familiar with. "We'll see. I don't want to think about Camilla right now."

And his hand slid between her thighs, cupping her pussy.

Audrey rolled over in bed to face him, her mouth

seeking his even as his fingers slid deeper, spreading her pussy and gliding over her clit. Even as she kissed him, she recognized the stalling tactic, and for some reason, it bothered her.

Why was it okay to talk business with brainless Camilla but not her? What made her different?

And why on earth did it bother her? She knew Reese was just a fling and had known that going into things. So why did she care now?

NINE

By the time Daphne and Cade returned from their long walk, Audrey had climbed out of bed with Reese, showered, and changed into new clothes. She read a book while Reese prepped dinner, and when that didn't hold her attention, she gave up on the book and simply stared out the window.

Her mood was pensive. She should have been happy, or at least content. She'd just had mind-blowing sex with an amazingly hot guy who found her sexy and attractive. Her sister was on the way to recovery for the moment. Life should have been good.

But she was bothered by Reese's confession about his finances. Had their fling ruined his business deal? If she hadn't had sex with him, would he be romancing Camilla right now and securing his business's future? Had she cost him a multimillion-dollar contract simply because she'd been flattered that he wanted to have sex with her instead of Camilla?

She should have been an adult about things and turned him away, told him to go hunt down Camilla and woo her simply because that was what he'd wanted to do. Camilla clearly wasn't the most logical person to reason with, and if his future depended on whether or not a flighty heiress was entertained, who was she to stand in the way?

But more than that, she was genuinely bothered by several aspects of it. And more than that, she was bothered by the fact that she'd cared so much. What had happened to her "nail and bail" plan? Reese was a player. She no more expected him to take this thing seriously than she expected Camilla to come waltzing back through the door again.

So why was it that she, Audrey, was acting like this was something real? Like it was more than wishful thinking on her behalf.

She was bound to get hurt if she let herself get tangled up into things too much.

As Daphne and Cade entered the house, laughing, Audrey forced a smile to her face for her twin. Even if Audrey was troubled, there was no question that things were looking good for Daphne. Her twin's cheeks, so sunken previously, now had color in them, and her eyes were bright and snapping once more, not glazed like before. Another few days and Daphne could be off the Xanax entirely, Cade had assured her, and that made her happy. "How was your walk, Daph?"

"Cold," Daphne announced, putting her hands on her cheeks as if to warm them. "What did you do while we were gone?"

Audrey held up her book in answer. "Just sat around." *And had dirty sex in Reese's bed.*

Daphne continued to smile, but her gaze turned curious as she watched Audrey. "I think I'm going to go out and smoke another cigarette. You want to join me, Twinkie?"

Audrey gave Daphne a puzzled look. Twinkie was one of their code words from when they were teenagers and developed hints for each other that only they knew. Calling her sister Twinkie meant that they needed to have a private talk. "Sure. Just let me get my coat."

They left the men inside and headed back out, Daphne clutching the pack of cigarettes in her hand. Neither sister said anything as they headed out to the dock at a leisurely stroll. When they arrived there, Daphne pulled out a cigarette and placed it between her lips, then lit it. Audrey said nothing at all, lost in thought.

Daphne glanced over at her. "So what's bothering you?"

"I'm fine," Audrey said automatically.

"Uh-huh," Daphne said in a voice that said she knew it was bullshit. "You can lie to a lot of people, sis, but not your twin. Spit it out." When Audrey hesitated, Daphne suggested, "Is it more man trouble?"

Audrey's smile was faint. "Something like that. You know, when I first heard we were coming out here, I thought I'd be spending all of my time with Cade and you. And I have to admit, while I was determined to get you clean, part of me was really, really excited to get to reunite with Cade."

Strange how that seemed so low on the priority scale now as Reese was looming in her thoughts.

Daphne looked stricken. "I've been kind of monopolizing him, haven't I?" She took another drag on her cigarette and then pulled it out of her mouth and stared at it thoughtfully. "I should have left him in the house with you today. I know you wanted to spend time with him."

And then she wouldn't have been able to have wild, crazy sex with Reese. Twice. No, it was a good thing that Daphne was keeping Cade distracted.

"I'm concerned that I gave you some bad advice,"

Daphne continued. "About nailing the hot bo-hunk and then forgetting about it after the fact."

Audrey laughed.

"I'm serious. In retrospect, I'm the last person who should be giving advice." She grimaced. "Here I am telling you to hit it with someone else when the man you love is in the house."

"You meant well," Audrey said calmly. "Don't worry about it. I'm the one who decided to nail him."

"Yeah, but . . ." Daphne scuffed one of her sneakers along the dock. "I didn't want to come between you and the man you've been dreaming about for years, you know? You and Cade would be so good together."

"That's kind of what I always thought," Audrey said absently. "Because we're so alike." Nothing like she and Reese. Their relationship seemed to thrive on mutual antagonism that ended up in a firestorm of lust. There was something so exhilarating about being with him. He drove her absolutely crazy, and she enjoyed every single moment of it.

"Oh, Audrey." Daphne sounded so sad. "I've messed this up, haven't I?"

"No, you haven't." Audrey reached out and squeezed her twin's arm comfortingly. "I'm equally to blame. It's funny, because I have dreamed about getting so much alone time with Cade again. Dreamed about it for years. And now that we're here, he spends all his time with you." She grinned. "Should I be jealous?"

She'd meant it as a tease, but for a moment Daphne looked stricken. She masked it quickly, and began to smoke her cigarette again, staring out over the lake.

"Well, I'm going to fix it," Daphne told her. "No more monopolizing Cade. I promise. He's your friend, too."

"Don't worry about it," Audrey said, not wanting to

seem too eager. She couldn't exactly say *Yes, please monopolize Cade so I can continue to crawl into the playboy's bed.* "We're here for you, remember?"

"I'm fine," Daphne said bluntly. She glanced back at Audrey. "We're heading into town for a few things tomorrow morning. I think you should go."

"Town?" Audrey echoed. "Oh?"

"Yeah. More cigarettes, some soda, things like that." She shrugged. "It'd get you some time with Cade."

"It would," Audrey agreed absently. But if they were gone for most of the day, she'd be alone with Reese. And since she'd won the bet, he'd have to be her servant . . .

Heat flushed through her and she began to picture all the delicious ways she could torment him. Walk around the house naked and make her lunch? Do her laundry naked? Run her a hot bath?

Better yet, massage and hot tub?

She wanted to tell her twin that she'd rather stay home with Reese, who was like her own special addiction. She knew he was bad for her and she just didn't care. But if she told Daphne that, it'd only make her twin more determined to keep them apart.

"Tomorrow morning, then," Audrey said, knowing full well she had no intention of heading into town.

Bright and early the next morning, Daphne nudged her twin. "Come on, sleepyhead. Time to go to town."

Audrey pulled the blankets over her head and gave a pained groan. "Can't. Migraine."

"Migraine?" Daphne looked concerned. "You want some of my Xanax? I can get Cade to give you some."

"Ugh, no." She was a little concerned that Daphne was

so quick to offer her heavy-duty drugs at the sniff of a headache. Maybe her twin wasn't as broken from her habits as she thought. Such an offhand suggestion for something so important? It was worrisome, to say the least. "I'll be fine. Just let me sleep. And leave the lights off."

Daphne didn't seem all that unhappy that Audrey was bailing on her. "All right. Cade and I will bring you home some chocolate or something." Daphne quietly got dressed and shut the door behind her, and all the while Audrey kept the blankets over her head and pretended like she had the worst headache known to mankind.

Total fib, of course.

The house was quiet for a bit longer, and then she heard the unmistakable sound of tires on the gravel driveway. Leaping out of bed, she peeked out the curtains and saw Cade's car heading down the road. *Perfect.* With a yawn and a stretch, Audrey dressed in her favorite leggings and oversized sweater, and then brushed her hair before pulling it into a tight bun, imagining how it'd drive Reese wild.

She was just about to head downstairs when there was a quiet knock at her bedroom door. On the off chance that it was her twin and she'd decided not to go to town, Audrey dove for the bed and pulled the covers over her head, feeling a bit like a naughty child. "Come in."

The door opened and there was a rattle of silverware, followed by the scent of pancakes. "I brought you breakfast," Reese said in a low voice. "Sorry about your head."

She pulled the blankets down and peeked out at him, unable to hide the faintly mischievous smile on her face.

"Though it's clear to me what happened," Reese said easily. "Your bun's on too tight."

She scowled and smacked him in the arm. "Not funny."

He rolled into bed and grabbed her, dragging her against him. "Neither's faking a headache."

She bit lightly at his earlobe, since it was so close to her mouth. "It was the only way I could get rid of Daphne. She wanted me to go into town with her and Cade."

"And you wanted to spend the day with me?" He seemed smugly pleased at the thought.

"Of course. You lost a bet, remember? Time for you to pay up."

"Ah, that's right." His hands slid over her body, then landed on her breasts, exploring. "Your slave for a day. I guess I'm off to a good start with breakfast in bed."

"You are," she agreed.

"But since you're not really sick . . ." He leaned over her and grabbed a pancake off the stack and took a bite out of it.

"Hey! Those are mine."

"Damn, Audrey. You're a good cook," he told her between mouthfuls. "You're going to make Cade a lucky man someday."

She snorted and plucked a pancake off the stack herself, taking a bite. It was plain, but still delicious. "I am, aren't I?"

"So what did you have in mind for your naughty slave today, O Mistress?"

She pretended to consider for a moment—like she hadn't already figured it all out in advance. "I think I'd like a full body massage, followed by more massaging in the hot tub. Then I'd like for it to be followed up by a nice round of oral sex."

"Demanding mistress," he said with amusement.

"A good mistress knows what she wants and goes after it."

"Indeed she does." He finished his pancake and licked his fingers in a way that made her get all hot and wet just watching him. "So when should we start?"

"Whenever you want to," she said breathlessly. They hadn't made plans to sneak out last night, and she hadn't realized how much she'd hungered for him. It seemed like forever since they'd last touched, but it had been less than a day.

Far too many hours.

"Mmm, after breakfast, then. I'm starving." And he nipped at her fingers as if to prove it.

They split the pancakes, eating quietly while cuddled on the bed. It was nice to just lay in Reese's arms and eat together, enjoying simply being together. It made them feel a bit like . . . the real deal.

Which, of course, was dangerous, since she was going to get her heart broken.

So she slowly raised one bare foot in the air and examined it thoughtfully. "It looks like it needs a massage, doesn't it?"

"Does it now?"

"I think so," she told him. "Time for my slave to spring into action."

He got out of bed and, to her surprise, disappeared down the hall. She frowned and reached for her cup of coffee, sipping it as she waited for him to return. Sure enough, he did a few minutes later and flung the blankets down on the ground, then scooped her into his arms.

She clung to him. "What are you doing?"

"Your slave remembers his orders," he said in a cheerful voice, heading out the door. "A nice full body massage in the hot tub and then oral sex."

"A nice full body massage and *then* the hot tub," she

corrected, beginning to squirm when he tromped down the stairs. "Put me down."

"I plan on it."

"When?"

"Soon," he said, and that mischievous look was back in his eyes.

"Reese," she said warningly. "You're supposed to be my servant today."

"And I'm going to obey your orders."

"*Reese.*"

He ignored her protests, opening the back door to the lodge and heading out to the hot tub.

"Reese, no!" To her horror, she saw the hot tub was uncovered and already on and bubbling. *That jerk!* He'd planned this.

"Into the hot tub for your full body massage, mistress," he said in a wicked voice, and then dumped her in, fully clothed.

Audrey gave a yelp as she splashed into the water, gasping. Her body had been braced for it to be ice cold, but it wasn't—it was incredibly warm and delicious. Too bad she was fully clothed, her favorite sweater and leggings sticking to her body. She glared up at him, wiping wet tendrils off her forehead. "You're such an ass sometimes."

"Most of the time," he corrected, and then quickly stripped his own clothing off, kicking it aside. She noticed he was already fully erect, and her pussy began to throb with excitement as he climbed into the hot tub next to her. "Ready for your massage, my mistress?"

"Only if you're going to undress me."

His eyes gleamed. "Why, I thought you'd never ask."

She snorted. Clearly that had been part of his plan all along.

Wet hands slid along her thighs under the bubbling water, and then she felt him push down her leggings until they pooled at her knees in a wet cluster of fabric. "Mmm," he groaned, rubbing his hands along her ass. "This isn't much in the way of servitude, if you ask me. I'd gladly rub your body down anytime."

"Next time I'll have to come up with something far more diabolical, then," she murmured, leaning back against him. She could feel the head of his cock brushing up against her backside as he curled her back against him and finished pulling her leggings off, her panties having gone with them. He fished the now-free leggings out of the water and tossed them onto the deck with a wet slap.

"Now your sweater," he told her. "Gotta free up those nice big breasts for their massage."

She raised an eyebrow at him but obediently lifted her arms above her head so he could tug the heavy, wet fabric over her. "Somehow I'm thinking you're going to get more out of this than I am."

"Oh, I intend for both of us to have a very good time," Reese told her, dragging the wet sweater over her arms and then letting it drop to the deck. Now she was in nothing but her bra, and it clung to her erect nipples, clearly outlining them. He reached out and gave her an experimental tweak that made her body jolt, and then he was undoing the clasp and rolling her bra down her arms. "Shall I begin?"

Her body was throbbing with need already. "Please do."

He grinned and put his hands on her shoulders, then turned her until her back was toward him. He spread his legs apart in the water and then backed her up against him, until she sat on the underwater bench, nestled between his thighs. "There we go."

She clasped her hands in her lap and waited.

Reese's hands slid to her neck and he began to gently knead her at the base of her skull. That felt wickedly good. She relaxed against him, suspecting that the massage was going to be less of a game than she'd anticipated. "You're good at that."

"I'm an expert when it comes to women," he murmured.

That bothered her, but she ignored it. She'd known that when she'd decided to sleep with him. So she closed her eyes and relaxed against him. They were just having fun together, nothing more.

His fingers worked her neck for a bit longer, getting her loose and making her muscles feel liquid. He fanned out a bit, working his thumbs against the base of her neck and her shoulders, stroking and kneading until she was ready to purr like a satisfied cat. Dreamy with pleasure, her eyes closed and she relaxed against him.

Reese's hands slid to her shoulders and then her arms, continuing to knead and massage. Every once in a while, his fingers would graze the sides of her breasts as he stroked her skin, sending little ripples up and down her body.

And then his arms slid from her sides up to her front, cupping her breasts, and her eyes flew open. She gasped when he gently massaged their weight in his hands, squeezing and kneading like he had her arms, and heat rolled through her body. She moaned when his fingers flicked at the tips and then carefully moved away, as if he wasn't massaging some of the most sensitive parts of her body.

"Feel good?" he asked, his mouth against her neck.

"Yes," she breathed, arching when his fingertips slid over her nipples again. She moaned in response, feeling the score of his fingernails over the sensitive tips.

But then he continued downward, stroking his hands over her belly, rubbing at her skin, and she reached backward, curling her arm around him until she could run her fingers through his hair, clench her fingers against his scalp, and let him know how much he was driving her crazy.

His kneading fingers stroked down her belly and pulsed over her mound, sending shockwaves skittering over her. She whimpered when he kneaded her sex with his hands, wanting his fingers on her clit. Her hips rolled against him in response, but he ignored it, continuing his soothing, stroking motions as if he were massaging any part of her body.

"Feel good?" he asked again.

She moaned in response, arching her breasts. "Please."

"A servant always tries to please his mistress," he said playfully, and nipped at her shoulder. "I need you to move to the other side."

She shook her head and clung to him. "No, keep touching me."

"I intend to," he said, a hint of amusement in his voice. "But I can't do your legs from this angle." His whisper tickled her ear, and she felt his tongue stroke the shell. "Don't you want me to do all of you?"

His words sent another ripple of need through her, and she moaned, obediently turning in the hot tub and sitting on the bench across from him. Now she could watch him, she realized in a daze, her gaze riveted as he gently picked up one of her feet and lifted it, his fingers beginning to massage it, his gaze on her.

Oh, God, she'd thought his fingers were good on her breasts? They were like magic on her foot. She moaned again, this time in sheer pleasure as he massaged the pads of her foot and stroked up her calf. She caught a flash of a grin on his face as he gently let her leg down and then picked up the other, giving it the same attention. Her body felt boneless between the tender massage and the delicious warmth of the hot tub, her eyes closing just a bit. She could go to sleep right now, if she wasn't so incredibly turned on.

"Almost done," he said in a low voice, lowering her foot to the water. "How are you feeling?"

"Amazing," she said dreamily.

"You look dazed," he said, moving toward her and reaching out to brush his thumb over her lower lip. "And aroused." His fingers skated over her face, exploring. "All flushed and rosy. Sexy as hell."

"I feel so good," she told him, leaning into his touch. "Your hands are incredible."

"I'm not done," he told her, and then patted the edge of the hot tub. "Put your belly here so I can do your back."

She eyed the sides of the hot tub. The lip of the tub on each end extended outward, long and flat and intended for sitting. They were more than long enough for her to bend over and stretch out. She supposed they were designed for additional people to sit on the edge, or to set down drinks or towels, but he wanted her to stretch out up there? "It's cold out of the water," she protested.

"I'll keep you warm." And he leaned over out of the hot tub and grabbed his trousers, then produced a condom.

The flush of her body rippled through her again, and she felt excitement building in her pussy. She knew what that condom meant, and God if it didn't make her wet. Obediently, she turned onto her belly and stretched over the far end of the hot tub. Her breasts tightened at the feel of the cold wood under her skin, her ass perched into the air. She hissed with surprise—and pleasure—when those glorious, magical hands began to knead her backside. "Ah, damn, Audrey. You have the softest, lushest ass I've ever seen. I'm almost sad I sent Camilla away instead of winning that bet, because I'd love to fuck this sometime." His fingers slid down the crease of her ass.

She shuddered against him, spreading her hips wider, biting her lip. She needed him so bad. She could feel how wet she was, could feel how slippery her pussy was. His hands skimmed along the planes of her back.

"So sweet, Audrey." His fingers coaxed her legs farther apart, and then she could feel the crown of his cock at her entrance. "Give me just a moment and I'll make you feel so good."

She heard him rip the condom open and her muscles clenched with anticipation. A moment later, she felt him return between her legs, and then Reese pushed in just enough to breach her.

A muffled gasp escaped her, and she pushed back against him, wanting more.

"Shhh," he told her, sliding his wet hand along her back. "Patience. I'm massaging you, remember?"

"This isn't like any massage I've ever felt," she managed.

"Inside and out. I'm a package deal," he told her, and slowly pushed in a little more, rocking his hips against her.

She whimpered, her fists clenching as she tried to remain still. She needed him deep inside her, pumping. Making her wild with need. Making her crazy. She squirmed when he paused again. "Reese," she groaned. "Please."

His hips did a little circle that made her absolutely delirious with pleasure, and her fingers curled as she tried to grip the wood for leverage. She wanted to thrust back against him, to drive him deep inside her and to ease the ache that he was teasing her with.

Reese palmed her buttock and gave it a light smack. "If

you could only see the view I've got. Fuckin' driving me wild." His other hand settled on her ass, and then he was cupping both cheeks. "Do you want me deep inside you?"

She bit her lip and nodded, her fingernails scratching at the wood underneath her hands.

"Tell me. Love to hear you say it."

A shuddering breath escaped her. "Need you deep inside me, Reese. So bad. Please."

"Love to hear that," he said with a groan, and sank to the hilt.

She gave a small cry at the sensation, the fullness deep inside her. It felt incredible, like nothing better . . . until he slid back and then thrust hard into her again, making her body bounce with the force of his thrust. Audrey moaned his name again, and he began to slowly pump into her, building a rhythm that made her wild with need. Back and forth, he slid in and out of her, dragging his cock out until only the tip was left inside her, then slamming back inside with a force that made her bounce atop the wooden cover of the hot tub. She was cold, her naked body almost entirely out of the water, but it didn't matter—the cold on her breasts made her nipples hard, and they scraped against the wood with every rocking slam of his cock deep into her.

And then she was coming. She felt her pussy tighten around him even as he continued to stroke into her, his drawn-out groan the only indication he'd felt her body react. Her legs trembled with the force of her orgasm, and a little sob of pure pleasure caught in her throat as she spiraled into bliss.

He came a second later, his thrusts wilder and harder, and then he groaned her name and fell over her back, pressing her against the wood. "Goddamn," he muttered after a moment, and hauled off her. "I'd intended to go a bit longer than that. I think I was overwhelmed by this beautiful ass."

And he gave her ass another light spank.

Audrey sat up, her entire body trembling with the aftermath. She remained on the edge of the hot tub, watching him peel the condom off his cock and then walk away to dispose of it in the garbage. When he returned a moment later, he moved back to her side and began to lightly kiss her mouth, his thumb stroking her cheek. "Sorry I didn't make that better for you. So much for being your slave all day, eh?"

She gave him a light smile. "The day's still young, and Cade and Daphne won't be back for hours."

His eyes gleamed. "Oh? What did you have in mind?"

"What *didn't* I have in mind?"

He laughed and dragged her into his arms again.

TEN

Though she talked a big game, Audrey began to get nervous around noon that the others would come back and catch them in bed. So she snuck out of Reese's bedroom while he napped and returned to her own, changing into a new set of clothing, and laundered her wet ones.

Reese woke up later and between stolen kisses and caresses, they cleaned up the lodge. She'd been straightening things, and when he'd caught her, he automatically helped out, then prepped a late lunch for them. Having Reese to herself was like a gift all its own—he was easygoing and fun to be around, and he was an incredible tease. That was okay because she teased back. By the time lunch was over, they'd chased each other around the kitchen twice, and ended up dry humping against the table simply because driving the other insane was such a turn on.

Late in the afternoon, Reese and Audrey were playing cards when they heard the car pull up the driveway. A stab of disappointment rushed through Audrey because having Reese here all to herself in the cabin, without having to worry about Daphne or Cade, had been so incredibly nice. Then she felt guilty for wishing her twin was anywhere but here.

This was just supposed to be a fling. So why did it feel more like a honeymoon than a fling? Especially when Reese grabbed her and pulled her against him for a quick, hard kiss before going to meet Cade and Daphne at the door? Audrey got up to follow him.

Cade and Daphne came up the stairs to the lodge, and Daphne had a cigarette hanging out of her mouth, her face pinched with stress. Cade was silent, too, but his look was thoughtful. Warning bells went off in Audrey's mind. "Everything okay?" she asked, taking a bag of groceries from her twin.

"Fine," Daphne said automatically. "Just tired. How's your headache?"

"Better." She gave Daphne a curious look, but didn't push. Maybe she was tired. It had been a hard time for Daphne and it could have been that she tired easily. But Daphne wasn't the sort to admit that she was tired, either. Curious, Audrey glanced at Cade.

Cade carried his packages into the house, and she trailed behind him, noticing for the first time that his form was more compact than Reese's. Reese had at least a head on his friend, and though Cade had a strong build, she liked the way Reese looked better. Maybe it was the dark hair and the roguish grin. The wicked gleam in his eyes.

Cade set his bag down on the counter, pulled something out of it, and offered it to Audrey. "Got you a present."

Surprise and pleasure swept through her. She glanced

over at Reese, before taking the small brown-paper wrapped package from Cade. "For me?"

"Of course." Cade gave her a soft, friendly grin. "Don't you think you're worth a present?"

She felt herself blushing like a schoolgirl. "Of course." With careful fingers, she tugged at the parcel string serving as a bow and slid it apart. Then she laughed to see the pair of romance novels enclosed inside. "My favorite author."

Cade grinned at her. "Daphne told me you'd finished your books. I thought you could use some extra reading."

"I'm going to go outside and smoke," Daphne announced, slamming the back door behind her.

Audrey turned and gave her twin a curious look. "What's going on with her?"

"It's a long story," Cade said, sounding a little weary. "Do you have a moment to talk, Audrey?"

"Oh, of course." She'd been about to head after her twin, but something in Cade's look made her stay. To her surprise, he glanced over at Reese, who leaned against one of the nearby couches, watching them.

"Yeah, well," Reese said in a flat voice. "I guess that leaves me to go check on Daphne, doesn't it?"

"If you don't mind," Audrey asked in a polite voice. "I'd appreciate it."

"Naturally," Reese said, a hint of snark in his voice. "We all live to serve you today, don't we?"

She frowned at his words as he left the lodge. That seemed to fit their playing as mistress and servant earlier today, but all the fun had gone out of it. He seemed irritated. She looked over at Cade. "What's going on?"

"Daphne's just in a mood." He leaned in and took her hand in his. "I wanted to talk to you."

"Oh? What about?" Cade was standing so close to her that she could see the flawless perfection of his tan, the golden highlights in his hair. He looked so perfect, his clothing crisp. He even smelled like a hint of mint.

"I had a long talk with Daphne today. And she . . . told me some things." Cade's blue eyes were utterly sincere, utterly kind. "I was wondering if you wanted to go to dinner. Just the two of us. You and me."

They were the words she'd been waiting to hear for so long. The words she'd dreamed of, from the man of her dreams. And for some reason, she glanced back at the back door for a moment before answering. "Of course."

"If you're up to it," Cade amended. "Daphne said you had a headache."

"Gone," Audrey replied swiftly. "When did you want to go?"

"Now?" He gestured at the front door. "There's a little place on the way to town that's cozy."

"Oh." Again, she glanced at the back door, imagining Daphne chain-smoking cigarettes down by the lake. "What about Reese and Daph?"

"Daphne knows I intended to ask you out." His smile was gentle, as was the hand he put at the small of her back, encouraging her toward the door. "I'm sure she'll let Reese know."

And wouldn't Reese tease her about this? The thought made her smile, and the butterfly returned to her stomach. He'd give her such a hard time, make her so flustered that she'd lose her mind—and then they could lose control together.

"Just let me grab my purse," she told Cade.

Cade glanced over the menu at Audrey. "It's nice to get out, isn't it?"

"Very nice," she told him with a smile, scanning the menu again. "Everything looks very good."

"It is. I took Daphne here when we dropped into town."

"Oh?" For some reason, she found that curious. "On a date?"

Cade gave a rueful grimace, and he shook his head. "Not exactly. Daphne's not in a place right now where she can date anyone."

"That's probably very wise," Audrey told him, and picked up her glass of wine, sipping it. "Wine's nice."

"Yes," Cade said, and took a sip of his own.

Audrey stared at the menu, trying not to feel strains of . . . boredom. They'd been at the small restaurant for about an hour, the place crowded with locals. There weren't many restaurants in the small mountain town, and this one was jam-packed. That was fine, though. They'd waited at the bar and sipped wine, chatting about the cabin and the weather and Logan's relationship with his new fiancée, Brontë, and the fact that her sister Gretchen had just moved in with Hunter Buchanan, another one of Cade's friends.

It was all very pleasant, like meeting up with an old high school buddy or a distant cousin and getting to know each other again.

It was nice. Just nice.

Audrey stifled a yawn behind her hand, blinking her eyes to focus them on the menu. So why was she so incredibly bored with everything? She should have been beside herself with excitement that she was finally getting some one-on-one time with Cade. Going out on a date with him? That was what she'd dreamed of for years. And yet she found herself jealous of her twin, holed up and cozy with flirty, playful Reese.

Kind of where she wanted to be, if she allowed herself to admit that.

"So what do you think Daphne and Reese are up to?" she found herself asking, then winced. God, could she sound any more obvious?

Cade glanced at her over his menu and smiled. "I'm sure they're fine. Don't worry about them."

"I'm not worried." A little jealous, maybe, but not worried.

"You don't have to fool me," Cade told her, setting down his menu. "I know you're a mother hen to Daphne. You worry endlessly about her."

And now all of this was making her feel guilty that she wasn't more worried about her twin at the moment, but instead she was thinking about Reese. What did he think of her being out with Cade? And why did that send an awkward squirm through her body? "She needs someone to take care of her," was all she said.

"She does," he agreed, and she heard a bit more passion in his voice. "Someone who has her best interests at heart. Sometimes I think her team doesn't think about what's good for Daphne in the long run, just how they can control her."

"I'd agree with that," Audrey said. Oh, great, now they were back to agreeing with each other again.

Cade looked troubled for a moment. "You know, she insisted on this."

"Insisted on what?"

"That we go out. She told me . . ." He toyed with one of the knives on the table. "That you had developed feelings for me. And it wasn't fair to you if I didn't give you at least a date to test the waters."

She wanted to smack her face with her palm. "Daphne has a big mouth."

He gave her another gentle look. "But she wasn't lying, was she? This must have been hard on you, all this time in the cabin with us and I never realized. I guess I've been preoccupied."

"Reese tells me I have a pretty good poker face," she said blandly. "So don't go blaming yourself. So you're here with me out of obligation?"

He said nothing, but the glint in his eyes was kind.

It should have bothered her or hurt her feelings. That he'd gone out with her simply to "test the waters" as a favor to Daphne. He did care for her and wanted to let her down gently, unless they had a wild spark tonight that surprised them both. And she should have been hurt by this, but all she felt was . . . relieved.

And still bored, if she was honest with herself.

Cade was nice. So nice. She could say honestly that he was the nicest man she had ever known. She was pretty sure there wasn't a mean or selfish bone in Cade Archer's body. He was thoughtful and kind and generous to everyone he met. And she'd known him since grade school, and he hadn't changed in the slightest. He was nice and responsible . . . just like her.

And that was why there wasn't an ounce of spark between them.

It had taken her so long, but she'd finally realized it—Cade wasn't exciting to her because he was just like her. He'd put obligation to friends and family first. He'd leap when someone needed help and be the first one on the scene to help organize and take care of things. And there was not a bit of attraction between them because she wasn't drawn to that.

She needed someone a little bit unpredictable to draw her out of her nice, wholesome comfort zone. Someone like Reese. He sparked her. Hell, he set her on fire with all the sparks he set off in her.

She should have realized this before dinner. Before things got all awkward between her and Cade thanks to her well-meaning twin. She hadn't told Daphne how she truly felt about Reese in comparison to Cade. Her twin thought she was simply lonely and "nailing" Reese to cover a broken heart over Cade.

Except Audrey hadn't given much thought to Cade since Reese had shown up. She should have indicated that to Daphne, but she'd been too busy lying to herself about things. It was hard to give up on a childhood dream, and Cade was the living embodiment of all of hers.

"Cade," Audrey began quietly. "I'm glad we're here because I do think we need to talk."

He nodded, waiting patiently. So patient, always patient.

"I've had a crush on you since we were thirteen," Audrey admitted with a smile. "And you gave me my birthday kiss. I thought I'd grow up and you'd notice that I'd grown into someone smart and intelligent and capable, and that I'd be the perfect assistant for you. That's actually how I started out as a personal assistant. I thought I'd get some experience in and wait for the opportunity to become yours, so we could work closely together. Silly, isn't it?"

His look was friendly, his eyes crinkling at the corners. "Not so silly. Logan tells me you do an admirable job."

"I am good at what I do," she agreed. "But that's because I like my job, not because of my crush on you. And it took me a while, but I realized that I was making myself into someone who I thought you might like—someone quiet and industrious and never causing any trouble. And I realized that while I like being that person, I like it even more when I let my hair down a little." She smiled at the metaphor, thinking of Reese. "And somewhere along the way, I've fallen for someone else. I hope you understand."

His shoulders relaxed and a real, genuine grin crossed his face. "Is it bad if I say that I'm incredibly relieved to hear that?"

She laughed and reached over the table to squeeze his hand. "Not in the slightest. Is it bad if I say I'm relieved that you're relieved?"

"I do love you, Audrey," Cade said seriously. "You're like the sister I never had."

"I feel the same way," Audrey said. "And I'm sure Daph does, too. You've always been there for us."

His smile faltered a little at Daphne's name, but he nodded. "It was her idea to bring us together, you know. She desperately wants you to be happy. I think she feels guilty that she was monopolizing my time at the cabin."

"I am happy," Audrey pointed out. "No sisterly interference needed. But I'd like for us to remain friends."

"Of course! Always."

She raised her glass of wine toward him. "To friendship?"

He lifted his glass and clinked it against her own, and they drank. Audrey relaxed and, oddly enough, felt a bit lighter. Strange how without her crush on Cade adding a layer of invisible pressure to her, she felt more free than ever. She hadn't realized just how much she'd strove to be so good and saintly that she'd crushed all the fun out of her life.

At least until Reese had shown up.

"So," Cade said, setting his glass down. "Do I know the man you're in love with?"

She fiddled with the edge of the tablecloth. "I didn't say *love*. We're more in the 'dirty fling' stages of things."

"No," Cade said. "I can see the look in your eyes when

you mention him. You light up and seem to glow with happiness. You're in love, Audrey." The look on his face became a little sad. "Trust me when I say I recognize it."

Audrey downed her wine, thinking hard. Was she really in love? How many days had they been at the cabin? She'd lost track because Reese had destroyed her phone. It was at least a week, probably more. Was that quick enough to fall for someone? Maybe so. All she knew was that she loved being with him, and he made her body sing. And she felt like a different—and better—person with him.

"Maybe love," she admitted. "I don't know yet. I want to give it more time."

"I understand," Cade told her.

"And it's Reese," she blurted. "I've kind of got a thing for Reese. We've been sort of seeing each other since the day you caught us."

"I thought as much," Cade told her, and the look in his eyes was troubled. "I didn't want to say anything before now, since I thought perhaps it wasn't serious, but . . ." He sighed. "I've known Reese for a long time, Audrey. Almost as long as I've known you and Daphne. Reese is . . . brittle when it comes to women. He doesn't commit."

"I know," she said simply.

"He's a playboy. He's out for fun and not much more. I just don't want you to get your heart broken over him."

"I know, Cade."

"He's dated a lot of women—"

"*Okay*, Cade. I get it." *Jeez.* "I knew Reese was a man-slut when we hooked up. Trust me. I'm well aware of the situation. I'm having fun with him, and that's all. If it means I need to strap on my big girl panties and take my licks when we move apart, then that's what I do. I understand this."

He still looked cautious. "If you're sure—"

"I'm not," Audrey admitted. "And that's part of what I like. I had my future all mapped out once upon a time, you know, and went after that. I like the uncertainty of not knowing. And I like that Reese pushes me past my boundaries. Whatever happens, happens. I can handle it." She shrugged. "And if we finish our thing and he moves on to someone else, I accept that, too. Like I said, it's just a fling."

Even as she said the words, they tasted sour in her mouth.

If we finish our thing and he moves on to someone else, I accept that.

Like hell she did. Just the thought made her chest ache.

It was too late for caution as far as she was concerned. She'd already fallen head over heels in love with Reese Durham, the biggest player in the entire world.

ELEVEN

They drank wine, ate a lovely dinner, and just chatted about family and friends and good times. It was pleasant to be able to sit out for the night and just relax with a drink, since the cabin was dry due to Daphne's substance abuse problems. They ordered extra plates of pasta for Daphne and Reese back at the cabin, drank a few cups of coffee with dessert, and then headed back to the lodge.

Audrey trotted up the stairs to the front door of the lodge, feeling curiously light. Now that Cade knew about her and Reese, and Daphne did, too, there was no more hiding. They wouldn't have to furtively sneak about and cop feels in the shadows or by the woodpile.

Not that she minded that sort of thing. But it'd be nice to be able to openly cuddle.

To her surprise, when she entered the cabin, Daphne was in the living room alone, curled up next to the fireplace and flipping through one of Audrey's new novels with a bored expression. She looked up as Audrey and Cade re-entered the cabin, her body immediately tensing.

"So, how did it go?"

"It went fine," Audrey said in a mild voice, and held out the paper bag. "We brought you dinner. Fettuccine and some breadsticks. Where's Reese? We got him something to eat, too."

Daphne got up, took the bag from her, and sniffed it. Her gaze strayed to Cade. "Was dinner romantic? Did you guys connect?"

"Dinner was nice," Audrey said as Cade set down his keys. "And we've decided to just be friends. You should have told me you were trying to hook us up. I would have told you not to bother. Where's Reese?"

"Not to bother?" Daphne's thin face looked stunned. She glanced back and forth between the two of them. "I don't understand. You've been dreaming of Cade for years. We talked about this earlier, remember? You said you'd been in love with him for as long as you can remember. I know I didn't imagine that conversation."

"I know," Audrey said. "But I was thinking in past tense, Daph. Not how I feel right now."

"Well, you didn't tell me," Daphne said, her fists clenching at her sides. "I thought I was coming between what you wanted. I put you two together so you could be happy together. You both deserve someone good. Someone who's right for you."

"We're not right for each other," Cade said gently, and gave Audrey's back a pat. "We're good friends, nothing more."

"But you told me that you wanted Cade," Daphne said, clutching the bag of food. She shook her head. "Remember? Bad advice Daphne?"

"Bad advice Daphne gave some good advice," Audrey told her. "I just didn't realize until we sat down at dinner that Cade wasn't what I wanted at all. I want Reese." She glanced around. "Speaking of. Where is he?"

Daphne bit her lip and glanced at Cade. "So, um, after you guys went to dinner, Reese seemed to be in a bad mood, so I had a little talk with him."

A sick feeling hit the pit of Audrey's stomach. "A talk?"

"I might have told him that I got you and Cade together because it was what you'd always wanted, and I'd encouraged you not to sleep with him anymore, since he was just a passing fling. I told him you'd agreed and decided to go out with Cade."

Audrey paled. "You didn't."

"I'm so sorry. I didn't know!"

Audrey glared at her twin and then rushed past her to Reese's room. Maybe he was still packing and she would have time to explain things.

But his room was empty, the bed sloppily made in true Reese fashion. Audrey sat on the corner of it and then sighed.

He was gone. Her fling was done. No more playboy. No more fireworks. No more butterfly in her stomach. He'd gone and left, and she knew he wasn't coming back. That wasn't Reese Durham's style.

Daphne appeared in the doorway, looking sad. "I didn't know, Audrey. I thought I was doing the right thing."

Audrey looked over at her twin. "What exactly did you say to Reese?" He wasn't the type to get easily offended, and that sick feeling in the pit of her stomach was growing.

Daphne twisted her hands. "I told him that we'd talked earlier today and you had mentioned that you were still in love with Cade, and that I'd set the two of you up on a date.

You looked so happy to go out with Cade, Aud. You really did."

Audrey groaned. "What did he say?"

"Nothing." Daphne paused, then wrung her hands again. "He looked really pissed, though. Called for a cab and left."

The thought of Reese being pissed because she was using him until she was bored with him and then running to Cade as soon as she had the opportunity? It was like a stab in the heart, all the more so because that was exactly what she had done. She just hadn't had a chance to explain to Reese how she truly felt. Torn between weariness and anger, Audrey shook her head. "Once again, you've screwed up my life."

Daphne flinched. "I was just trying to help—"

"No one wants your help, Daphne! Look at you. You can't even help yourself." She headed to the door. "How do you possibly think you can help me when you're such a mess?"

Daphne blinked her large, hurt eyes.

But Audrey wasn't going to be moved by Daphne's sad face. Once again, her twin had messed up, and once again, Audrey was paying for it. "Sometimes I think you don't think of anyone but yourself, Daphne. Did you want Cade and I to come home and shower you with thanks for putting us together? Was that why you did it?"

"No, I—"

"You know what? I don't even want to hear your excuses," Audrey said, raising a hand to silence Daphne. "Next time, just stay out of my business, okay? When you feel like you need to help? Don't. Just don't. You've screwed up enough." Audrey shut the door in her twin's face and called out from the other side. "I need to be alone now."

"I'm sorry I'm such a screwup," Daphne said in a soft voice.

Audrey ignored it. She was mad at her twin at the moment, but she was mad at herself, too.

She crawled into Reese's bed and sniffed the covers. They still smelled like him. Disappointment furled in her belly. She didn't have her dream of Cade anymore, and that was all right. But she'd thought that she'd have a bit longer with her dream of Reese. Maybe a few more nights with him before they went their separate ways.

This was too early. Way too early. And he'd left because she'd jumped at the chance to go out with Cade. Except she hadn't known her own heart until she'd been given what she thought she wanted.

Audrey pulled the blankets over her head and closed her eyes. Maybe if she tried hard enough, she could dream about Reese tonight.

After all, she didn't have much of anything else left.

"*Daphne! Daphne! Wake up!*"

Audrey jerked awake, disoriented. There was a vague feeling of something being *wrong* but she couldn't put her finger on it. Her dreams had been disturbing, too. Unhappy. She automatically rolled over and looked for her twin, then realized she was in Reese's room.

"*Daphne, please!*"

That was Cade's voice. And he sounded terrified. Ice settled in Audrey's chest and she leapt out of Reese's bed and went to the room she shared with Daphne. It was empty, the bed still made. Confused, she headed down the hall. Cade's door was shut, but the lights were on underneath.

She knocked. "Cade? What's going on?"

"Audrey? Oh, God. Audrey, she won't wake up." Cade's voice sounded frantic.

She pushed open his door, not bothering to ask for permission. Cade knelt on the floor, a blanket pooled around his hips. He was naked. So was the sprawled form of Daphne on the floor, mixed with the blankets. It was clear that they'd slept together.

Cade looked up at Audrey, his face ravaged. His fingers caressed Daphne's slack cheek. "She won't wake up."

Numb, Audrey went to Daphne's side and knelt by her, pressing her fingers under her twin's nose. Daphne was breathing, but it was slow and irregular, so faint she could barely make it out. Her lips were tinged blue and when Audrey pried back one of her eyelids, her eyes were rolled back in her head. Audrey raised her hand and her fingernail beds were faintly blue, too.

Another overdose. Goddamn. Why wouldn't Daphne learn? Heart aching, she cradled her twin closer and began to lightly tap her cheek. She had to stay calm. Had to. Cade—sensible, sweet Cade—was a mess. "Call an ambulance. She's had an overdose."

He bolted out of the room, forgetting that he was naked, and Audrey didn't even have the heart to look. She simply pulled her frail twin closer and rocked her against her chest, stroking the too-thin arms.

She'd thought Daphne was getting better. Her twin had seemed more alert, more happy than usual. And yet they'd fought tonight, and that was all it had taken for Daphne to revert back to her old ways.

Daphne hadn't changed. She ran from her problems straight to the pill bottle. Audrey couldn't even feel panic, not this time. She'd seen Daphne overdose too many times.

She just felt weary. As if she'd already lost her twin.

Cade returned a few moments later, a towel wrapped

around his hips. He scrubbed at his face. "They'll be here as soon as they can. Should we drive to the hospital—"

"No." Audrey hugged Daphne close and then checked her mouth for obstructions, making sure that her twin could breathe. "No, we'll stay here so they know where to find us." She considered Cade's nakedness. "Where's her clothing?"

He bolted for the other side of the bed and grabbed at a pile of clothing on the floor, then offered it to Audrey with shaking hands.

She should have encouraged Cade. Should have told him everything was okay. But there was a hollow ache in her gut that wouldn't let the words out of her. She was calm. Oh so calm. And she was furious at Daphne on the inside. "How did she get the drugs?"

"It can't be drugs. I—" He raced into the bathroom, then returned a minute later, defeated. The prescription pill bottle was empty. "How did you—"

"Because I've seen this before," Audrey said flatly. "You think this is the first time she's overdosed?"

Cade buried his face in his hands for a long moment. "She seemed so sad tonight. I just . . . I hugged her and then she kissed me, and the next thing I knew . . ."

"She knew you had her pills," Audrey said in a hard voice, eyeing Daphne's skinny jeans and T-shirt. She wouldn't be able to dress Daphne since she was unconscious, so she grabbed the blanket and wrapped it around her limp form. "She used you to get to them."

The look on Cade's face was bleak. "I should have known."

You should have, she wanted to say, but she could see the agony in his face. And she realized just how blind she'd truly been.

Cade was here for Daphne because he loved her. Of

course. Vibrant, happy Daphne who was like sunshine itself when she was sober. Cade wanted her to get better because he loved her and because he'd carried a torch for her all these years, just like Audrey had carried a torch for him. And she'd been too blind to see it for herself. Too wrapped up in her own thoughts to realize that he was spending all his time with Daphne, holding her hair back as she'd thrown up. He'd gone above and beyond friendship levels and it had never occurred to Audrey.

Daphne must have known it, too. That was why she'd been so stricken when she'd sent Cade and Audrey out on a date. She was being a martyr, pairing together the two people she cared for most in the world because she thought that was what Audrey wanted and what Cade deserved. And when she realized she'd just made things worse for everyone, she'd tried to take the easy way out again. She'd approached Cade and seduced him because she'd known he wouldn't be able to resist.

It was always the same old song and dance with Daphne.

And Audrey realized, for the first time, that she couldn't save her twin, no matter how much she loved her. So she simply pressed her cheek to Daphne's and held her, waiting for the ambulance to arrive.

TWELVE

"I'm here."

Audrey looked up from her spot in the waiting room of the hospital to see Gretchen rushing down the hall, two cups of coffee in her hands. Gretchen looked like a mess—her dark red hair was pulled into a messy ponytail, and she wearing a grubby sweatshirt, yoga pants, and flip-flops despite the chilly weather.

At the sight of her older sister, Audrey gave her a wan smile. "Hey, Gretchen. I'm glad you could make it."

"Make it? My fucking junkie little sister's in the hospital. Of course I made it." Gretchen scowled at the woman seated next to Audrey who was on the phone, a camera around her neck. "Move it, sister, or you're going to be eating that telephoto lens."

The woman glared at Gretchen, but discreetly vacated the seat, going to talk to one of the other photographers hovering in the waiting room.

"Jesus," Gretchen said, flopping into the chair and handing a coffee to Audrey. "I see the paps didn't waste any time getting here. Who clued them in?"

"My guess is him," Audrey said tonelessly, gesturing at the man in the corner. He was dressed in a slick, pinstriped suit despite the late hour and was chatting animatedly to one of the paparazzi while he texted on his phone.

"So who's that douchebag?"

"One of her managers."

Gretchen grunted. "Surprise, surprise. He probably thinks all this publicity is fabulous."

"Probably," Audrey said in a tired voice.

Gretchen wrapped an arm around Audrey's shoulders and pulled her into an awkward hug. "How you hanging in there?"

"I'm fine," Audrey said in her brightest, most efficient voice. "Cade is struggling, though, so I'm trying to keep him calm. I sent him off to talk to one of the board of directors about donating a wing if they'll give Daphne privacy while she recovers. He liked that idea."

"Clever," Gretchen admitted. "But I was asking about you."

"I'm fine."

"You don't seem fine."

My sister overdosed because I blamed her for my love life troubles, I'm not in love with Cade like I thought I was, and I fell in love with a guy who abandoned me. "I'm fine."

Gretchen gave her a disbelieving look. "You do realize that this is one of those times that it's okay to be emotional?"

Audrey simply sipped her coffee, ignoring Gretchen. Her sister talked a big game, but she knew as soon as they heard word on Daphne, Gretchen would fall apart like she always did. Her big sister had a heart of gold, but she was impulsive and incredibly emotional. Couple that in with Daphne's self-destructiveness and Cade's restlessness as he sought to be able to do something—anything—to assuage his guilt over Daphne using him to get to the drugs? It was just best all around if Audrey kept her head together. Someone had to.

Later on, in the privacy of her own apartment, she could break down if she wanted to, but there would always be more to do. People to call, arrangements to make for Daphne's car, managers to scold, her boss to check in with . . .

Someone had to be the practical one in all of this. The dependable one. And it was exhausting, but it needed to be Audrey. Longingly, she thought of Reese and the way he always pushed her into showing emotion. The way he'd laughed as he'd tossed her into the hot tub and bent her over the edge to made love to her.

Tears pricked her eyes and she blinked them back. This was not the time to dissemble. At least she had some really good memories of their interlude, before it had all gone to shit.

"Miss Petty?" A doctor entered the crowded waiting room and immediately the half dozen paparazzi and reporters stood up, readying their cameras. Audrey stood and raised her hand quietly and, true to form, Gretchen burst into emotional tears, just like Audrey had expected.

The doctor eyed Gretchen and moved to Audrey's side, leaning in to whisper. "Your sister is in intensive care, but we feel she's out of the woods. She's awake and alert and can receive visitors."

"Good. Thank you," Audrey said. She squeezed Gretchen's hand consolingly as she mopped at her face with Kleenex.

"You can't bring those," the doctor said with a sniff, gesturing at their coffees.

Gretchen automatically handed hers to the reporter sitting next to her. "Here, make yourself useful," she said in a watery voice.

Someone pushed through the double doors nearby and then Cade was sprinting at them, his blond hair mussed and his clothing wrinkled. He looked like hell, dark circles under his eyes, and pocketed his phone. "I'd like to see Miss Petty."

"I'm sorry," the doctor said. "Family only."

Cade looked at Audrey, raking a hand through his hair in frustration.

"It's fine, Cade. Go home and get some sleep," Audrey told him in her easiest voice. "I'll handle it from here."

"I need to see her."

"I know you do," she said soothingly, and gave him a hug. She whispered in his ear, "Maybe tomorrow. I'll work on the doctors, okay?" When she released him, he nodded and then sat down in one of the waiting room chairs.

The man with the suit approached the doctor and handed him a business card. "I'm Miss Petty's manager. I need to see—"

"No," Audrey said at the same time as the doctor.

"I'm Miss Petty's manager," the man in the suit repeated. "The label—"

"I'm her legal guardian," Audrey interrupted. "And she doesn't want to see him."

The doctor shook his head. "It doesn't matter. Right now we are only allowing immediate family to visit." He looked at Gretchen and Audrey. "If you will follow me."

Gretchen shot the manager the bird when they left, and Audrey pretended not to see it.

They followed the doctor through the maze of corridors in the intensive care unit. "We're keeping her under heavy monitoring," he explained. "Her system was compromised by the amount of drugs, but with time and proper care she'll make a full recovery."

Gretchen began to loudly sniffle again, and Audrey handed her more Kleenex. "Thank you, doctor."

He gave Audrey a pointed look. "I don't need to tell you that that young woman needs serious help."

"We know."

"She told me she was trying to get clean. You know I must recommend constant psychiatric observation and a detox facility where she can be monitored at all times. She is a danger to herself right now."

"I can force her to go," Audrey said quietly. "But it won't work unless she wants it. It has to be her decision."

"I realize this. As a professional, though, I'm recommending it strongly. I don't know that Miss Petty could survive another overdose. Do you understand me?"

"I do."

The doctor nodded and led them to a door. The room's blinds were down and the door was closed. Isolated. Private. "I'm Doctor Howell. Please let me know if you need anything else."

"Thank you, Doctor," Audrey said, her voice calm as she shook the doctor's hand. "We will."

Gretchen sniffed loudly.

The doctor turned and left. When they were alone at the door, Audrey turned to Gretchen. "I'm going to say some unkind things to Daphne," she warned her sister. "But I need you to support me in them, understand? It's for her best interests."

Gretchen's eyes widened but she nodded. "I'll follow your lead."

Audrey opened the door and they went inside.

The lights in the intensive care unit were turned off so Daphne could sleep. Her twin's frail form was hooked up to multiple monitors, all beeping and flicking with her vital signs. Intravenous medications hung from her skinny arm, needles taped into it. As they shut the door, Daphne opened her eyes and gave them a wan smile. "Hey."

Gretchen burst into tears again. She sat down next to the bed and took Daphne's hand in hers, squeezing it. "Hey, baby girl. It's your slutty sister come to visit."

The corner of Daphne's mouth quirked, as if she were trying to smile and didn't have the energy. "That's an odd greeting."

"You told me I was a slut the last time I saw you."

"I did? Huh. I don't remember." Daphne's voice was soft, tired.

"It's because you were drunk. And high. Both," Gretchen told her.

"That explains it." She turned to look at Audrey. "I guess I caused you a little trouble, didn't I?"

Anger flared in the pit of her stomach, but she tamped it down. Anger wouldn't reach Daphne. It'd just make her run harder. "You caused everyone a bit of trouble," Audrey said, her voice mild. "Your manager's here, along with every paparazzi he could round up at this hour."

"I don't want to see him," Daphne said in a tired voice. "Tell the doctors not to let him in."

"They won't," Audrey reassured her. "Cade's waiting to see you, too."

"I don't want to see him, either." Tears welled in her

eyes and trickled down the sides of her face. "I can't look at him right now."

"Because you used him to get to the pills?" Audrey said coldly.

Daphne sighed. "You don't understand."

"I don't," Audrey said calmly. "I've never understood it. You have the life you've always wanted and you're tossing it away."

Daphne said nothing. She squeezed Gretchen's hand as Gretchen continued to mop fresh tears from her cheeks. "Don't lecture me, Audrey. You don't know how hard it is to be me."

Audrey moved forward and put a hand on Gretchen's shoulder. "You're right, Daphne. We don't know what it's like to be you. We'll never know. That's why it's time for us to say good-bye."

That got her twin's attention. Daphne's gaze focused on Audrey, her eyes widening a little. Audrey felt Gretchen stiffen under her grasp, but she didn't speak up to contradict Audrey.

"You're my twin," Audrey said in a soft voice. "I love you more than anyone else on the planet. And I thought that by supporting you through everything, no matter what happened, that I'd be doing you a favor. That you needed someone to lean on."

"I do—"

"But I see now that I'm not doing you any favors," Audrey continued. "I've always let you do what you wanted, even when I didn't think it was the right decision. All those times you bailed out of rehab early? I let you. All those times you went right back to that bad situation? I said nothing. And this last time? When you promised to get clean and then overdosed as soon as my back was turned? That's my fault because I supported you when you said you didn't want to go to rehab."

Tears began to pour from Daphne's eyes. "I was doing better," she protested. "Yesterday was just a bad day."

"There are always going to be bad days, Daphne," Audrey said bluntly. "Some are going to be worse than others. That doesn't mean you run for the pill bottle to fix things. That doesn't mean you use a man who loved you simply to get your way." She felt no pleasure at Daphne's flinch. "And it doesn't mean that I'm going to continue to support you while you make bad choices. So this time, instead of supporting you, I'm offering you a choice. You can go back to rehab—"

"No—"

"And you can stay there until I've met with all your doctors and I've decided that you're clean." Audrey turned her calm to Daphne, ignoring her tears. "Or we can say good-bye now."

"Good-bye?" Daphne choked.

"If you do this again, the doctor says you won't live," Audrey said bluntly. "And I already feel like I've lost the sister I used to know and love. I won't go through this again. I won't hold you on the floor and worry if you've killed yourself. If you won't get help, this is where Gretchen and I leave you behind. You can destroy your own life, but you can't destroy ours, too, Daph. And watching you kill yourself slowly is ruining all of us."

Daphne said nothing as tears poured down her cheeks.

"I'm sorry," Audrey said. "But this is the way it has to be. You know I love you, Twinkie. You know I do. But I can't watch you destroy yourself. Come on, Gretchen. We're leaving."

"Oh, but—" Gretchen began, looking at Daphne and Audrey. After a moment her face screwed up like she was trying desperately not to cry again, and she leaned in to hug Daphne. "I love you, too. I hope you make the right decision."

"Audrey," Daphne said piteously, now sobbing openly. "Don't go. I want to talk to you—"

Audrey shook her head, her heart breaking into a million pieces in her chest. "You make your decision, Daphne. And if it's the one where you choose to live, then we can talk. But for now, Gretchen and I have to go." She turned to the door, then looked back at her sobbing twin. "I love you, Twinkie."

"Aud, wait—"

Audrey opened the door and ushered Gretchen out.

They walked down the hall in silence. After a moment, Gretchen looked over at Audrey, her eyes red from weeping. "Sometimes you are stone cold, you know that?"

"I know," Audrey said, feeling heavy and aching with sadness. She wanted to run back in there and comfort her twin, but she knew it was the wrong thing to do. This was the only way she could think of to get Daphne to turn her life around. So she had to be firm, even if it meant she had to be cruel.

"You're not even crying!"

"I've shed enough tears over Daphne for now," Audrey said. "I've got to be strong."

Someone had to. There was so much to do. Someone would need to talk to the paparazzi and downplay the story. Talk to Daphne's management team and discuss how to proceed. Call family and friends who would see the news and worry. Straighten out her work, Daphne's insurance, and a million other small things that someone had to think about. She didn't have time to be emotional or needy.

But for a brief, weak moment, she wanted to curl up

into someone's arms and just cry and weep and be a blubbering baby. Someone like Reese, who didn't mind if she wasn't strong all the time.

But Reese wasn't here.

They returned to the waiting room, Gretchen sniffling the entire time. Cade met them at the door, the look in his eyes worried.

"She doesn't want to see you," Audrey told him gently. "I'm sorry."

"I'll wait out here," he said. "Until she wants to see me."

"You might be waiting a while," Gretchen told him tearfully. "These twins are the most hardheaded women you'll ever meet."

A ghost of a smile touched Cade's pale face. "Oh, I know."

Reese poured himself another drink and considered the cards in his hand. Nothing but garbage. *Eh.* He swallowed his scotch and tossed his cards on the table. "I fold."

"Gotta stay in to make some money, Durham," Jonathan Lyons teased him, raking the pile of chips toward him. "Unless this is some new tactic you're trying."

Normally, Reese would have risen to the bait. But his mood was foul tonight, so he just grunted and poured himself another scotch.

"You're in a bad mood," Logan observed, taking the scotch bottle from Reese's hand and refreshing his own drink. "Business trouble or women trouble?"

"Are they ever separate?" Reese asked with a grimace and tossed his drink back. Women were *definitely* trouble. Upon returning to the city, he'd approached Camilla in a strictly business manner about the cruise line. She'd refused to see him. So he'd gone to her father, only to be stonewalled once more.

His business was fucked, all because he wouldn't pork a bored heiress. *Goddamn.*

Hunter snorted at his side. "For most people, yes, women and business are separate."

Reese made a face at the scarred man. Hunter was usually silent. Count on him to chime in for that. Reese glanced around the table at his friends. Logan was to one side, Hunter to his other. Across the table, Jonathan was carefully stacking his pile of chips while Griffin dealt the next hand.

Cade was nowhere to be seen.

"Where's the golden boy?"

Griffin shrugged and continued to deal. "You're his keeper. You tell us." His cultured, European accent made the insult sound almost pleasant. "Weren't you vacationing with him for the last week or two? We had to cancel three meetings because of you two being out of town."

Reese grunted again. "We were busy. And we're not joined at the hip. I'm not his keeper." If he was, he wouldn't have let Cade near Audrey.

Audrey, who'd lit up shyly at the thought of going on a date with Cade. Who'd forgotten all about him an instant later. Audrey, who'd just been using him for sex to pass the time, her sister had informed him as soon as they'd gone. Daphne had gone on to confess to him that Audrey had told her hours earlier that she still wanted Cade and not Reese.

And that ate at him. He stared down at his empty tumbler and considered refilling it again. Maybe he needed to get good and blasted.

It wasn't like him to get all hung up on a woman. But then again, Audrey wasn't like most women. He thought of that tight little bun and her prim shirts covering those big, lush breasts, and that fiery passion she showed in bed. He clenched his jaw in frustration.

Fuck. The one woman who didn't bore him within a week and his best buddy scored her right from under his nose. It fucking sucked to be him.

There was a bang at the top of the stairs. Automatically, all five men glanced up.

"Isn't Bruno up there?" Logan asked Hunter.

"Always," Hunter replied.

"No, miss," they could hear from upstairs. "You can't go in there."

"Fuck off, Bruno! I can, too. Let me in!" The voice was familiar.

Reese turned to Hunter, who groaned and rubbed a hand on his scarred face. "Is that who I think it is?"

Hunter glared at him and got to his feet, approaching the stairs just as the door flung open and a disheveled Gretchen Petty stumbled her way in, brandishing her purse like a weapon. She bounded down two stairs, glared back at Bruno, and then brightened at the sight of Hunter waiting at the foot of the stairs for her. "Hey, baby!" She peered at the others sitting around the table, her gaze going to the cards and poker chips, and a wide smile crossed her face. For a moment she looked so much like Audrey that Reese's chest ached.

"Thank fucking God," Gretchen said a moment later, spoiling the vision. "Poker night. With the way Bruno was acting, I thought I'd wander in on some secret sausage party or something." She tripped down the stairs, ignoring Griffin's choked sound of outrage, and kissed Hunter on his unsmiling mouth. "But then again, I know Hunter doesn't like cock, so that couldn't be it."

"Hello, Gretchen," Logan said in a flat voice. "Did Brontë set you up to this?"

"No." Gretchen's eyes widened. "Does she know about this? That little hussy. She never said a word." She moved to Cade's empty chair and sat down, inviting herself to the table. "I was wondering where my lover had to run off to when I was clearly in need of more comforting, and I got nosy, so I tailed him here." She looked over at Hunter and wiggled her eyebrows at him.

"Way to go, Hunter," Reese said sarcastically. "Maybe we should invite everyone's girlfriends to show up and hang out. Fuck privacy, right?"

Hunter moved to Gretchen's side, putting his big hands on her shoulders and ignoring Reese's foul mood. He stood behind her, showing his support for her presence, along with the stony expression on his face that just dared someone to say something.

"Jeez, why is everyone so pissy?" Gretchen looked around at the table of irritated men. "You sure I didn't interrupt a circle jerk?"

Hunter leaned down and whispered something into Gretchen's ear.

Her eyes widened and she studied the group. "A secret society? Holy shit! Do you guys all have the same tattoo that Hunter does?"

Griffin groaned and threw his cards down. "What's the use of keeping a secret anymore?" He pointed at Logan. "I hope you have some more of that nondisclosure paperwork that you made Brontë sign."

Hunter glared at Griffin. "It's fine."

"It's not fine," Griffin protested, taking the words out of Reese's mouth.

"So do you guys meet here every week?" Gretchen looked excited at the prospect, picking up one of the poker chips and examining it. "I bet Hunter never wins, huh? He blushes like a schoolgirl. It's a total tell."

As if on cue, Hunter turned red, his scars showing livid against the flush.

"The meeting's screwed this week anyhow," Reese said, setting his empty tumbler down on the table and pushing it away. "Cade's not here so it's not like we can start anyhow."

"I imagine he's still at the waiting room of the hospital," Gretchen said. "He wouldn't leave as long as my sister was in there."

Blood roared in Reese's ears, and he felt all the color drain out of his face. His heart lurched sickeningly in his chest. Audrey was in the hospital?

His Audrey was hurt?

He got to his feet. "Where's she at? I have to see her."

Gretchen gave him a puzzled look. "Daphne?"

"Audrey," he growled, his fists clenched. He wanted to hit something, the rage burning through him. Audrey was hurt and he hadn't been there to protect her. He should have never left. It took a moment to sink in and he looked at Gretchen, confused. "Wait. Daphne?"

The disheveled redhead gave him a curious look. "She overdosed a few days ago. Cade won't leave her side."

Relief staggered him and he collapsed in his chair, burying his face in his hands. "Ah, fuck. Thank God."

The room was silent.

"Well," said Gretchen after a moment. "That wasn't *my* reaction to hearing my sister overdosed, but okay."

"You feeling all right, Reese?" Logan nudged the scotch bottle toward him again.

He took it and didn't bother to use the glass. He drank

straight from the bottle, letting the amber liquid burn right to his gut. Audrey was all right. His Audrey.

And Cade wasn't in a relationship with her. *Good.* The vicious thought startled him. Cade was his best friend. He should have been happy that his buddy hooked up with someone as intriguing and delicious as Audrey. It shouldn't have been eating at him.

But it drove him fucking crazy. He thought about it every night when he went to sleep, picturing Audrey with her sexy hair down and tumbling around her shoulders, kissing Cade, pushing those lush breasts against him.

She should have been with *him*, damn it.

"Your sister overdosed?" Logan asked. "The problem one?"

"Yeah," Gretchen said, her voice sounding a bit wobbly. As Reese looked up, he saw Hunter's hand tighten on Gretchen's shoulder, and she placed her hand against his, as if seeking comfort. "Been a rough week. At least for me, anyhow. I just keep crying."

Logan grunted. "Audrey didn't say anything. She's been back to work for two days. I didn't realize there was anything wrong."

Reese sat up straighter, his attention captured. Audrey was back at work with Logan? So she wasn't with Cade and Daphne?

"Yeah, that's Audrey for you," Gretchen said bitterly. "Audrey just smiles and takes things calmly and puts our lives back in order. She hasn't cried a lick since Daphne went into the hospital, even though it has to be hurting her."

Reese ached at that. His Audrey wouldn't, no. She'd wear her hair in that tight little bun and starch her clothes within an inch of her life because she liked to hide all her fire and emotion behind that outer serenity. She must be raging on the inside.

And she had no outlet. Cade wouldn't know how to act with her. He wouldn't know how to draw all that emotion out of her, to make her human again, and to help her let all that pain out. She needed someone to goad her beyond her boundaries, to make her forget that she was trying to be so self-contained. So she could let loose and just be herself.

But no one would understand that about his Audrey but him, because no one saw past the surface but him.

And suddenly, he needed to be at her side. She would need comforting. A strong arm to lean on. Someone to irritate her out of that icy shell she always put on.

Reese jumped to his feet, but the room spun and he wobbled. "I need to see her."

Logan braced an arm on Reese, steadying him. "You're drunk, man. Sit down."

"See Daphne? They're not letting anyone see Daphne," Gretchen said. "Once she's released from the hospital, she's going straight into rehab for God knows how long. Haven't you seen the papers? They're having a field day with this."

"See Audrey," he told them, trying to get to his feet again and ignoring Logan as he pushed him back down again. "Need to talk to her." She had to be hurting, and she wouldn't let anyone see it.

She always thought she had to be so strong and capable. She was the opposite of him in so many ways, but they were so alike, too. Here he was letting his business fall down around his ears simply because he had too much pride to ask his friends for help.

Ah, fuck. Reese sat down and slumped in his chair, rubbing his face. *Damn.* The realization hit him like a ton of bricks. He was a fucking fool sometimes. "I need to see Audrey. She has to be hurting."

"Not tonight," Logan said in that voice of authority. "And not while you're drunk."

Gretchen watched him with a curious gaze. "Why do you want to see my sister?"

It was on the tip of his tongue to tell her that it wasn't any of her business, but judging from the stony look on Hunter's face, he wouldn't get very far if he told Gretchen off. So he ignored her and turned back to Logan. "You said she's back at work?"

Logan's jaw clenched as he considered Reese. "You're not coming to my office to harass my personal assistant."

"Fuck it, man. I just want to see her, all right?"

"Then come to the cocktail party on Thursday like you intended. She'll be there in a professional capacity."

"Good. That's good." Reese sighed and took another drink from the bottle.

"Wow, he's a bit of a sloppy drunk," Gretchen said in a mock whisper. "Now's the time to clean him out if you're really playing poker down here."

"It's business," Griffin said in his stiff, aristocratic voice. "Something you clearly don't know much about."

"Watch it," Hunter said in a warning voice.

"Speaking of business," Reese said, setting the bottle down on the table and shoring up his courage. He rubbed his eyes and then regarded his friends. Audrey had told him to trust in his friends, and he'd been too blind to do it. No longer. "I need your help . . ."

"I'm not taking it," Brontë said with a stubborn look on her face, arms crossed over her chest.

Audrey pushed the foot-long velvet box toward her again and wiggled it. "I'm not your assistant, I'm Logan's. He said that the gentleman here tonight has an interest in antique jewelry, and it'll reflect well on him if he has you kitted out properly."

"He's full of crap," Brontë complained, but took the box from her. "You know he's constantly coming up with new excuses just to be able to buy me jewelry." She snapped open the case and groaned. "This even matches my dress. Did you pick this out?"

"Absolutely not," Audrey said with a smile. "And your dress looks lovely." She might have taken a picture of the green satin sheath so Logan could purchase the appropriate jewelry, but she wouldn't have bought it and passed it off as Logan's idea. Brontë was too good a friend for that. "Do you need help putting it on?"

"No, I'm fine," Brontë grumbled, tying the waterfall of emeralds at her neck and then peering into a nearby mirror. "God, the man has expensive taste."

"But good taste," Audrey corrected, and then gestured at the double doors down the hall. "Shall we join the party, then?"

"If we must," Brontë said cheerfully, straightening her skirt.

Audrey smoothed a hand over her tight, professional bun and adjusted the earpiece she wore over one ear, the microphone curved to her mouth. That small item, along with her plain beige business suit, would tell anyone who tried to talk to her that she was there in a strictly professional capacity. Not that it would be a problem, Audrey thought wryly. Strange men never tried to pick her up at these parties. The occasional one would try to headhunt to replace his assistant, but for the most part she was invisible unless someone needed her to dictate notes on a whim.

She followed Brontë into the party, scanning the crush of guests. The ballroom was owned by Hawkings Conglomerate, and they kept it reserved for the frequent parties that Logan threw for his business associates. This party was like many others, so things were running smoothly as usual. She kept an eye on the waitstaff as they passed by with glasses of wine and champagne, then strolled past the hors d'oeuvres table, which was neat and still relatively clean. The rich didn't eat much at these parties. They drank like fish, but most of the food went home with the staff.

The ice sculpture at the center of the table was a woman's bust, the long, swan-like neck of the bust ornamented with a thick diamond choker that had its own security guard standing at hand. And the guests tonight glittered like stars, since it was a party celebrating the acquisition of one of the largest and oldest jewelry chains in America by Hawkings Conglomerate. The man had been trying to get Logan to buy his business for some time, but Audrey suspected that Logan only had interest after acquiring a fiancée.

Which was kind of cute, really.

It made her wistful, too. Wistful that someone would look at her and think of her like that. That she would be at the forefront of someone else's mind at all times.

And utterly wistful that that person was Reese Durham. Which was more than wishful thinking. Reese wasn't the type to settle down with someone, especially not someone like her. Reese dated heiresses and movie stars and women who could do things for his career, not a nobody personal assistant who wore tweed and tight buns, no matter how compatible they were in the bedroom.

It just wasn't meant to be. She'd known that all along, but it didn't mean she didn't wish it had been something different.

Audrey turned toward the kitchen, intending on checking out the wine stock to see if they needed to order more at the last moment. This crowd was drinking heavily and Logan wouldn't like it if supplies ran out early. When people were a little tipsy, their tongues got looser. And when tongues got loose, a lot of interesting information was passed in conversation and Logan listened like a hawk.

As if her thoughts had conjured him from midair, a tall, handsome man stepped out of the crowd and began to head toward her. Reese.

Her heart thudded in her chest and her eyes widened. She stopped in mid-step and turned and headed the other way, pressing a hand to her earpiece as if she'd just gotten an important message. *Look busy*, she told herself. *Look busy.*

"Audrey, wait."

Her steps sped up, her cheeks burning, until she was practically running out the double doors of the ballroom and down the marble-tiled hall, doing her best to escape him. *Damn it.* She should have known he'd be here at a party that Logan threw. Of course he would be. She was foolish to think that just because he'd ditched her back at the cabin that she wouldn't have to run into him again.

The footsteps got faster, and then a hand tugged at her arm. "Audrey, I said wait."

She turned, jerking her arm out of his grasp, and gave him a scowl. Then she straightened her suit and smoothed a hand down the front of her beige jacket. "Do you mind?"

He let her go and a smile curved his mouth. "Not at all, actually."

"You almost ripped my sleeve."

"Now that would have been a shame, wouldn't it? Not that I'm averse to ripping your top off." And he gave her a lascivious look that made her blood heat and her temper rise. "I seem to recall that you enjoyed ripping mine off my chest."

Audrey put on her most professional expression. "Can I help you with something, Mr. Durham?"

"Yeah." He regarded her for a long moment. "You can tell me why you have that stick up your ass when you're talking to me. I thought we were past that."

She didn't blink an eye but merely clasped her hands and waited for him to continue.

He sighed, looking disappointed. "I heard about Daphne. I wanted to see how you were doing."

"I'm fine," she said automatically, then moved to step past him.

Reese grabbed at her sleeve again, then tugged her back into place, ignoring the baleful frown she leveled at him. "Don't pull that with me."

"Pull what?" She attempted to leave again, but this time he stepped in front of her, which only made her glare harder.

"You know exactly what I mean," Reese told her, the look in his eyes still full of concern. For her. "The whole 'I'm being the stable, responsible twin because I'm too proud to ask for help' thing. Gretchen said you haven't shed a tear since Daphne went in the hospital. She said that you're keeping busy and being strong. Except I know you, and I know what you're like underneath, and I wonder how long it is before you break down and start screaming."

Audrey continued to stare at him with that too-tight, too-professional smile that was starting to hurt. "Can I go now? I'm sure Mr. Hawkings needs me."

"No, he doesn't," Reese said in a husky voice, and his hands moved to her waist, grabbing her and pulling her close. "I need you. And I think you need this."

To her surprise, he pulled her into a hug. A warm, friendly hug that assumed nothing and simply gave comfort. Audrey stiffened for a long moment, waiting for the inevitable—for Reese to crack a joke, for him to reach out and pinch her ass, something.

But he just held her.

And she felt her knees weaken a little. Her eyes stung. She bit her lip, trying to maintain her composure.

Reese's hand stroked her neck. "You're just like me, see," Reese told her in a soft, husky whisper. "You're so busy being capable and not needing anyone that you forget that you need things, too. And I'm guessing that right now you need a shoulder to cry on. You've had a really rough week, and everyone's expecting you to be strong and handle it all because they can't. And I'm guessing that's the last thing you want to do."

Audrey burst into tears.

Great big, ugly sobs ripped out of her throat, and her fingers curled in the lapels of his black jacket. She clung to him while he stroked her neck and whispered soothing things, holding her and simply comforting her.

"It's all right, firecracker," he said in a soft voice. "I'm here for you. I'm the one person you don't have to be strong around. You just have to be yourself with me. I'll never ask you to be anything else."

Eventually, Audrey's tears stopped and she gave her swollen eyes a swipe, though she didn't pull her cheek from Reese's shoulder. It felt too good to be huddled in his arms, her face against his neck, breathing in his scent. She felt vulnerable with him—vulnerable and yet oddly protected.

Like he was there to take care of her. Was this how Daphne felt when Audrey stepped in and handled things? If so, she suddenly understood why her twin let her shoulder all the burdens. It felt good to have someone to lean on.

Audrey pulled away from Reese's shoulder and smoothed his jacket, frowning to herself at the wrinkles she'd left in the fabric. "I've ruined your suit," she said with a note of alarm. "If you're going to return to the party, let me call someone—"

"Shh," Reese told her, and cupped her cheek. "I was only at the party to see you."

Her heart thudded. "Me? Why me?"

He grinned. "Because Gretchen wouldn't give me your cell phone number."

"I still have to get it replaced," she said, and the prim tone returned. "Someone threw it into a hot tub, remember?"

"I still think that's one lucky hot tub."

"Why did you come looking for me?"

"Because I left without saying good-bye," Reese told her. "And I needed to fix that."

And he leaned in and gently kissed her mouth.

The feel of his lips against her own brought back a rush of memories of their time in the cabin. Oh, and his scent was so divine. Why did Reese always smell so incredible? She whimpered when he grazed his lips over hers, and then his tongue brushed against the seam of her mouth, demanding entrance. She had no choice but to part her lips for him and let him stroke inside her mouth. His hand cupped her nape, dragging her against him, and her hands splayed on his chest for support as he gently and sweetly plundered her mouth. His kiss drugged her senses and made her forget everything, the world beginning and ending with his lips and tongue.

The kiss slowly ended, and Reese pressed one more soft caress on her mouth. "I want you in my bed, Audrey," he murmured, sending skitters of fireworks through her body, the butterfly returning to her stomach.

"I—"

"Reese, there you are, darling!" a woman's voice cooed down the echoing hallway. "Why did you leave the party? Minka and I were just saying that I—"

The woman's voice stopped. Audrey peered over Reese's shoulder at the beautiful blonde in a slinky ice-gray dress, accompanied by a gorgeous brunette. They stared at Audrey in surprise, then at Reese.

Audrey looked up at Reese's face and saw the annoyance in his eyes.

She pushed away from him. How had she forgotten who he was? He was the ultimate playboy, the quintessential player. She was a nobody who was a bed warmer. Of course.

"You should go back to the party," she said in a brisk voice, straightening his lapels.

"Audrey," he began, following her.

"Just leave me alone," Audrey said, shaking her head. She walked down the hall to the elevator and hammered at the button.

"Reese? What's going on?" one of the women asked. She had a thick and sultry European accent. "Are you coming back inside?"

The voices down the hall lowered to a murmur, and she could hear Reese's low baritone mixing with the women's voices, though she couldn't make out what they were saying.

Audrey pushed the button again. It didn't arrive fast enough for her. With a hateful glare at the elevator, she headed to the fire exit and began to head down the stairs.

She just had to get out of there. Away from Reese and the inevitable women who crawled all over him. Away from the party and Brontë's happiness that ate at her.

Away from the memory of that comforting hug, and that wonderful kiss. It was nice that Reese wanted her in his bed, but she couldn't deal with the women crawling all over him.

Not when he wasn't hers. Not when her heart would break every time he dated someone else, because she'd given her heart and he hadn't. She couldn't do it.

In retrospect, taking the stairs in a pair of heels—no matter how sensible—from the thirtieth floor? Not her best idea. But she continued to trudge down the stairs, her heart heavier with every flight. By the time she got to the bottom, she was exhausted—mentally and physically.

Which was why, when she opened the door to the fire escape and saw Reese standing there alone, she groaned. So much for her legendary composure.

Reese grinned at her, holding the door open. "Get your exercise in?"

"Shut up."

"The rest of the world takes the elevator."

"Just shut up."

"Not until you and I have a little talk."

She sighed, then crossed her arms over her chest. "What could we possibly have to talk about? We slept together. It was no big deal. You left. End of story."

"I left because you went out with another man," he said

flatly. "And you were excited about it. So how about we talk about that?"

"You're blaming me?" She gave him an incredulous look. "Are you serious? You're the one who ran like a chicken."

His jaw clenched. "Is that so?"

"Yeah, that's so."

"Who's the one who just took the stairs for thirty floors?"

She gritted her teeth.

"Now quit changing the subject."

"I went out with Cade because he asked, all right?" She jabbed at his chest with a finger. "And I didn't realize that I'd fallen for someone else until I couldn't stop thinking about you at dinner."

His hard expression softened, and that roguish grin returned to his face. "So you fell for me, huh? I bet Cade hated that."

Her face flamed with color. Should she backtrack on her story? Or just keep going? "Cade was relieved because he thinks of me as a little sister," she said in a matter-of-fact voice. "And then he slept with Daphne later that night."

Reese leaned against the stairwell, propping one arm up against the door. "I can think of someone who was at that cabin that didn't think of you like a little sister."

"So can I," she said wryly.

"So how is it that you fell for all this"—he paused and gestured at himself—"and yet you still keep running away from me?"

"Because I can't do this, Reese. Just because I was stupid enough to fall in love with you doesn't mean that I want to end right up in your bed again when I know it's not a permanent thing. And I wouldn't try to force you into anything because that's unfair. One-sided romances always are."

He reached out and touched her cheek, then pulled her close. "So you fell in love with me, huh?"

She weakly pushed at him. It felt too good to have his arms around her. "Reese, don't."

"What if I told you that I haven't been able to stop thinking about you?" He leaned in and grazed his lips against the shell of her ear. "What if I told you I keep comparing every woman I meet to you and they all come up lacking? What if I told you that I haven't even given the thought of another woman any consideration since I left your side?"

A wry smile touched her mouth. "It's only been a week. I'd say you're a normal man."

"Ah, but I'm not a normal man. I'm the billionaire gigolo Reese Durham," he teased. "Your words, I believe. And a week for me is an eternity, especially when it's a week without you." He leaned in and lightly kissed her jawline. "And what if I told you that maybe I'd fallen for you the moment you kissed me like you wanted to make me never forget you? What would you say then?"

She shivered, leaning into his mouth. Her fingers curled at the lapels of his suit again, but she said nothing. She didn't want to break the spell.

"What if I told you," Reese murmured, kissing along her jaw until he got to her mouth,"that I was willing to try a committed relationship with you? Just you and me against the world."

A tremble swept through her. "I'd say not to lie about things like that."

"Firecracker, you know I'm many things, but I've never been a liar." He lightly kissed her mouth. "How about it?"

She twisted her hands in the front of his suit and kissed him hard. "I'd say let's go for it."

He groaned and his hand slid to her hip, then he tugged her leg around his waist. "Ah, that's my girl." The kiss became brutal and fierce. She wasn't quite sure who was leading—her or him—only that they desperately needed each other in that moment. She moaned with need, pressing her body against him, her leg locking around his waist. Her skirt was hiking up and she didn't care.

"So fucking sexy when you're dressed up all subdued like this," he groaned against her mouth. "Do they even know how fucking hot you are when you get riled?"

"Only you," she breathed. "Only for you."

"Good," he growled, and kissed her hard again, pressing her against the stairwell door.

A throat cleared, and Audrey and Reese broke the kiss for a moment to look around. A bellhop stood in the doorway, giving them a red-faced look.

"Can I help you with something?" Reese asked, his hand not straying from Audrey's hip.

"Sir, you're in the middle of the hallway," the bellhop protested.

Audrey bit at Reese's ear, then whispered, "There's a storage closet on the thirtieth floor, across from the ballroom."

"Now you're talking," he told her. "Think we can make it up thirty flights?"

"How about we take the elevator this time?" She smoothed a hand over her bun and was thrilled when his gaze went there and got even hotter, as if she'd stroked his cock in public. Keeping a cool look on her flushed face, Audrey moved to the elevator and pushed the button, straightening her skirt. Reese followed behind her, and they waited, patiently. Quietly.

The elevator eventually dinged. They got in. No one else did. The door shut.

As soon as the door shut, they were all over each other again. Hands sliding under jackets, mouths locked, moans filling the air. Her hand stroked the front of his pants, feeling the hard length of his cock and glorying in it.

"Goddamn," Reese growled when she did it again. "Fucking slowest elevator ever."

"That's why I took the stairs," she said with a giggle.

The doors finally opened and they stumbled out, hands still on each other. The hallway was blissfully empty, and Audrey headed down the hall in the opposite direction of the ballroom, toward a storage closet that held party decorations and cleaning supplies. Sure enough, the door was unlocked. She pushed it open and then gestured for Reese to follow her in.

"How'd you know this was here?"

She shrugged. "I usually have to keep an eye on the staff when there's a shindig, and there's *always* a shindig. You never know when someone's going to need an emergency mop."

"You're so handy," he said, and it sounded like the sexiest thing in the world.

She shut the door and locked it, a flush rolling through her body. "You say the sweetest things."

He pulled her close and began to kiss her again, his mouth hot on hers. After a moment, he groaned and pressed his forehead against hers. "Fuck."

"What is it?"

"No condom."

"That doesn't sound like you," she teased.

He chuckled in the darkness. "I wasn't planning on scoring. I just wanted to talk to you. Didn't give a shit about anyone else."

Her hand stroked along the front of his pants again. "I'll take a chance. I'm feeling the need to gamble. I need you. Don't care how."

"You sure?"

"I'm sure." Her hand slid to the front of his pants and slid his zipper down.

"Think I can get up that sexy little skirt of yours?"

She laughed as he pinned her against the wall. "You mean this sensible beige knee-length skirt?"

"The one that clings to your luscious ass and makes me think of all the dirty things I could be doing to you? That's the one." His hands dragged it upward, exposing her panties. "Ah, thank God you're not wearing pantyhose."

"It's just me under here," she agreed. She moaned when his fingers dipped into her panties and stroked her clit teasingly. "Oh, God, Reese, I need you so bad."

"Then drop these," he murmured.

She did, and then he was between her legs, his own pants around his knees. She felt the heat of him nudge against her a second before he slid deep, and she cried out in sheer pleasure. "Oh, Reese!"

"Ah. Fuck. Firecracker, you feel too good." He groaned and pressed his forehead against hers again. "I think I need to go bare into you from now on. You feel amazing."

"I'll get on the Pill," she assured him.

"Good thing we're in a committed relationship as of five minutes ago," he told her. "Because I think I'm in heaven." He thrust deep, shoving her up against the wall, and she cried out and clung to him. His strokes were hard and fast, and it was clear he wouldn't last long. And she wanted it to be as rough and wild as he could make it, because she needed him so badly.

So she slid her hand between them and rested her finger against her clit. Every time he slammed into her, her finger rubbed against it, making her moan.

"Damn, firecracker," he groaned. "Touching you drives me insane. Not gonna last long."

"No," she breathed, and then bit back a scream when she began to come, her pussy clenching.

He growled her name and thrust again. Then he was coming, too, jerking hard and rough against her. She felt the wash of his seed inside her, and she shivered again.

When she tried to slide her leg down his hip and back to the floor, he stopped her. His hand continued to hold her in place, locked around his hip. As if he wanted to stay there forever. That was fine with her.

He leaned in and kissed her again, slow and tender. "I might have just made you pregnant," he told her. "That was irresponsible of someone who prides herself on responsibility."

"What can I say? You bring out the wild side in me," she said, pleased and dopey from his loving. "Plus, that would be really bad luck."

"Doesn't matter," he told her, and kissed her again, as if he couldn't stop. "I might bring out the wild side in you, but you bring out the responsible side in me."

"I do?" That made her pleased, oddly enough.

"Yeah. Did Logan tell you that he and Hunter are investing in my cruise line?"

Her hands tightened on his jacket in excitement. "They are? You approached them?"

"I got some good advice from a very sensible woman," he told her in a husky voice. "A very sensible woman who has a naughty side. And it's the woman I happen to love."

"You do?" Her voice was even softer, as if she couldn't quite believe it.

"Yeah. Except she loses her head around me," he said in a teasing voice, then pressed a kiss on the tip of her nose. "Which is why I think I'm going to have to marry her."

Her breath stopped. "You . . . what?"

"I mean it, Audrey." He kissed her again, this time coaxing her mouth open with a lick of his tongue. "Marry me. Be my wife. I don't want anyone but you. I love you. I love your spirit and your pride and that sexy figure of yours, and I can't stand the thought of you getting away from me again. And if we've made a baby, then I want to marry its mother."

"Aren't you jumping the gun just a little? I thought I brought out your responsible side."

"You do."

"Proposing marriage after a few weeks isn't very responsible!"

"I said you brought out my responsible side," he said with a chuckle. "I didn't say how big it was." He leaned in and kissed until she was breathless. "Say yes, firecracker."

She considered it a moment, then returned his kiss. "Tell me you love me again."

"I love you," he said, and it was husky and achingly sweet. "I love your good side and your naughty one." He kissed her neck. "Especially your naughty one."

She smiled. "It might be stronger than the good one from time to time."

"That's what I'm counting on." He nipped at her collarbone again. "Now tell me you'll marry me."

"Yes."

His hand clenched around her thigh, and he pressed his hips against hers. She felt his cock still buried inside her, still hard, and he began to thrust again. A moan built in her throat.

"I love you, Audrey," he told her. "Wanna elope to Hawaii?"

She bit her lip, moaning with pleasure. "Is this a ploy to get me to agree to anal again?"

"Mmmm. Now that you mention it, we can save that for the honeymoon."

She giggled.

"Now don't distract me, woman. Do you, or do you not wanna elope to Hawaii?"

He was kissing her and his hips were rolling against her own in a way that was driving her to distraction. "I . . . I'll have to ask for the time off."

"I'll talk to Logan," he told her. "Or you can ask him at poker night."

"Poker night?" she echoed, confused.

"Yeah. I'll explain some other time, but it involves a non-disclosure."

She was going to ask him exactly what he was talking about, but then he began to stroke deep inside her again, and Audrey found she didn't care much about poker night or any other night at all.

As long as she was in Reese's arms, it didn't matter.

EPILOGUE

3 months later

Despite their closet declarations, they held off on any sort of commitment for several months.

It had been Audrey's idea. Reese had been totally gung-ho about heading out to Hawaii the next morning on his private jet and dragging Audrey into a makeshift wedding. Except there had been Daphne to look after, and she didn't feel comfortable leaving her twin while she was still in intensive care.

And then a few days later, she'd gotten her period, which eliminated any fear of pregnancy. After that, there'd been no need to rush, so Audrey had asked Reese if they could postpone for a little while. He'd agreed . . . as long as she'd move in with him.

So she did, and their lives returned to normal.

Well, for the most part, Audrey amended with a wry

smile, looking out the small window of the jet at the clouds below them. There were some things they still didn't see eye to eye on. She looked over at Reese, sprawled on the leather chair in the private jet, and extended her hand. "I'm going to close my eyes and count to ten, and when I open them, my phone had better be back in my hand."

"No." And he wiggled his eyebrows at her, that infuriating man.

"Reese Durham," she said in a warning tone. "I need to check my email and make sure there's nothing that requires Logan's immediate attention."

"You told me yourself that Logan hired two additional assistants. Let one of them handle it." He put a finger to his goatee, as if coming up with a brilliant idea. "Or, I know. You could quit and spend more time with your soon-to-be husband."

She rolled her eyes at him and got up from her chair. "Don't make me search you."

"What a terrible prospect," he said in a dry voice, and put his hands behind his head. "Do with me as you will, firecracker."

"You are a frustrating man," she told him, and began to pat him down, searching for her phone.

"And you're a frustrating woman," he said, dragging her down on top of him and ignoring her squeal of protest. "I told you that you work too hard."

She flailed against him for a moment, but when his hands went to her breasts, she made a soft sound of pleasure and slid down next to him on the couch. "I'm not working too hard."

"You are. Look at how exhausted you've been lately." His fingers stroked her cheek absently. "Last night when I came home, you were asleep already."

She yawned at the thought. "Your poker game ran late."

"Not that late," he told her. "I told Logan he's working you too hard and I'm going to fuck him up if he runs you into the ground."

Audrey groaned, burying her face in his shoulder. "You did not. Reese, he's my boss!"

"I can be your boss."

"No, you're going to be my husband, remember?"

"All the more reason for you to quit."

"You're trying to get me all pissed off so we can have angry sex, aren't you?"

His hand caressed her breast, idly teasing the ultra-sensitive nipple through the fabric of her top. "If I was trying to get you angry, firecracker, I'd show you that white bikini I got for you to be married in."

"Reese," she said in a warning tone. "I'm not wearing a bikini on a public beach."

"It's a good thing it's a private beach, eh?"

She should have protested. Pitched a fit. She knew he'd bought it purely to get a rise out of her. It was probably ridiculous—something with a string for a strap and a thong in the back. He seemed to think she was some sort of nubile ubervixen . . . not that she minded, really. But laying against him made her sleepy, and his hands felt so good on her breasts that she didn't even complain.

"See?" he murmured, kissing her hair. "You're exhausted. That does it. I'm letting Logan have it when we get back to New York."

"No, you're not," she said softly. The reason for her exhaustion had nothing to do with her job.

She was pregnant.

It was, in retrospect, a bit of a nightmare. After that initial torrid interlude in the closet, she'd gotten on the Pill.

Unfortunately, she hadn't gotten on the Pill quick enough, and by the time her next period had rolled around, it didn't happen. She blamed it on stress and the Pill itself because her life had been turned upside down. Stress from moving in with Reese, Daphne's enrollment into rehab, juggling her job—all of it would have driven a normal person insane. But when she missed her period for the second month in a row, she went back to the doctor. Sure enough, she was pregnant.

And she didn't know what to do. She hadn't told Reese yet. Part of her was utterly terrified that he'd look at it as her trying to entrap him into a long-lasting relationship. She wondered if he'd blame her because she was supposed to be on the Pill. And she was, but she'd still somehow managed to get knocked up.

She had to tell him. Before they got married, so he could still get out of things. But she'd put it off. She'd meant to tell him before they'd left for Hawaii, but it had never been just the right time. Reese had been busy with plans for the new Durham Industries cruise line, along with the investment into an exclusive line of high-end luxury cars he'd partnered with Jonathan Lyons on. Once his billionaire buddies had heard about his financial issues, they'd leapt in with both feet to assist him, and Reese was doing better than ever.

Busier than ever, too.

She hugged him a little closer, resting her cheek against him.

"Why so sad, baby?" Reese ran his thumb over her lower lip, caressing her. He constantly touched her when they were together, something she found she enjoyed quite a bit. It was as if he couldn't help himself and had to be touching and caressing her at all times. "Is it Daphne? Are you regretting our bet?"

She gave his abdomen a light smack. "You know I never back down from a bet."

Dares and bets had become their thing. It was a fun way to get the other riled up, which led to passionate sex and then even more sex. Audrey dared Reese to invest in something he didn't want to. Reese dared Audrey to wear something low cut. The stakes changed frequently, from kisses to public makeouts to anything and everything they could think of.

One stake frequently ended up on the table, though: anal sex.

Audrey was pretty sure Reese brought it up constantly as a trump card. But he hadn't won a bet in which anal had been brought into play. They hadn't explored that part of their relationship yet, but she had a bottle of lube in her carry-on that she hadn't told him about. They'd joked that they'd save it for the honeymoon and it was here.

Today's bet had included anal, too. Reese had bet her that she couldn't go without calling Daphne while on their honeymoon. She bet that she could. If she lost, they would have anal sex. If she won, he owed her a full body massage every day for a month.

She was dangerously close to losing the bet already, and the plane was still somewhere over the Pacific. Because right now? She desperately needed to talk to her twin. Despite being in extended on-location rehab, Daphne had been allowed a private cell phone that only had one number programmed into it—hers. It was her only condition on going into rehab, and one that all parties had given into gracefully. The twins talked on the phone daily, sharing secrets and discussing how Daphne was doing, how Audrey's relationship was going, and everything in between.

Audrey had her sister back, and it was the best thing in the world.

She stroked a hand down Reese's flat stomach. Well, tied for best thing in the world.

"You hungry?" Reese asked her, still running his hands over her body.

"Mmm, I could eat."

"You lay here and I'll let the attendant know we want lunch." He slid off the couch and headed to the front of the private jet, where the attendant and pilot were located.

She waited for him to disappear, and then as soon as he did, she jumped up and ran to the bedroom and shut the door behind her. Since he still had her phone, she'd have to use the one in the bedroom. She had time for a quick call, too; Reese was good friends with the pilot and often stopped up to the cockpit to chat with him for a few minutes.

Audrey quickly dialed Daphne's number.

Her twin picked up on the second ring. "I was wondering when you'd call. How's it going?"

"Reese bet me that I wouldn't call while we were on our honeymoon," Audrey said with a sigh. "So I have to make this short."

"That's fine. I have group in about ten minutes anyhow." Daphne's voice was cheerful and strong. Gone was the thready uncertainty, the shaking, and the sullenness. The rehab seemed to be working, but Audrey wasn't going to get her hopes up too much. She'd give it time. If Daphne could stay clean for a year, then maybe this had a chance. Three months made her optimistic, though. More than that, Daphne herself seemed to be changed. For the first time she truly, genuinely seemed to want to get better. She'd cut ties with her label, citing that she needed a career vacation. She still had two albums under contract with them, but since she'd been clear that she wasn't interested in the money or fame any longer, they'd negotiated down to a remix album and a greatest hits album—for a much smaller price tag. Daphne hadn't minded it at all.

She said she was done with music. Audrey didn't know if that was the case, but she liked this new aspect of her twin.

"So did you tell him?" Daphne asked, excitement in her voice.

"Not yet," Audrey said, a trembling note in hers. "I'm scared."

"Don't be a baby. Just suck it up and tell him. I . . . are you crying?"

"No," Audrey said, and then ruined it with a watery sniff. *Damn it.* The pregnancy hormones were making her insane. She'd cried three times in the last week over stupid stuff.

"Well, you need to stop," Daphne said sensibly. "Especially if you want to keep this a secret. If he sees you crying, he's really going to think something's up."

"I just don't know what to do, Daph," Audrey said, wiping away her tears. "What if he doesn't want it?"

"Then the two of us raise that baby with Twinkie power," Daphne said stubbornly. "It can have two moms. Or just one. We can pitch-hit and switch out. I'll put on some boring clothes and re-dye my hair and the kid will never suspect a thing."

Audrey gave a weepy giggle. "Great. Don't forget that you need to put on some weight, too."

"This is true. You have bras bigger than the dress I wore to last year's Grammys."

The comment made her think of the white bikini Reese

had bought her, and she burst into new tears. A white bikini for their wedding. What if he didn't want to get married when he found out she was pregnant?

"Oh, jeez," Daphne said soothingly. "It's going to be okay, Twinkie. Calm down."

"Audrey?" Reese stood in the doorway of the bedroom, frowning at her.

"I gotta go. I'll call you later," she whispered to Daph, and hung up.

"Why are you crying?" Reese shut the door behind him and strode across the bedroom to her, a black look on his face.

"It's nothing."

His fingers swept over her cheeks, brushing away her tears. She looked up at him and the edges of his mouth whitened with anger. "It's not nothing. Is it your sister?"

"No, Reese—"

"I'm going to fucking kill her if she's pulling another one of her stunts. It's bad enough that she's stressing you out. What did she do this time?"

"Reese, she didn't do anything—" Her hands brushed his aside.

"I'm going to turn this fucking plane around and then I'm going to go choke her by her scrawny neck for making you cry again. Goddamn, I—"

"Reese! Shut up!" Audrey exploded. "I'm pregnant, okay? I'm pregnant and I'm freaking out."

As soon as the words left her mouth, she clapped a hand over her lips. *Oh, hell.* That wasn't how she'd wanted to tell him. How did he always manage to rile her so much?

"Pregnant?" Reese stared down at her, stunned. "You're sure?"

"That's why I'm tired," she told him in a dull voice. "And that's why I'm crying. Hormones, for the most part. So yeah. Pregnant. I guess I didn't get on the Pill fast enough." Her stomach was tying in knots of anxiety, and she had to force the next part out of her throat. "I wanted to tell you before we got married. So, you know, you had time to change your mind. I know we were relieved when—"

"Audrey?"

"Hmm?"

"Do me a favor and shut up."

Her mouth snapped shut.

Reese leaned in and kissed her on the nose, his hand clasping the back of her neck. "A baby, huh?" A wide grin crossed his face. "Damn. I must have some incredible sperm."

She snorted and gave him a light thwap on the abdomen. "Now you're just trying to make me laugh."

"Is it working?" He leaned in and kissed her again, this time on the mouth, and this time with more excitement. "You know I can't stand to see you cry."

"Well, I'm going to cry for the next seven months or so," she said in an irritable voice. "So if you are going to stick around, you might want to get used to it."

"Stick around? What the fuck does that mean?" He sounded genuinely offended.

Audrey sighed. "It means I won't force you to get married, Reese. I know this isn't what we wanted."

"Audrey," he said softly, and dropped to his knees in front of her. He wrapped his arms around her waist and buried his face against her stomach. "How can you think that I don't want you or our child?"

She started to get weepy all over again. Reese was being

so sweet, so wonderful. "I don't know. It doesn't really match the playboy lifestyle."

"Neither does getting married," Reese pointed out. "But I've been bugging you to marry me for the last three months. You're the one dragging your feet."

She was, it was true. Audrey sighed and brushed her fingertips through his hair. "You're not upset?"

"Upset? At the thought of little ginger babies? Hell no." He got back to his feet and grabbed her by the waist and swung her around. "Holy shit. We're going to be parents."

"Reese." She tapped on his arm, torn between laughing and throwing up. "Can you put me down?"

"Absolutely." He moved to the bed and dumped her on it, and then a moment later he was crawling over her before she had a chance to get up. He began to kiss her with fierce, sweeping movements of his tongue, and she responded immediately, growing slick with desire. He settled between her legs and she immediately wrapped them around his hips, tugging him against her.

"I love you, Audrey," Reese told her between kisses. "That hasn't changed a bit." He raised his head for a moment and looked down at her, stunned. "Holy shit. We made a baby."

"We did," she said in a small voice, beginning to feel a little better about things. His excitement was genuine, and his excitement was making her excited. And then she smacked him on the arm. "Ginger baby?"

He grinned and cupped one of her breasts in his hand. "Are these beauties going to get bigger?"

"Yes." They were already and her bras were fitting tight.

"Hot damn, I'm in heaven." Reese kissed her again. "Big breasts and anal sex in an airplane on the way to Hawaii."

She laughed at that. "I thought we were waiting for the honeymoon."

"We were," he said, then wiggled his eyebrows at her again in a cocky gesture. "But someone dared me that she couldn't call her twin, and she lost. That makes me think she wants me pretty badly."

Audrey gave a soft sigh, staring up at him. "I'll always want you, Reese. I love you."

"I love you, too, firecracker." He kissed her again, this time soft and with wonder. "I love you and our baby."

She smiled at him, her eyes brimming again.

And then he kissed her one more time. "But there's no way you're getting out of this bet now."

And she laughed.

First comes love, then comes marriage . . .

Turn the page for a special look at

the first book in Jessica Clare's new

Billionaires and Bridesmaids series

Marjorie Ivarsson adjusted the bow on her behind and craned her neck, trying to look in the mirror at the back of her dress. "How is this?"

"Fucking awful," said the redhead next to her in an identical dress. "We look more like cupcakes than bridesmaids."

"Do you guys really hate the dresses?" Brontë asked, wringing her hands as the women lined up and studied their reflections in the mirrors.

"Not at all," said Audrey, who Marjorie knew was the extremely pregnant, nice one. She elbowed the not-as-nice redhead next to her. "I think they're lovely dresses. What do you think, Marj?"

"I love it," Marjorie lied. Truth was, all that red and white made her look a bit like a barber pole with a bow, but Brontë had worked long and hard to pick out dresses and had paid for everything, so how on earth could

Marjorie possibly complain? She'd seen the price tag for this thing. Apparently they'd been custom made by a fashion designer, and the price of just one dress cost more than Marjorie would make in months. Brontë was spending a lot on her wedding, and Marjorie didn't want to be the one to kick up a fuss.

So she adjusted the bow on her behind again and nodded. "It's beautiful. I feel like a princess."

"Oh, you're so full of shit," Gretchen began, only to be elbowed by the pregnant one.

"I think I need this let out a bit more on the sides," Audrey said, waving over the dressmaker. "My hips keep spreading."

A woman ran over with pins in her mouth, kneeling at Audrey's side as Marjorie gazed at the line-up of Brontë's bridesmaids. There was herself, a six-foot-one Nordic blonde. There was Gretchen, a shorter, curvier woman with screamingly red hair that almost clashed with her dress, except for the fact that she was the maid of honor, so her mermaid-cut gown was more white than red. There was Gretchen's sister Audrey, who was a pale, freckled redhead and heavily pregnant. And sitting in a corner, beaming at them as if it were her own wedding, was a frizzy-headed blonde named Maylee who was currently being stitched into her bridesmaid dress. Apparently she was a last-minute addition to the wedding party, and so her dress had to be fitted on the fly.

Gretchen fussed with the swishing tulle gathered tight at the knees by decorative red lace. "My wedding is going to be in black and white, I swear to God, because this shit is ridicu—"

"So what made you decide to have a destination wedding, Bron?" Marjorie asked, trying to be the peacemaker.

She was a little disturbed at Gretchen's rather vocal opinions about the dresses, and sought to change the subject.

Brontë beamed at Marj, looking a little like her old self. "This is where I met Logan, remember? We got stuck here when I won that trip from the radio and the hurricane hit." She grabbed Maylee's hands and helped the other woman to her feet as another tailor fussed over the hems. "Logan bought the island and decided to renovate the hotel. He pushed for them to have it done this week so we could get married here. Isn't that sweet?"

"Sweet," Marjorie echoed, adjusting the deep vee of her neckline. Truth be told, her brain had stopped processing once Brontë had said "bought the island." Marj was still weirded out by the fact that Brontë—quirky, philosophy-quoting Brontë—had dated a billionaire and now they were getting married. In her eyes, she always saw Brontë as a waitress, just like herself. They'd worked together at a fifties sock-hop diner for the last year or two . . . at least until Brontë had moved to New York City to be with Logan. It was something out of a fairy tale—or a movie, depending on which was your drug of choice. Either way, it didn't seem like something that happened to normal people. "You're so lucky, Brontë. I hope I can meet a guy as wonderful as Logan someday."

"Hope is a waking dream," Brontë said with a soft smile. "Aristotle."

Gretchen snorted, only to be thwapped by her sister again.

"Bless your heart, Brontë, for paying for everything so we could all be here with you," Maylee gushed, striding forward to line up with the other bridesmaids. "Look at us. We're all so lovely, aren't we?" She put a friendly arm around Marjorie's waist and beamed up at her. "Like a bunch of roses getting ready for the parade."

"I believe they are floats in a parade, Maylee," Gretchen said dryly. "Which, now that you mention it—"

Marjorie giggled, unable to stifle the sound behind her hand.

"So who are we missing?" Audrey asked, counting heads. "I know Jonathan and Cade are also groomsmen, right? That's five groomsmen and I only count four bridesmaids here? What about Jonathan's ladylove? What's her name?"

"Violet," Brontë added. "And I offered for her to be in the wedding, but she declined since we're not familiar with each other, truly. Logan wanted me to add her to the bridesmaid lineup to make Jonathan happy, but Violet insisted on simply attending." She strode forward and adjusted the lace band under Marjorie's bust. "Does this look crooked to you? Anyhow. Angie's flying in but her kid was having dental surgery today, so she's not coming in until tomorrow."

Marjorie smiled at Brontë meekly. She'd feel a lot better when Angie was here. She, Brontë, and Angie had all waited tables together (along with Sharon, but no one liked Sharon) at the diner. Angie was in her forties, motherly, and wonderful to be around. They often went to bingo together.

Gretchen nudged Marjorie. "So do you have a date for the wedding? Bringing yourself a man in the hopes he'll catch the garter?"

"I do have a date," Marjorie said. "His name's Dewey. I met him playing shuffleboard."

"Dewey? He sounds ancient."

"I believe he's in his eighties," Marjorie said with a grin. "Very sweet man."

"Ah. I getcha." Gretchen gave Marjorie an exaggerated wink. "Sugar daddy, right?"

"What? No! Dewey's just nice. He's on vacation because his wife recently died and he needs a distraction. He seemed so lonely that I invited him to be my date at the wedding. Nothing more than that. He's a sweet man."

"Leave her alone, Gretchen," Brontë said, butting in. "Marjorie always finds herself a sweet old guy to dote on." Brontë gave her a speculative look. "I don't think I've ever seen her out with anyone under the age of seventy."

Brontë knew her well. Marjorie smiled at that. "I guess I'm pretty obvious. I just . . . you know. Have a lot more in common with guys like Dewey than most people."

It was true. She didn't really *date* older men. She just spent her time playing bingo with friends, and shuffleboard, and going to knitting circles and volunteering at the nursing home when she could. Her parents had died long before Marjorie could remember their faces, and so she'd been raised by Grandma and Grandpa. Marjorie had grown up quilting, canning, watching *The Price Is Right*, and basically surrounded by people four times her age. It was something she never grew out of, either. Even at the age of twenty-four, she felt more comfortable with someone in their eighties than someone in their twenties. People her age never sat and relaxed on a Saturday morning with a cup of coffee and a crossword. They never just sat around and talked. They took selfies and got rip-roaring drunk and partied all night long.

And that just wasn't Marjorie. She was an old soul in a really long, lanky body.

That was another thing that the elderly never made her feel weird about—Marjorie was tall. At six foot one, she was taller than every woman and most men. No one wanted to date someone that tall, and most women looked at her like she was some sort of freak of nature. Not her grandma and grandpa. They'd always made her feel beautiful despite her height.

So, yeah. With the exception of Brontë and Angie, all of Marjorie's friends were living in retirement homes.

"Well, I think we're good on the fitting for now," Brontë said as the tailors finished their measurements. "Everyone out of their gowns. Go enjoy the day and I'll see you ladies tonight for the bachelorette party?"

Maylee giggled and Gretchen high-fived everyone. Audrey only patted her rounded belly. "Guess I'm the designated driver."

They shimmied carefully out of the fitted gowns and changed back into their clothing. Marjorie had brought her beachwear with her just in case, and changed into her polka-dotted one-piece swimsuit, then wrapped a sarong around her hips, stuffing her clothing into a bag.

It was a lovely day for a walk on the beach, and she had a few hours before afternoon shuffleboard started up, anyhow.

Jessica Clare also writes as Jill Myles and Jessica Sims. As Jessica Clare, she writes sexy contemporary romance. You can contact her at jessica-clare.com, or at twitter.com/_jessicaclare, facebook.com /authorjessicaclare, or pinterest.com/jillmyles.

From *New York Times* Bestselling Author

Jessica Clare

and *USA Today* Bestselling Author

Jen Frederick

LAST HIT

NIKOLAI

I have been a contract killer since I was a boy. For years I savored the fear caused by my name, the trembling at the sight of my tattoos. I am the hunter, never the prey. But with her, I am the mark, and ready to lie down and let her capture me. I will carry out just one last hit, but if my enemies hurt her, I will bring the world down around their ears.

DAISY

I've been sheltered from the outside world all my life. Nikolai is part of my new life, but he's terrifying to me. He's the only man who has ever seen the real me beneath the awkwardness. With him, my heart is at risk . . . and also, my life.

M1576T1014

FROM *NEW YORK TIMES* BESTSELLING AUTHOR

JESSICA CLARE

ROMANCING *the* BILLIONAIRE

A Billionaire Boys Club Novel

Jonathan Lyons. Playboy, billionaire, and adventurer, he lives life on the edge. When he hears that his mentor, Dr. Phineas DeWitt, had a secret journal that leads to a legendary artifact, Jonathan takes action. It stirs his blood, but it comes with a heady challenge: DeWitt's daughter, Violet. She has what Jonathan needs. And she's not giving it up to the man who broke her heart many years ago . . .

jessica-clare.com
facebook.com/AuthorJessicaClare
penguin.com

M1575T1014